Will the light that

Special Forces ve nightmares that keep him in the shadows, exiling himself from human companionship as he wrestles with his demons. Walking the night to outrun his memories of those he wasn't able to save, he comes to the rescue of a small, valiant woman who puts herself in danger to save a young runaway.

Jilly Sullivan's life is dedicated to making a difference for the poor, championing one hopeless cause after another, spending time in the worst parts of town. When a desperate criminal overpowers her and a nameless hero saves her from harm, both their courses are altered forever.

Gabriel finds himself drawn to the vibrant light that is Jilly, and she lures him from the darkness in which he's most comfortable. The more time they spend together, the more powerful their bond becomes. He comes to the defense of a young boy victimized by a brutal drug dealer, and when that drug dealer assaults Jilly in retaliation, Gabriel rescues her but quickly retreats to the darkness where he believes he belongs. Can Jilly, rocked by her brush with evil, convince this man to believe that he deserves to live in the light?

BOOKS BY JEAN BRASHEAR

SWEETGRASS SPRINGS:

Texas Roots

Texas Wild

Texas Dreams

Texas Rebel

Texas Blaze

Texas Christmas Bride

The Book Babes

Texas Hope

Texas Strong

Texas Sweet

Be Mine This Christmas
Texas Charm
Texas Magic
Be My Midnight Kiss

THE GALLAGHERS OF MORNING STAR
(cousins of the Sweetgrass Springs clan)
Texas Secrets
Texas Lonely
Texas Bad Boy

LONE STAR LOVERS
Texas Heartthrob
Texas Healer
Texas Protector
Texas Deception
Texas Lost
Texas Wanderer
Texas Bodyguard
Texas Rescue

THE MARSHALLS
Texas Refuge
Texas Star
Texas Danger

THE GODDESS OF FRIED OKRA

SECOND CHANCES series
Guarding Gaby
Bringing Bella Back
The Price He Paid
The House That Love Built
The Road Back Home
Dream House

DANGEROUS TO LOVE collection
The Light Walker
The Choice
Mercy

Texas Rescue

Lone Star Lovers
Book Eight

Jean Brashear

© Covers by Lee Hyat Designs
www.leehyat.com

Formatting by BB eBooks:
bbebooksthailand.com

Chapter One

"We're behind schedule," Teo Hernandez said.

"I'm not worried," Jilly Sullivan replied to her construction foreman, smiling into the phone as she walked to her car.

"Of course you're not," he grumbled. "You're the eternal optimist."

"With the two of us working together to make the Marin family's dream come true, how could anything possibly go wrong? You have to think positive."

"Trying to build a home with volunteer labor in a neighborhood that's…challenging, to say the least—want me to add to the list of what else can go wrong? Then you go and promise we'll be done by Halloween?"

"This is not the toughest job we've done, and look at the bright side—it's our fourth house in that neighborhood, and the residents are getting excited about how things are sprucing up. I can't wait to see what got finished today."

"It's eight at night and you're just now leaving work? Don't you ever keep regular office hours? Pretty girl like you ought to be out on a date."

Well, at least she'd distracted him from the litany of woes, even if she'd turned the spotlight squarely on herself. "I was brainstorming a fundraiser."

"With who?"

"With myself, if you must know."

"You need more help. College kid interns aren't enough. You go on home. You can see the house tomorrow."

"I've been stuck in the office since seven this morning. Plus I don't live that far away—oh! I almost forgot! I might have a line on a new volunteer, a plumber—awesome, right?"

"A licensed one?"

"Teo…"

"Okay, okay. You produce a plumber so I can stop getting down on these old knees, and I promise that I'll be so sunny you'll need dark glasses."

She laughed as she got in her car. "Admit it. I'm good."

"No one in their right mind would try to say you're anything but hard-working. Okay, and hard-headed."

She heard the chuckle in his voice. "Thanks a lot, Mr. Grumpy." She couldn't be fonder of him and knew how fortunate Foundations for Families was that he was so devoted to the cause. He'd retired several years ago as a plumbing subcontractor, intending to kick back and do nothing after a lifetime of hard manual labor, but that had worn thin very soon, and, as he'd put it, his wife had told him—not completely in jest—to find something useful to do or one of them had to go.

Jilly thanked her lucky stars daily that Teo was a failure at idleness. He'd originally come to see if he could help part-time and now supervised each job from start to finish.

"I just call it like I see it, Sunshine. You know it's true. Sure you won't go on home?"

She grinned, hearing Teo use her father's pet name for her. "Just a quick drive-by first, then I'll be in bed and snoozing. It's just…this family is special to me."

"Everyone is special to you, girl. You take on every sad

case that crosses your path."

Her family said the same and despaired of the fact, though she thought they were proud of her, too, even if her four overprotective big brothers tended to treat her like she was still a little girl. "I love my work. Neighborhoods invest when we locate a project there, you know that. Everyone draws hope from it."

"They do." He sighed. "Okay, good night, Sunshine."

"Goodnight, Teo." She disconnected and started her car.

In a few minutes she was approaching the newest project of Foundations for Families, a fifteen-hundred square foot home being built for the Marin family: single mom Lucia, her four children ranging in ages from fifteen to two, and her widowed father, Alberto Gonzales. As required by the program, the adults contributed labor, even Alberto, who was badly crippled from the ravages of rheumatoid arthritis but still gamely worked alongside the crew. Lucia's two eldest, fourteen-year-old Beto and fifteen-year-old Lili, worked on weekends, as well.

As she neared the pale yellow one-story, she smiled. Every home warmed her heart, but this one was especially meaningful to her. Lucia was barely older than Jilly's own twenty-nine and she'd dropped out of high school when she'd gotten pregnant with Lili—an old story, but Lucia hadn't given up there. She'd received her high school equivalency certificate while juggling two small children and a night job housekeeping in a motel, then she'd managed one or two classes a semester at Austin Community College as she'd risen to a supervisor's job. When her husband had left her after the fourth child, Marisa, was born, she'd still never admitted defeat. She was now accounts payable supervisor for a small chain of five motels, and she'd taken in her father when he was widowed.

How could you not root for someone like that?

Eagerly anticipating the progress she'd see, Jilly's heart took a tumble when she got close enough to spot the broken front window.

Oh, no. Lucia would be so upset. She was extremely proud of her home.

Jilly hoped the break had been an accident Teo had forgotten to mention. She couldn't bear to think it might be vandalism. She rolled down her window to get a better look.

Just then, a young man came around the side of the house and stalled in surprise, his hands full of electrical wire. The copper in it was a valuable commodity that could be sold.

"Hey!" She held out her phone. "Drop that, or I'm calling the police."

Then she recognized him. A friend of Beto's who'd showed up to help last weekend. "Freddie?"

She emerged from the car. "You don't want to be doing this." Poor kid. She'd seen the ragged condition of his clothes, the too-prominent bones. "Put it back. Beto and his family deserve better. He's your friend. How can you do this to them?"

"Miss Jilly…I…" His eyes were scared and confused.

"It'll be okay, Freddie. Just set it down and go on home." Where did he live, she wondered? And why was he out on a school night? "Are you all right? Go on, take it back, and we'll work something out."

His jaw firmed. "I can't."

"Freddie…" She held up her phone. "I don't want to have to call the police, but you can't do this to the Marins. I know you don't want to hurt them. You've worked hard here. Return that wiring, and let me take you home. We can pick up a snack on the way and talk."

He looked as though he might cry as he cast a quick

glance behind her.

A hand clapped over her mouth while the other snatched away her phone. "I don't think so," said another voice she didn't recognize. "What the hell you doin' here, *puta*?"

Whoever this was, he was taller, older. When she resisted, he tightened his grip painfully.

She tried to shake him off, but instead his fingers dug into her cheeks.

"Stop that. Go on, Freddie," he barked. "Get your ass in gear. Give me a piece of that wiring first."

Freddie froze in place.

"Move it!"

With a look of apology to Jilly, Freddie complied.

Jilly struggled. Her captor threw her phone to the ground and grabbed her hair in his free hand, yanking it so hard her eyes watered.

Okay, then. He might think she was weak because she was small, but she didn't have four brothers for nothing. She cast her eyes down to gauge the level of his knees, then took a backwards kick aimed at crippling him.

"Shit!" He grunted but didn't let go. Instead, he yanked her right arm behind her, brutally tight.

She jammed her left elbow into his gut. He bent double and lost his grip on her.

She ran for her phone, scooped it up and raced toward her car—

He recovered too fast and charged. Knocked her to the ground. "Oh, you shouldn't have done that…"

Jilly screamed loudly with what air she could summon.

The man cuffed her head, and her ears rang. "Get over here, dumbass," he shouted at Freddie.

"Freddie, run!" She wriggled frantically to get free, but the man outweighed her significantly.

"You be still, or you ain't gonna like what happens."

Though it went against the grain, she complied while her mind raced over every last self-defense tactic she'd ever learned.

Gabriel Coronado couldn't exactly date when he'd become a night creature. He only knew he hadn't slept for more than four hours since he'd left Iraq.

He spent his nights outrunning his memories, becoming adept at navigating his way through the darkness and its blessed balm of concealing shadows. The heat in his brain cooled when night fell, and he could think more clearly. Most people troubled by nightmares feared the darkness, but to him it was a comforting friend. In the night, others passed you and went on their way, eager to get to their destinations.

In the daylight, people wanted to talk. Expected you to be normal.

He couldn't remember the last time he'd felt normal.

But he knew exactly when his former life had ended. Nineteen Iraqi children lying massacred in the sand in retribution.

Because of him. Because he'd believed he could make a difference. Oh, he had, all right. Just not the one he'd intended.

No. He would not think of it now, not when he had a choice. The night was for calm, not for thinking. Not for memories. He redoubled his pace, intent on finishing his ten miles with at least two minutes shaved off his pace.

Then he heard the scream, clearly feminine.

He angled to the right toward where the sound seemed to

have emerged, and kicked up his pace, covering almost a block before he spotted the small blonde lying on the ground, held there by a knee jammed in her back, while her attacker waved a knife in her face.

For a second, he felt the sting of sand. Heard the rumble of armored vehicles, the whip of the wind…the screams of the women, the groans of the injured…the dying…down a long, hollow tunnel drawing him into the vortex—

No. He squeezed his eyes shut—hard. *No.*

Then he opened them again. Night. Trees. *Here, not…there.*

He braced one hand against a trunk, let the bark dig into his skin and ground him.

The knife was far too close to the woman. She could be hurt before Gabriel could get in range to disarm her assailant. Gabriel had no weapons except the one that always traveled with him—his own body, a formidable and well-honed defense, courtesy of the United States Army Special Forces.

There was concealing shrubbery a few feet away, so he edged backward and made his way with all the stealth he'd had years to perfect. He noted the cell phone lying on the ground near the woman. He had foregone most of what others considered civilization, living without telephone or television, gladly cutting himself off from what most people believed to be a minimum level of connection to the outside world.

He'd had enough of the world and avoided people whenever he could.

So he could make no convenient calls to the cops. Unless a neighbor had heard her scream, this woman had only Gabriel to depend on.

He emerged from the vegetation five feet behind the man who appeared agitated, likely hopped up on something, cursing and gesturing with the knife. On cat feet, Gabriel closed in one more long stride, then launched a well-aimed kick that sent the knife spinning away. He used his momentum to topple the assailant, then pin him to the ground. He spotted wires lying on the ground and swiftly restrained the man at both wrists and feet.

"Are you all right?" he asked the woman.

"Yes." To her credit, her voice shook only a little.

"You have no business out here alone at night."

"Yes, I do. This is my project. I know the neighbors."

"Didn't help you much, did it?" He glanced around at closed front doors, at the absence of a single person. "I don't see anyone rushing to your aid."

Just then they both heard the sirens, and she turned to watch for the police to come. "See? The neighbors called for help."

Damn it. He didn't want to talk to the police, didn't want to be making statements or appearing in court. He didn't look at her again, but he didn't need to. She was pretty and naïve and valiant, a sure recipe for trouble. Instead he tugged his ball cap down lower over his eyes as he edged back into the cover of darkness, still near enough to watch over her until she was safely in someone else's hands.

But not close enough to be spotted.

The moment the police cars stopped and officers emerged, he slipped away as quietly as he'd arrived.

"Ma'am? Are you hurt?" one officer asked.

"No—no, I'm fine, just…" Now that it was all over, Jilly found herself shaking and wrapped her arms around her middle. Her brothers had each had experience with danger, but her life had been free of any trace of violence. It was astonishing how her heart was racing, how her knees wanted to give. She straightened her back and locked her knees to support her.

"What's your name?"

"Jilly Sullivan."

"You live around here?"

"Not far. Closer to South Congress."

"Someone I can call for you? Sure you don't want the paramedics to look you over?"

"No!" she said quickly. "I'm fine." Or she would be.

"You do this by yourself?" the patrolman asked, pointing to the man lying on the ground, trussed like a roasted bird by the very wire he'd been stealing.

"Oh, no, he did—" She turned and pointed.

At the empty darkness.

"Who?"

She scanned around her for the stranger who'd come to her aid. "There was a man…I don't know where he went."

"Come on out," ordered the cop. "Sir? Come out now."

Nothing but silence.

"Where did he go? When did he leave?"

"He was just here. He saved me."

"Who was he?"

"I have no idea. I've never seen him before."

The second cop glanced at the man on the ground, then exchanged looks with the first. A quick frown. "Can you describe him?"

She had only the briefest impression of a tall, powerful body and shaggy dark hair, a thick black beard obscuring his features. "Not really. He had on a cap that hid his eyes, and—" An unexpected shudder shook her. "—I was on the ground face down when he showed up." She stared at the spot, at the man who'd attacked her. "This guy had a knife and was waving it at me," she said, pointing to the man on the ground.

"Would you like to sit down, ma'am?"

"No, thank you. I'll be fine." She would be, even if the shock of this had her a little shaky inside. Her size always made people think she was weak, but they were wrong. She was the head of an organization that survived at least in part through the sheer force of her will.

"All right then. Can you tell me how it all happened?"

"Gladly, but first, may I ask a favor?"

"Sure thing."

"I have friends and relatives in the police department. Is there any way to keep them from hearing about this?"

"Don't you think they'd be worried?"

She gave a half-laugh, then sighed. "Well, you see, that's sort of the problem. They're a bit overprotective."

"They're right to be that way. Young lady like you shouldn't be here at night, all alone."

"I know all the neighbors. I'm here almost every day."

"Wouldn't be letting my sister come here at night."

Jilly resisted another sigh. "If I promise not to do it again, would you please keep this as quiet as you can?" Her brothers and father already wanted her tucked inside bubble wrap and could barely stand the less than desirable location of her office, the parts of the city she frequented. "The publicity would be very bad for our efforts to recruit volunteers and obtain funding. I'm trying to do good work here, and I actually do trust the people in this neighborhood. Tonight was a unique occurrence."

She glanced back at the man being pulled to his feet. "I've never seen him around before." She returned her gaze to the policeman. "These are good hardworking people we're helping, folks just trying to get ahead against long odds. Please? Could we avoid any unnecessary publicity?"

"You know you're lucky not to be seriously hurt. I don't know what that guy's on, but he's wired on something and wouldn't think twice about hurting you real bad."

But for the intercession of her unknown savior, things could have ended much worse, she acknowledged. "I've never had any problems before, but I will be alert, I promise."

"Don't tell me you're not going to press charges."

She thought for a moment about how frightened Freddie had seemed. He had disappeared, but if she pressed charges, he might be drawn into it. She didn't think he made a habit of this sort of activity. She couldn't imagine Lucia letting Beto spend time with someone who did. "If you find drugs on this man, I won't have to, will I?"

"Your family is right to worry, miss. Don't be foolish."

She knew her family thought she was a bleeding heart, but she also fervently believed that she could make a difference, that she was doing so already. This young man—she could see now that he was barely past a teenager himself—might be just like Freddie. If no one ever believed in boys like them, they'd lose any opportunity to climb out of the world in which they'd been trapped by the simple fact of birth.

If she couldn't live her beliefs, then what good were they? "I'll wait until you see what he has on him."

The cop shook his head and walked away. A couple of minutes later, he was back. "Yeah, we found enough on him to take him in, but you should still press charges."

She saw the young man look at her and frown. She crossed the distance between them, stopping a few feet away. "You don't have to live like this. There are people who will help."

His lips twisted in a sneer, but she wasn't going to give up on him easily.

"Not everyone is your enemy, you know." She nodded

toward the house. "We're doing this to help a family in need. We can always use volunteers."

The young man stared at her but didn't say a word.

"Just remember what I said." She stepped back, and the second cop put him in his squad car, then drove away.

"Do you have a good flashlight?" she asked the officer beside her. "I only have a penlight on my key chain."

"I do. Why?"

"I want to put this wiring back inside. We're behind schedule already, and we can't afford the expense if this wiring could possibly be reused. I have a key."

"It won't be very safe with that broken window."

"There might be something inside I can cover it with. You don't have to help me, though."

The cop sighed. "Let's go." He retrieved a powerful flashlight from inside his car.

She smiled at him. "Thank you."

He even helped her carry the wiring into the living room, which was untouched. They conducted a survey of the house, and Jilly was starting to feel hopeful.

Until they reached the kitchen. It was a shambles, another window broken, the sheetrock torn out so that the wiring would be accessible. "Hell of a mess," the cop said.

"It is."

"Might not be too bad, though. I've done a little remodeling with my brother-in-law."

"We can always use help on these projects."

His eyebrows rose. "Uh…"

"Isn't the department all about community policing? It's a great way to meet the neighbors in a positive setting."

He shook his head and grinned. "You're good at this, aren't you?"

She smiled back. "I am. But I'm also serious."

"I've got a new baby at home, and the wife works shifts as a nurse, so we're juggling a lot."

"I understand."

"But I'll think about it. Tell the guys."

"Any help will be much appreciated."

He helped her wedge some sheetrock in the broken window frames, but without tools on hand, that was all that could be done. It was late now, and she didn't want to wake Teo to come help her board up the windows. She would just have to live her belief that the neighborhood would respect what they were trying to accomplish here.

The cop walked her to her car and waited until she was inside. "Miss, I'm not saying I don't admire your principles, but you know the chances are a lot higher that this guy will be out in a few days, getting high and stealing again."

"I know that, but if we give up on everyone, then what does that say about us as a society? I appreciate your perspective, but I can't afford to share it."

He tapped the roof of her car. "Lock your doors, miss, and you'd best be getting on home."

"Good night, officer. Thank you for your help—and thank you for protecting all of us."

He seemed stunned for a moment, as though he seldom heard such sentiments. He tipped his cap. "I appreciate you saying that."

As Jilly drove away, she noted that he waited until she was back on the street before getting in his vehicle and returning to duty.

Her brother Dane and his fiancée Vanessa, who had become one of her own dearest friends, lived along her route home in the boutique hotel Vanessa had created from a rundown mansion. For a moment, she thought very seriously about stopping there instead of going home all alone. She loved her little cottage, but tonight some company would be welcome. She couldn't seem to stem the jittering inside her, and despite what she'd told the cop, a good dose of family was exactly what she craved right now.

If she did that, however, the night's events would spill out because she was terrible at keeping secrets—and then the whole family would descend upon her. Her mother would try to understand, but she would worry, and her dad would redouble his efforts to convince her to move back to West Texas where he and her brother Rafe could watch over her. At best, the male family members who lived in town—Dane and another brother, Alex, along with her sort-of brother-in-law Saint, an APD detective—would dog her every step. Her movie star brother Liam would insist on hiring a cadre of bodyguards for her.

No one but her mother saw her as anything but the baby of the family, and much as she adored every last one of them and understood exactly how lucky she was to be so loved…sometimes Jilly thought she would suffocate from all the devotion.

So she would go home alone and lock her doors, try to put the night away where it belonged.

But her savior…Jilly took a moment to send up thanks for his bravery. She could still feel the bite of rocks on the ground she'd been thrown on, still feel the ache in the shoulder that had been wrenched behind her.

She'd never been struck by another human being, and the ugliness of it shook her.

Without the mysterious stranger, Jilly admitted to herself, if to no one else, she wasn't sure how much worse things could have gotten. Who could he be?

She couldn't help but wonder about a man who intervened but slipped away before he could be recognized for his courage. He'd been unarmed, yet he so easily disarmed the assailant who was threatening her with a wicked-looking knife, one she could still see so very close to her own skin. Jilly shivered and turned on the heat in her car, though the night was mild. She couldn't seem to stop replaying the young man's tensile strength, the acrid scent of his agitation, the unnerving feeling of her own fear…

Stop. Now. Don't think about it any longer. It was over, and she still believed she'd done the right thing. Not everyone could be saved, but a lot of the people she encountered only needed a hand up instead of being written off.

She very much wished, however, that she'd had the opportunity to properly thank the man who'd rescued her. Whether or not she'd recognize him again, she fervently hoped she'd get another chance.

Regardless, she suspected she would be wondering about him for a long time.

Once she was safely away, Gabriel stretched again and resumed his run. Discipline was important in maintaining balance. He could keep all the doors in his mind safely closed as long as he didn't allow himself to stray outside the boundaries he'd created to seal himself off from others.

The kid's eyes… Eyes told you so much. He'd seen them in every guise, every state known to man. Desperation…agony. Grief. Fanaticism. Hatred. For too many years of his existence, he'd lived in a world of violence and the suffering that always accompanied it. The weak, the innocent…those were the ones who suffered when others resorted to brutality and violence.

But even in those dark times, he'd seen eyes alight with joy, with kindness, with compassion. Sometimes even hope, though he could count those instances on his fingers.

The small blonde's eyes had exhibited fear, yes, but they'd held determination, as well. She might not reach his shoulder, but there was courage within her. Believing in good when the world contained so much evil wasn't easy. He saluted her for her faith.

He just didn't have a lot of conviction that her faith would be rewarded. In the end, it seemed that evil always had its day, always claimed its due.

At last he reached the broken shell of the house his grandmother had left him, even after he'd abandoned her. Some repayment for years of devotion—instead of coming home to her after his discharge, he'd been too restless, too uneasy, and hadn't wanted her to see how much he'd changed, how he didn't know what to do with the gaping hole that was his future. He'd never expected to leave the world that had been his whole life since the day he left high school—and he likely never would have, if not for the chopper crash that had left him fighting to survive.

He'd been a lifer, that simple. A Master Sergeant who had refused to be promoted because advancement meant no more leading teams, staying behind to plan and supervise instead of being in the thick of the action. Adrenaline junkies, one guy's girlfriend had called them all, and she wasn't wrong. The life was hell on relationships, but man, it was a sweet one, otherwise. You were risking grave danger, you were using your body and your mind to the limit, and you knew what you were doing mattered.

Then one day the chopper delivering his team far into the mountains had crashed, and half his team had died. He'd emerged from several months in the hospital with a new raft of scars, a leg full of pins and a ban on further parachute jumps, a death sentence to an operational team member.

He'd fought the ruling, battled his way back into shape so that he only limped when extremely fatigued. Hell, he could have outperformed any guy fifteen years younger, but the docs wouldn't lift the ban, and just like that, he was done. Washed up. No idea what to do with himself unless he went back in as a private contractor.

No deal. There was a need for those guys, sure, but being a mercenary was not for him.

Neither, it seemed, was there a place for him back in the real world. He'd never been all that sociable, never bonded with anyone but his team, and when he returned, he didn't fit. People talked about things that meant nothing—how the hell was he supposed to care who could sing best on some TV show when he could still hear little Sayidah's pure crystal voice turn to screams of terror? Couldn't anyone see how ridiculous life was, how even the poorest person over here had ten times more than so much of the world's population?

And there were people whose lives were dedicated to destroying this country, yet over here, the ordinary citizen acted as though a person could simply walk the streets with impunity, as if there was something magical about being an American that would protect them.

He knew, though, that violence could touch anyone…anywhere. He carried the taint of it like a parasite beneath his skin. His Mama C, his *abuela* Carmen Coronado, had been so good, so kind, so relentlessly positive by nature that he couldn't expose her to the mess inside his head—it would have troubled her so, and her life had been hard enough already because of him. So he'd struck out for parts unknown, wandering for months and seldom touching base with the only parent he'd ever had. Every day that passed without contact made the prospect of explaining himself more difficult to contemplate.

He'd been trying to spare her from the despair that dogged his every step, yes—but the reality was that he'd broken her heart.

And still she'd never given up on him. When he'd finally made his way back to Austin, he'd learned that she was dead, that she'd left him the house he'd grown up in.

As penance and tribute to the love she'd given him all his life, he'd begun to restore the house bit by bit, as if somehow that would make up for his neglect of her.

He didn't live in it, though. He couldn't. Instead, he camped out in the garage. He wasn't sure when he'd ever feel right about making himself at home in the place he should have returned to the day he stepped back on U.S. soil.

The run hadn't helped this time, he realized as he stood outside the small frame house. Guilt and violence were a nasty mix.

He was still working on both.

So, right there on the grass where a boy had once played, Gabriel removed his shoes and stood motionless, letting his bare feet feel the coolness and allowing the sensation to calm his uneasy mind. *Deep, slow breaths, in and out. This moment. Only this.*

A slight breeze rustled in the leaves of the pecans and the live oaks, a peaceful brush over his skin. When at last his mind was emptied of all but the now, Gabriel slid into the unhurried movements of the tai chi he'd practiced for years.

The night surrounded him, settled him. The darkness that was his friend once more carried him away into a place where he could live with himself, where he could forget about all he'd done wrong, where he could simply…be.

Chapter Two

As dawn's light first cast its faint glow, Gabriel returned to the house where the woman had been assaulted. A couple of neighborhood dogs barked, but otherwise the houses were quiet.

He circled the structure and peered in the windows. When he reached the back and saw the state of the kitchen, he frowned. Another window was broken back here, and sheetrock had been destroyed so that the thieves could get at the wiring.

He carefully picked the glass shards from the window frame, pushed back the sheetrock scrap wedged there and climbed in, though getting his six-foot-two frame inside was a struggle.

He couldn't stay long, but he couldn't forget what he'd heard from the woman before he'd slipped away in the darkness.

I'm trying to do good work here, and I actually do trust the people in this neighborhood.

Then she'd moved closer to the guy who'd been ready to knife her, for heaven's sake. *You don't have to live like this. There are people who will help.*

Naïve, dangerously so. And too damn valiant for her own good, just as *Mama C* had been, so trusting when the world was so full of evil.

This woman was small, too, only a few inches over five feet, he'd bet, and she looked like a teenager with that ponytail. *They're a bit overprotective*, she'd said.

Hell, they needed to be. If he knew who *they* were, he'd contact them himself.

Methodically he picked up shattered fragments of sheetrock from the floor and placed them in the dumpster outside. He stood there, hands on hips, and examined where the wiring had been cut, thinking about what would be required to fix it. His efforts to rescue his grandmother's house from decay had made him pretty good at a lot of areas of construction. He didn't have his tools with him, however, and regardless, there wasn't time to rewire before the workers showed up, even if he'd had enough light to see. Besides, some of the wire itself had been damaged by the idiots who'd tried to steal it.

He grabbed the broom resting in one corner and swept up the debris, using a piece of sheetrock as a dustpan. Then he heard a car start up nearby and realized the light outside was much brighter now and he risked discovery by staying.

Time to go.

Jilly knew Teo always arrived by seven to be the first person onsite, so she made sure she was there before him, to ease him into the news from last night. She'd just made it to the front door when she heard him drive up and get out of his truck.

"What on earth happened?" He nodded toward the broken window in the front.

She turned. "This was here last night when I came by."

"Why didn't you call me?"

She looked away. "I handled it." She could handle much more than anyone gave her credit for.

"Jilly?"

"They were stealing wiring. There were two of them."

"How would you know that?" His expression turned pained. "Unless they were still here when you arrived? Please don't tell me you confronted them."

"They were just kids."

"Kids kill people in this neighborhood. You called the cops, right? They arrested the thieves?"

"It's taken care of, Teo." She opened the door. "The damage was confined to the kitchen, except for the window in front." She moved ahead of him, eager to change the subject.

"Wait a minute, missy. You did call the cops, right?"

"Someone did. And they came."

"Why do I hear a *but* in there somewhere?"

"There's a big mess, a lot of sheetrock torn in here and—" Jilly halted abruptly.

Teo walked around her. "You cleaned up already?"

She could only stare and shake her head. "I just got here right before you."

"So who…?"

"Surely not," she murmured. "He left."

"Who left?" Teo faced her. "Jilly, give me the facts—all of them. Who did this, and are they in jail? Exactly what went on here last night?"

"I'm not sure…I need to think about this."

"Jilly…"

Just then the front door opened. "What happened to the window?"

The voice was Lucia's, and the fear in it snapped Jilly out

of her absorption. "We can talk later, okay?" she said softly to Teo. Without waiting for his response, she moved past him to soothe the woman whose dream had just been damaged.

Mama C's kitchen was the most difficult for Gabriel to consider remodeling, mostly because the room was filled with memories for him. The entire house was badly outdated, but to make major changes seemed a betrayal of the life he'd been given, the woman who'd sacrificed so much to care for a lost boy. The house might not have been much, but Carmen Coronado had put her heart and soul into it, every wall, every floor, every window bearing traces of the woman who'd come to this house a young bride and survived being widowed early. Who'd raised a daughter who'd gotten pregnant too young.

Then, when she'd deserved to relax and take life a little easier, instead she'd started all over, raising Gabriel from the time he was four, after his mother had left them, disappearing one day with a boyfriend who didn't want children and never coming back. His father—whoever he was—had never been in the picture.

The two-bedroom house had only one bathroom, a living room, the kitchen and a tiny enclosed storeroom, plus a small screened-in back porch where a washing machine had rocked on the uneven wood floor. Carmen had supported both of them with a beauty parlor she'd created in the storeroom with the help of a neighbor who'd managed to install the deep sink she needed by tying onto the kitchen plumbing. Gabriel could still remember her pride as she'd given him the first shampooing.

Many pots of *frijoles* had simmered in this kitchen, countless tortillas had been cooked on the cast-iron griddle. Outside his grandmother had grown a large garden of tomatoes, peppers, squash and onions, plus assorted herbs and two peach trees. She'd raised chickens to provide them with eggs, as well as the occasional bird for the pot. Every summer of his life, they'd sweated through long evenings to preserve the extra produce that would tide them over the winter.

They hadn't had much in a material sense, but every morsel Gabriel had consumed had been produced with love.

As he looked once again at the faded linoleum counter, at the ancient stove and outdated refrigerator, Gabriel knew he had to confront the future, what he would do with this house that had been his only home. So far he'd focused on shoring up the foundation, on replacing windows, tearing off old shingles and making the roof safe from the weather—all things he wished he'd come home and done for his grandmother while she was living, instead of logging endless empty hours in unfamiliar towns and long, lonely roads in a futile effort to outrun his nightmares.

If he was going to sell the place, he needed to transform it, to erase the familiar sights and scents of his memories and make the shabby place shine.

But he didn't need the money, not yet at least. He'd saved virtually all his pay, and with careful spending, he could last a long time before he had to re-enter the world seeking income. If he would stay here, replant the garden, follow the example of self-sufficiency he'd been taught, he could stave off that day even longer.

Right now, he was stuck, nearing the end of the needed structural improvements and unwilling to make the cosmetic ones that would forever alter the house that had sheltered a small, scared kid.

In truth, he was stuck in more ways than one.

As he entered the garage where he was camping out, Gabriel threw himself down on the cot he'd been using when he pretended to sleep. He stared up at the unfinished wood ceiling and tried to will himself to unconsciousness.

But as he did, the image of a small, fierce blond warrior kept intruding.

She really was like Mama C, he realized. He wasn't the only pitiful creature his grandmother had taken in. Though she'd worked countless hours to support him and many more hours taking care of him, she had also been the first to cook food for the hungry, to take in a woman running from the brutal hands of her man. Her home was small, but there was always room for a sick child whose single mother couldn't afford daycare or an old man with no one to watch over him. She'd insisted on Gabriel having his own room after being dragged around to so many dirty, miserable places by a mother who couldn't settle, but a big wooden blanket box that doubled as an altar was filled with quilts she had pieced and afghans she had knitted. Those had formed many a pallet on the living room floor for the transient in need.

She'd expected him to pitch in, and he had, sharing his toys with the children, delivering meals to neighbors, helping her in the garden. As an older boy and a teenager, he'd helped out with the children because kids always seemed to flock to him. He'd also assumed the chores that required heavy lifting, doing whatever he could to shoulder burdens an old woman shouldn't have to carry.

Maybe it was inevitable that Gabriel would reach out so unwisely in Iraq. The plight of the common people had moved him. They had suffered under a dictator, and they continued to suffer after being freed, buffeted around by the ill winds of warfare and tribal hatred.

It was the children whose plight affected him most. He'd

been one of those small ones who had no one to watch over them—until his lost mother had brought him within range of the old woman who would save him.

But he'd been naïve when he'd tried to do the same for others, and the Iraqi children had been the battleground. Ahmed, whom he'd first met when the boy was being beaten after trying to steal a bag of rice to feed his sister, would have been better off if Gabriel had never entered his life trying to save it. In the end, the boy had died because of Gabriel's notion of being some kind of hero.

The small blonde was courageous and compassionate, but she was not wise. She needed to take off her rose-colored glasses and see the world for what it was, a dark and lonely and dangerous place.

Or the world would eventually teach her that lesson.

Let it go. Sleep. Finally, he drifted off.

Small, torn bodies carelessly tossed like a child's rejected toys across blood-soaked sand…

Ahmed's eyes on his as the life drained out of him—

Picking his way through the bodies, stumbling…

A sound, a click.

He whirled, weapon ready, already firing—

No one there. He tripped, righted himself.

Looked down

A body. A woman, a small one…

Strawberry blonde.

Heart thundering, Gabriel bolted from his cot, lashing out, screams echoing in his ears. The battery-powered lantern tumbled to the ground. He was lost in darkness, fumbling for his weapon—

Street sounds filtered in.

A dog barked.

Slowly he began to come back, to feel dirt beneath his feet, not sand…

Realized the shouts were his.

The adrenaline surge waned, leaving him shaky and sick…and so damn tired of being a freak.

He wrenched open the door and charged into the sunlight, standing still while his heaving breaths slowed… glanced at the house, searching for the real.

His shoulders sagged. He hadn't had such a bad one in weeks.

The strawberry blonde head…where had that come from?

But he knew. Another innocent who needed protection.

But not his.

No more sleep would come now. He raked his hands over his head, clasped them behind his neck. If only he could wash away all of this filth, this misery that tainted him…

He looked up. The house. The only cure he'd found was pounding nails or focusing on solving electrical problems or…

But he couldn't start on the inside of Mama C's house. Not yet.

Then he knew what he was going to do, however much it went against every move he'd made since he'd returned.

Hadn't he learned you couldn't really save anyone?

He would stay out of sight, and he would not get involved.

But he had to know more, he realized. Had to understand what she was up against, this small, unwise champion.

"We can handle this, Jilly," Teo said. "Go on to the office."

"As you can see, I'm not dressed for that." She wore jeans and sturdy shoes. "I am perfectly capable of managing my workload, and right now, getting this job back on schedule is at the top of the list." She put her hands on her hips. "Begging for money can wait for another day, Teo. You could use more hands, and it's sure not my first time to do manual labor. I didn't grow up on a ranch for nothing. I even know a thing or two about remodeling a house, since most of my family is obsessed with doing that. I've been slave labor more than a few times."

"You're too little, girl."

Nothing could fire up her temper more. "Go tell Celeste Sullivan that small women are weak. Come on, I dare you. My mother will serve you on toast for breakfast."

Teo chuckled and shook his head. "Okay. Tell me what you're best at."

"Whatever I need to be. I don't have as much experience with electrical or plumbing, though I've helped my dad do both, but I can swing a hammer, and I can paint. I've even done some taping and floating."

"You could never lug a sheetrock panel."

"No, but once it's up, I can take it from there. Or I can clean up or sweep or...just put me to work, Teo. I don't care what I do."

He studied her for a long moment. "You need gloves."

She whipped a well-worn pair out of her back pocket. "Not my first rodeo, I'm telling you."

"We are behind," he admitted. "But it would be better if you focused on finding more volunteers."

"I've already put out some feelers, and my intern April is doing follow-up for me. I've got my phone in my pocket if anyone responds." She put on her gloves and fisted her hands on her hips. "So?"

Teo shook his head. "All right. Lucia wants flowerbeds in front, but first we have to get the area cleaned up so she has decent soil to work in."

Her face split in a wide grin. "I'm on it, boss."

The older man walked away, chuckling.

Jilly got to work.

That night on his run, Gabriel thought about what he'd witnessed from the invisibility of the rampant vegetation surrounding the site. *We are behind*, the older man had said. *You're too little.*

Gabriel would agree, except that his grandmother had been even smaller than this woman…this Jilly, she was called. And he'd seen few challenges Mama C wouldn't tackle.

Jilly. He hadn't been sure of the name when she'd answered the cop that night, though he'd caught the name of her street that wasn't far from his own.

Her name somehow fit with the red-gold ponytail that bounced from the hole in the back of her ball cap. The one that said *Recovering Blonde.*

He smiled. And was aware that his mouth wasn't accustomed to the motion. He'd watched her joke with her coworkers and smile as she worked, as though sunshine was her normal habitat, and he was aware of a strange sensation he couldn't quite put his finger on. Then it had struck him.

A door had been opened into his solitude.

He didn't like it much, but he couldn't seem to close it. And the sunshine was dispelling the soothing darkness that had become his life. He couldn't quite get comfortable there now, couldn't relax and slip into the unconscious ease he'd come to count on.

It was all her fault. For whatever reason, the small blonde, this…Jilly…had trespassed into his solitude as she had his thoughts.

He wanted her out.

Dragging himself back to the night, he realized he was nearly in front of the home under construction. Before he passed it, he spotted a figure walking toward the house and ducked behind a tree to observe. Under the streetlight, he saw that it was a kid, his movements both furtive and awkward as he circled the house, heading for the rear.

Gabriel followed with stealth. The kid craned his head to peer through a window, then shook his head and reached for the back door knob.

"I wouldn't if I were you," Gabriel said.

The kid gasped, looked back, and took off.

Gabriel gave chase. The boy was fast, but he was panicked. Gabriel caught up with him quickly and took him down.

The kid started crying. "I wasn't gonna hurt nothin', I swear. I wanted to see was it okay."

Gabriel turned him over and remained crouched above him. "Who are you?"

The boy's chin jutted. "Ain't nothin' you need to know."

"The police will." The kid didn't have to know Gabriel had no way to call them. "What are you doing here?"

"I ain't talkin' to you. Who you think you are, anyway?"

If Gabriel hadn't dealt with scared kids before, he might have bought the bluff. "You don't need to know," he echoed.

Their gazes locked.

The boy looked away first. "Miss Jilly, she helped me," he said quietly. "She let me go. I just—I never wanted to do it, but Mako tell me he hurt my kid brother if I don't do what he say."

Ah. Now he got it. "You were one of the thieves from last night."

"Didn't wanna be."

"And Jilly let you go." Anger stirred. "So you left her with that guy, that Mako?"

"I had to." His throat worked. "I got a kid brother to watch out for. Can't go to jail."

"You saw he had a knife on her and you *left*?"

Again the kid's eyes shifted.

"Answer me."

"Yeah."

"Mako could have killed her." Forcibly Gabriel throttled back on a simmering rage. "You abandoned her with him."

"She okay. I asked around. She didn't get hurt."

Gabriel's voice went deadly soft. "He knocked her to the ground. He tied her hands behind her. He held a knife to her throat. You don't think that counts as hurt?"

"I'm sorry." The kid started crying. "I was scared. I didn't know what to do. Damien got no food all day, and he little. Mako say he split the money, say insurance take care of it, nobody loses."

What kind of world was it where children were so often the ones to suffer the worst?

And why the hell had another abandoned kid crossed his path? He didn't want this, didn't want to care.

He held the boy's eyes with his. "Tell me your name."

"Freddie."

"Where do you live, Freddie?"

The boy's eyes shifted. "We got a place."

Yeah. But the same place every night? Doubtful. "Where's Damien right now?"

"He with his mama. She not working tonight."

"She's not your mother?"

The boy shook his head.

"How old are you?"

"Fifteen."

"Why'd you pick this place to rob?"

His head drooped in shame. "Belong to my bro Beto. I helped work here one day. Gonna be real nice."

Gabriel stared at the top of the boy's head and sighed. He rose, held out a hand and helped Freddie to his feet. "Mako's wrong. This house is being built by volunteers with the money coming from donations, did you know that? You owe them for what you did. How do you plan to make it right?"

A quick jerk showed panicked eyes. "I ain't got no money. I can't pay."

"You know how to work, right?"

"Don't matter. Nobody want to hire me. Got to be sixteen."

"You think the world hates you? You don't have a family to take care of you, so you think you have to give up?"

The boy only shrugged. "Don't matter what I want."

"It does, Freddie. What you want very much matters. You can change all this."

"You sound like Miss Jilly. She nice, but she don't get it. She's a pretty white lady who thinks talk can fix things." The boy's eyes were ancient.

"I never knew my father," Gabriel said. "My mother left me when I was a kid."

"No shit?"

"No shit. But I had someone a lot like Miss Jilly who believed in me. You know she never told the cops about you?"

"That what Mako say. He think she stupid. Say she deserve to get robbed."

"Forget Mako. What do you think?"

Freddie was silent a long time. "Be nice if she was right about how the world can be, but she ain't right. She just don't get it."

Gabriel didn't disagree, but to simply let the matter go like that was a disservice to the woman. "Maybe the rest of us have to look out for the folks like her."

"Huh?"

"Even if her way can't fix everything, Beto and his family are getting a new house because people like Jilly believe. Is it better for her not to believe?"

Sullen shake of the head. "I guess not."

"So how do you think you can repay her for not turning you in?"

"I ain't stupid. You tryin' to get me to say I'll come back here to help, right?" He looked away. "I don't know, man."

"Did it ever occur to you that you could learn some skills helping out here, skills that could help you get a paying job?"

Freddie blinked. "No."

"You afraid of hard work, Freddie?"

"No."

"Then show up here tomorrow and see what you can learn."

The boy's head cocked. "You working here?"

"No." No way. Too many people. Too much noise.

"Don't know how to do this work, neither? Maybe you should show up and learn, too."

He nearly grinned. The kid had stones, that was for sure. For a second he was reminded of Ahmed's audacity, of how the younger boy faced down bigger tormentors.

The reminder wiped away any smile. "I already know how."

"So, what, you got another job, that it? Maybe I could come there. Think they'd pay me?"

Gabriel wasn't taking anyone home with him. It wasn't home, anyway. Not now. "No."

"You sure good at saying no." Crestfallen, the boy turned away.

Every rib showed through the back of his dirty t-shirt.

No. I don't want this. He only wanted to be left the hell alone.

"I'm outta here. Don't try to stop me." But loneliness and reluctance rode every line of the boy's frame.

Damn it. "I'll come for one day, but that's it."

Freddie turned. "For real?"

"Don't ask me again." His voice was too sharp, he knew it, but he hated this. Wasn't the kid's fault, though. "You're going to help me fix what you tore up."

"You know how to do that wiring shit, seriously? Like you can hook up lights and stuff?"

"Yeah."

"Sweet!"

"How do you plan to live in the meantime? This work doesn't pay."

The boy's shoulders stiffened. "Not your worry, man. I take care of myself."

He was probably trying to, but he was losing the battle. There wasn't an ounce of fat on his frame. Inwardly Gabriel sighed. Handouts weren't a good long-term solution, but this boy had to eat. He reached for his wallet and withdrew a twenty. "There won't be any more of this if it isn't used for food for you. Eat a good breakfast and be here by 7:30. You have a place to stay?"

"Yeah."

Gabriel doubted he had much of a place, but the boy wasn't his problem. "I'm not a sucker like Jilly. You get a good night's sleep, eat a filling breakfast and be here ready to work. Show these people you can work hard, and maybe the foreman will have some ideas about where you can get a job." He proffered the bill. Freddie took it and folded it carefully, sticking it deep into the pocket of threadbare jeans barely hanging onto his butt.

And pull up your pants, he wanted to say, but like food and a place to sleep…he did not want to be involved.

"Seven thirty. Now get the hell out of here."

The boy lingered. "Mister, you crazy like Miss Jilly? Think you can change things?"

Gabriel snorted. "Not hardly. I know you're thinking you just copped twenty easy bucks and have no plans to show up tomorrow."

"Hunh." The boy smiled a little. "Guess we'll see."

"Yeah."

"Okay, well, I'm outta here." But he hesitated.

Gabriel didn't move, and finally the boy took off.

Before he could resume his own run, another car drove by, one he recognized. His temper stirred when he realized it was Jilly. *You'd better not even stop, much less open the door*, he warned her silently. *Tell me even you are not that naïve.*

When she drove on past, he released the breath he hadn't been aware of holding.

He shouldn't give her a thought. It was none of his concern if she chose to be stubborn and foolish and reckless. Jaw tight, Gabriel stared after the red taillights vanishing in the distance. *Not my problem*, he reminded himself. *None of them are my problem.*

But he'd promised the kid one day. If he was going to

commit that insanity, he needed to change his appearance so she would not recognize him.

He continued staring sightlessly for a long time.

Chapter Three

As he slid into the tai chi move High Pat on Horse, Gabriel's gratitude renewed. His body was not the same as it had been before the chopper fell from the sky, but it served him again in a way he'd been warned it never would. His transitions in the tai chi Twenty-Four Form were executed with an ease that had seemed impossible even months before. The regimen had reconditioned his core and brought stability back to his spine. His were no longer the movements of a man who sought to be the best in the art of war, no longer focused on the stealth and strength required to slip through the shadows and surgically remove threats from existence, no.

Now they were all about keeping the world at bay, about seeking the place where he could exist without the clamor chaos and guilt had wrought. Once he'd held complete mastery of his mind every bit as much as his body. He'd commanded men with sure confidence and unerring focus. He'd been able to quiet his mind in the midst of the most tense situation, under any sort of pressure.

Then innocent children had been murdered by zealots, and his focus had buckled.

A few days later, the chopper his team was in had plunged from the sky, and though he'd made it out of the wreckage and dragged two of his men with him—not that he remembered doing it—he'd been thrown into an existence where he controlled nothing. Not whether he lived, not what his future would be. The military career he'd loved had been a casualty, and months had been consumed by his recovery.

And now here he was, getting involved with a messed-up kid who probably wouldn't even show up today. Yet by returning to the jobsite and revealing himself, Gabriel would be creating expectations. Obligations he didn't want. Responsibilities.

Once he'd lived to tackle any responsibility and excel, to exceed any expectation, to prove himself.

He closed his hands into the final prayerful pose and went completely still. Brought crisp morning air into his lungs and order into his mind as ripples rose from the depths.

He settled on the cool, damp grass, legs crossed beneath him, a miracle of its own that they would do that so easily now. He focused on slow, steady breaths that cleansed him, that eased him into that place where he wanted nothing, where he let go of need, of worry, of desire for anything beyond the still, quiet pool he'd worked very hard to find inside himself.

Some time later he emerged, rising into consciousness with his senses renewed, hearing the lone mockingbird chattering in the pecan tree at the edge of the yard, the low hum of far away morning traffic as the city awoke…the bark of Mr. Cantu's dog down the block.

Refreshed by the peace, muscles loose from his workout, in recent days Gabriel would have sought his bed for a few hours of sleep that more often now were undisturbed by dreams.

The cat meowed, and he opened his eyes. "*Buenas días*," he said to Chico, the ancient three-legged cat Mama C had sheltered and who always reappeared to observe Gabriel's morning routine. He extended his hand, and the old tom made his halting way over for a good scratch.

After the feline was reduced to a purring puddle, he rose more smoothly than either he or the doctors had imagined he'd manage, and walked to his makeshift quarters, the cat trotting alongside. Though Chico had survived on his own before Gabriel's return, now Gabriel supplemented the animal's diet of small creatures.

He would feed the cat and feed himself. Then he'd head to the jobsite to fulfill a rash promise.

It was after lunch before Jilly could drop by the site that day. She'd gotten caught on the phone with one of their donors, dealt with questions from the city inspection department and left voicemail messages for her brothers who lived in town. Both were very skilled with all types of construction, and even though Alex was now an artist of growing fame and Dane a renowned adventure photographer, they had been raised like her, never too proud to get their hands dirty. Both were self-employed, so she figured she could tap them for a short stint of help to get this project caught up, if need be.

She changed into work clothes she'd taken with her to the office, and when she showed up, it wasn't empty-handed. She'd stopped at a little Mexican grocery not far from her office and picked up *pan dulce* as a treat for the crew. Good for morale and good for the family who owned the grocery. Jilly bought as many of her own supplies there as the store could provide. She had grown up in a small town in far West Texas and understood the importance of supporting local businesses.

When she made her way inside, she was greeted with smiles, even from Mr. Grumpy. "Hey, Teo, who spiked your water with happy juice?"

"Come into the kitchen and you'll see."

Curious, she followed. Her eyebrows lifted. "Wow. Wiring. What happened?"

Teo nodded toward the far wall. "He did. Hey, Gabriel, I'd like you to meet someone."

A man who'd been fishing wire between studs completed his task, then turned.

Wow was right. And she wasn't only talking about the wiring.

"Jilly Sullivan, this is Gabriel Coronado. He's a new volunteer, and man, he's good. Even brought his own wire to replace some of what was damaged."

Tall. Dark. Gorgeous. The words rattled around in her brain and clogged up her throat.

"Ms. Sullivan," he said in a deep, resonant voice, nodding. Then he began to turn away.

Teo frowned at her.

"Oh—sorry." Jilly gathered herself and extended a hand in welcome. "Thank you very much for helping us out here."

He stared at her hand, then finally shifted the coil of wire from his right hand to his left and returned the shake, withdrawing quickly. "Sure." Immediately he turned back to his work.

But not quickly enough that she didn't notice the strength in his fingers, the calluses that backed up his experience. To register that this man had a presence to him, a gravity that was unusual. A look into his beautiful dark brown eyes told her little, only that he was very, very guarded.

She glanced at Teo and mugged. *What's up with him?* Teo

shrugged back.

Okay, so he wasn't much of a talker. He was still a godsend.

"How did you know?" she found herself asking him.

He went on working as if he hadn't heard.

"Mr. Coronado?"

Slowly he turned. "What?"

"How did you know we needed an electrician? Or wire?" Teo was frowning at her again. Hastily, she reassured them both. "I mean, I'm sure not complaining. We really do need your help, and we're very grateful to have you. I just wondered how you found out."

He'd already returned to his work. "I heard about what happened."

"Where?" Who else knew? She'd managed to skim over the details with Teo and the Marins, but had the cops been talking?

"Word gets around." He revolved halfway. "Is that a problem, Ms. Sullivan?"

"What? Oh, no—no. Neighbors…that's…fine. Just fine."

Both the men were looking oddly at her, and she realized she probably sounded like a lunatic. "Well, I'll just get to work now. Thank you so much. And please, call me Jilly."

As she walked away with Teo, however, she couldn't resist a glance back. There was something about the man…

"Don't you hang around long, you hear me?" Teo said, yanking her back to the moment. "I remember that tonight is your Girls' Night Out."

"But there's still catch-up to do."

"We've made big strides today, I'm telling you. That Gabriel does the work of two men. You take that night off, missy. You need it."

After a restless night and a strenuous day, Jilly thought the smartest plan might be to go home and get some sleep to catch up.

But Teo was right—tonight was Girls' Night Out, and as its founder, Jilly made it a policy to never miss.

For now, though…time to get back to work.

Gabriel couldn't get out of here soon enough. Freddie hadn't shown…not that he should be surprised. However ticked off he was, he understood that kids like Freddie were seldom good at simple courtesies most people took for granted. When you were scrambling to survive, things like appointments and responsibilities went by the wayside. From what little he knew about the boy, Freddie clearly was dealing with a lot of garbage.

The fault was Gabriel's for abandoning his resolve and getting involved. He couldn't backslide. He already felt too exposed simply being with all those people today, being introduced, having them pay attention to him. The irregular popping of the nail gun, too reminiscent of small arms fire, had his every nerve on edge, and all the talking…

He was more comfortable as a creature of the night. He'd spoken to others so seldom since his return that sometimes he'd wondered if his voice still worked.

He never should have come out of hiding. He wasn't ready to be friendly. If not for Jilly, he'd still be enjoying his solitude, and for that, he couldn't thank her.

As for letting himself get boxed in by sympathy for the kid, well…apparently he'd needed a reminder.

"A good day, friends," Teo said. "Let's wrap it up."

Lucia, who'd only arrived two hours before because her job ended at three p.m., paused in her painting. "I could work another hour."

Jilly could see the concern on her face. She desperately wanted to be in her home by November first as planned. She'd told Jilly what it would mean to her to celebrate *Dia de los Muertos*, then Thanksgiving and Christmas in her first home.

"Teo? I could stay with her," Jilly offered.

"No," said the new man's deep voice, one she'd hardly heard all afternoon. "Not a good idea."

She whirled, hands jammed on her hips. "Excuse me?"

"You heard." He turned away.

"You just started today. What do you know about anything?"

"I grew up not far away. A woman shouldn't be here at night." He disappeared around the corner.

"Hey—" She started forward, but Teo intervened.

"Lucia, it's a school night, right?"

Lucia nodded. "But—"

"One of the things I admire about you is how you're there for your children." He smiled reassuringly. "We're back on schedule—a little ahead, actually, thanks to Gabriel here."

All three of them glanced over, but the man named Gabriel was nowhere in sight.

"Where did he go?" Jilly asked.

"He's getting in his truck," said one of the other volunteers.

Another Houdini, like the man from the other night.

Jilly frowned. The other night.... For a second, Jilly was struck by the notion, though it was surely a stretch. Still, she mentally tried to superimpose this man over her memory of the other... Gabriel Coronado was clean-shaven where she recalled a heavy beard on the other man, but both were tall with powerful builds... She'd been so unnerved, plus it had been very dark...

The only thing she could say the two definitely had in common was that both liked to give her orders.

But that could describe all the men in her family. Half the men she met, simply because she was vertically challenged.

"I hope he'll come back," Teo said fervently. "He finished all the wiring and even improved upon what had been done, plus he secured the broken windows, since the new ones won't be here until tomorrow. Then he climbed on the roof and inspected all the flashing." He leveled a look at Jilly. "He's really good. We'd be lucky to have him. Anybody know where he lives or how to contact him?"

Every head shook.

"He said he grew up not far away," Jilly said. "That's not much help."

"Well, we'll just have to cross our fingers," Teo said. "At any rate, what he did today was fantastic." He returned his attention to Lucia. "So we're in good shape. Shoot, if that guy comes back, we might finish in record time. And I happen to know that this little girl here—" he pointed toward Jilly, who stuck her tongue out at him "—has plans with her friends every Tuesday night. So you'd be doing her a favor to go home, Lucia, and be with your family."

"We're really doing all right, in spite of...?" Her quandary was evident.

"We really are," Teo assured her. "Now everybody take off, and I'll see you in the morning, bright and early."

"He's a good man," Lucia said after he walked off.

"Teo's the best," Jilly responded.

"But you are no little girl. You do good for so many, Jilly. We say prayers for you every night, my family."

Jilly gave her a hug. "Thank you, Lucia." Then she grinned. "My family will be relieved to know that someone besides them is praying over me."

"If they understood the good you do, they would know that the Good Lord watches over you already."

Jilly didn't know what to say to that except, "Thank you."

"We will add Gabriel Coronado to our prayers tonight. He is an answer to them, is he not?"

Jilly stared out the window, wondering about the elusive stranger who'd arrived like a blessing. "He certainly is."

Then she shrugged and started picking up her tools, so she could go home and clean up for Girls' Night.

A couple of blocks down the street, Gabriel rolled his shoulders, fingers tapping on the steering wheel. He was sweaty and tired, edgy from trying not to react to each sharp noise or the sound of so blasted much talking.

He wanted an hour-long shower and a cold beer and endless days by himself.

Then he spotted Freddie. Slammed on the brakes and launched himself out of the truck. "Why the hell didn't you—"

The startled boy's gaze shot up. His nose was bleeding, and he had a split lip, a gash over one eyebrow running blood as well. His threadbare shirt was torn, his jeans streaked with dirt and grease.

"What happened?" Gabriel closed the distance between

them. Freddie's eyes darted to the side. He poised to run.

Gabriel held up his palms. "Hey, easy now. Who did this to you?"

"Nobody."

"Well, *nobody* did a hell of a number on you. Where else are you hurt?"

A slight shrug. "Nowhere bad." But he wouldn't meet Gabriel's gaze. "Look, I gotta go."

Gabriel halted him with one hand lightly on his shoulder. "Not just yet. Talk to me. Who did this?" At least now he understood why Freddie hadn't shown up for work.

The boy's Adam's apple bobbed as he swallowed convulsively. He still wouldn't look up.

A teenage boy's pride was fragile at the best of times, and Gabriel knew only too well the humiliation of having the crap beat out of you. He hadn't always been this big. He took mercy and dropped the subject.

For now.

"Come on. Let's get you fixed up."

"I don't need no doctor."

Kid, you probably need that and more. A whole lot more than Gabriel wanted to get stuck providing. "That's good because I'm not one." Though all Special Forces had some medical training, and Gabriel could manage a lot more than simply cleaning him up.

He gestured to his truck.

Freddie hesitated.

"I can probably still catch Jilly. Want her getting involved? You'll be in the emergency room before you can say boo."

"No. Don't need your help neither."

"I'm not offering much. I'm not your nanny."

That generated a tiny smile. "Ow," the boy said as his cut lip flexed. But some of the stiffness left his frame.

"C'mon, kid. Sooner we get you cleaned up, the sooner you get the hell out of my hair." He guided Freddie to his truck, and the boy showed only token resistance as Gabriel opened the passenger door and gestured him inside.

"C'mon, kid. Sooner we get you cleaned up, the sooner you get the hell out of my hair." He guided Freddie to his truck, and the boy showed only token resistance as Gabriel opened the passenger door and gestured him inside.

Chapter Four

"Shady Grove rocks! I do so love Austin," enthused Annabelle Quinn, the newest member of Girls' Night Out. She clinked her margarita glass against Jilly's, then settled back in her chair with a sigh. "Live music under the trees, sinfully good nachos, wonderful family and friends…ah, the joys of normal life."

Jade Sandoval, married to Jilly's brother Alex, grinned. "Yeah, and you're so normal and all."

The most famous actress in America stuck out her tongue and shoved the sunglasses she was using for disguise back up on her nose. "Vanessa promised I could be one of the girls."

"And I meant it." Vanessa cast a reproving glance at Jade, but the sultry redhead's mischievous grin didn't falter. "Annabelle is family now, or the next thing to it, now that she's with Sean. And she is normal."

"Because normal is the byword of all Sullivans and anyone in love with them." Jilly snickered. Her brother Liam was Annabelle's male counterpart in Hollywood—two-time Sexiest Man Alive and top box office draw. Rafe was a former Special Forces medic and now a *curandero*, practitioner of a healing tradition dating back to the Aztecs. Alex was once an FBI agent and now an artist commanding thousands per canvas, and Dane was a world-famous adventure photographer.

Only she was just…Jilly. Kid sister.

Normal. Disgustingly so.

"On the topic of love," Jade spoke up. "How's Patrick, Jilly?"

"Patrick?"

"Cute guy? Legal Aid lawyer? Been dating a couple of months?"

"I know who you mean." But she shrugged. "He's okay. We went out last week."

The others exchanged looks.

"Don't do that."

"Do what?" Vanessa asked.

"Not you, too, Vanessa. You were my best friend before you became my prospective sister-in-law."

"I still am, sweetie."

"Look, I can't help it if no one measures up. I'm not going to settle." She had lived all her life with the knowledge of what love could be, beginning with the deep and true bond between her parents. Her brothers had taken their own sweet time, but they, too, had found their soulmates. If she couldn't have that, she would prefer nothing.

She wanted it, though, more than she would ever let on.

"And you shouldn't," Annabelle concurred. "You'll find him, Jilly."

What did Annabelle know? She was gorgeous and famous, the object of fantasies.

Jilly was…sunny. And plucky. Everyone said that.

Big woop.

She dated. She tried. She didn't compare men to her remarkable brothers—they were freaks of nature. She didn't expect that from a man. But she did expect that zing, that click of a key in a lock…and she had yet to meet a man who spoke to her heart at that depth.

She was beginning to think she never would.

But she had a good life, didn't she? She was doing work that mattered, she was helping people. She had lots of friends and made more every day. She would be fine. It wasn't like her life wasn't filled with love…just not that kind of love.

"I pity the man," Jade said. "Whoever it is has to run the whole *he's not good enough for our baby sister* gauntlet."

"No kidding," Jilly muttered. She'd had that up to her eyeballs since her first date. Who could stand up to the pressure of being with a girl who had a ring of giant redwoods surrounding her? Glowering giant redwoods, to boot?

She couldn't stand the subject anymore and switched topics. "Just over three weeks until the wedding, Miss Vanessa. Everything on target?"

Annabelle snorted. "On target? It's micromanaged within an inch of its life." She lifted her glass in salute. "You are a wizard, Vanessa. You can take over planning my life anytime."

"Dealing with the hotel and Dane's travel schedule is enough, plus…" Vanessa lightly touched a hand to her pregnant belly.

"You're feeling all right?" asked Clarice Valdez, another member of the extended family. Her sister Diana was married to Jilly's eldest brother, Rafe, and Clarice's detective husband Saint was on the Austin police force with Jade.

"Couldn't be better. Once the morning sickness left, everything smoothed out." Vanessa made a moue. "But this baby's growing so fast that I can only hope I'll still fit in my dress by the time of the wedding."

"There was a cure for that, you know—you could have put my brother out of his misery long ago," Jilly reminded her.

"Dane wasn't ready, either," Clarice remarked gently. "And it's not that simple for those of us who didn't grow up cradled in the loving arms of the remarkable Sullivan family. Trust doesn't come so easily to everyone, Jilly."

Subtle shame pervaded her. Jilly had thought she knew how lucky she'd been to grow up surrounded by love—even overprotective love—but the incident at the jobsite had been an awakening. It was one thing to care about others who were touched by violence, but even her relatively mild scare had her looking at the toll in a new light. Jade had been held hostage by a madman twice, once as a teenager, then again when she was working undercover trying to hunt down a serial killer. Clarice had been taken prisoner by men who were after Saint. Annabelle had been captured by human traffickers to use as leverage, and Sean had nearly died trying to save her. Even Vanessa's life had been altered forever by tragedy when she'd lost both her parents and her own young family.

Only Jilly had skipped through life without even a brush with harm…at least until the other night. But still, she'd escaped anything serious, thanks to her mysterious savior. She had no scars to compare to any of theirs, but for a moment she really wished she could talk the experience through with these women who were like sisters. Could speak of what had happened, about how she felt.

But they were the last people she could confide in, not only because they'd be worried and want to take some kind of action, but because they would spill their guts to the very same overprotective males she did not want learning about the incident. Her family counted on her to be okay, to be sunny and happy and carefree.

She was okay, really. She might not have saved herself, but she hadn't panicked, either. She had taken action. And she was dealing with the aftermath.

But she also wasn't in the habit of hiding things from her beloved family. Thanks to her savior, though, nothing really bad had happened, and she would be more careful next time. She planned to drive past the jobsite as she went home because she refused to let one bad experience cow her, but if she saw anything, she wouldn't leave her car and would instead call for help.

"Jilly? Hello?" Clarice prompted.

Before she could blurt out anything she'd regret, she jumped to her feet, seizing the music for a distraction. "Hey, check it out—the band's coming back from break. Who wants to dance?" She grabbed Jade's hand and headed for the dance floor before any more questions could be asked.

Gabriel couldn't take the boy with him to Mama C's. Wouldn't. That was his place, his refuge.

Instead he pulled in at a nearby drugstore, next to the neighborhood convenience store.

"What are we doing here?"

"Getting supplies. You coming or staying?"

Freddie glanced around, then froze. "Coming."

Gabriel followed the direction of his gaze but didn't see anything. "Fine. Get a move on." He stalked inside, grabbing adhesive bandages, butterfly bandages, peroxide and antibiotic ointment. He found some hand wipes and added them to his stash.

Freddie was alternately dogging his heels and falling far behind.

Gabriel kept his eyes peeled on the glass of the front door. The kid was spooked, and they weren't that far from where Gabriel had found him.

He paid at the cash register, on impulse throwing in a

candy bar. The boy might need a reward by the time he was through.

Freddie clung to him like a shadow as they left, putting Gabriel between him and a group of gangbangers loitering between the two stores.

Gabriel faced them straight-on. Most bullies were actually cowards, he'd long ago learned. He easily picked out the leader and stared him right in the eyes, lifting his brows.

The leader stared back.

But he looked away first. The group huddled, shooting glances back at Freddie, both posturing and threatening…but from a careful distance.

"Get in," he told Freddie. "But don't you look away. They don't get to win."

"But they—"

"No," he snapped. "You're predator or you're prey. That simple." He cast back one last look before he opened his door.

They were gone, in search of weaker foes.

He started the truck. He'd intended to do the bandaging right here, but that would embarrass the boy. Instead, he headed to the nearby hike and bike trail along Lady Bird Lake. After parking, he emerged from the vehicle and sought the shelter of trees and a big rock just off the path. He set out supplies. "You want to clean it yourself?"

Freddie shook his head. "Can't see to do it."

"Then don't cry when it hurts."

"As if." Freddie snickered, and Gabriel found himself grinning, too.

But when he started cleaning, Freddie's face was replaced by Ahmed's.

No. Don't do this.

The Iraqi boy had been smaller, if close in age, and Gabriel had stupidly tried to clean the dying child's face of the blood, even as he knew there was nothing he could do to save the boy.

"You okay?"

Freddie's voice jolted Gabriel back to the present. He grappled for balance. For sanity. *I'm here, not there. It's over.*

He squeezed his eyes shut and concentrated on slowing down his heart.

"I don't even know your name, man."

"What?" Gabriel's head whipped back.

"Your name. You sure you okay? You on somethin' or what?"

"I'm fine." He clenched his jaw. Breathed. In. Out. "Name's Gabriel Coronado. Stand still so I can get this done."

Hurt rode high in the boy's eyes. His shoulders stiffened. "I'll do it. Go on." He snatched at a box of bandages.

Gabriel yanked them from his grasp. "I said stand still." His voice was too harsh, and the kid didn't deserve it.

Abruptly Gabriel set the box down and walked away a few feet, staring out at the lake that wound through the center of Austin.

He heard the boy's footsteps moving away and cursed. *Pull it together.* He took a deep breath that filled his chest and turned.

The boy hadn't gone far, only behind a tree where he stood, his posture sheer dejection.

"Freddie," he called. "It's… Sorry. Not your fault."

When the kid didn't move, he waited him out. "Let me get you fixed up. Least I can do for being a bastard."

When the boy emerged from behind the tree, Gabriel could see the high color in his cheeks, the moisture hastily brushed from his eyes.

You are a bastard, all right. Kid deserves better.

That was the crux of the issue, that he was no good to anyone, that people would be better off if he'd just go away.

If only he could figure out where *away* was. He'd traveled half the country looking for it.

Freddie lifted one shoulder. "I've seen worse."

Once again the kid made him want to smile. That was, what, three times today? A personal record.

"Maybe if you weren't such an ugly mug, I wouldn't get all pissed off," he said gruffly.

Freddie's eyes lit at the teasing. "Don't matter what you think. The ladies like me fine. You got you a lady?"

At Gabriel's silence, the boy continued "Didn't think so. I could give you pointers."

"I'll keep that in mind." Then Gabriel focused on the task ahead, ruthlessly rejecting any side trips to other times and places. Other injured faces.

"Ow!" Freddie hissed when the peroxide went on.

"C'mon. Peroxide doesn't sting."

"How you know?"

"I've had a nick or two." Or a body full of scars.

When Gabriel pushed together the cut above Freddie's eye, then taped it tightly with butterfly bandages, Freddie hissed. "That hurts. You sure ain't no nurse."

"Fill out a form in the complaint department. Be still."

But Gabriel could see the twinkle in the boy's eyes. Sass was good. Better than fear anytime. If the kid could still complain, he wasn't beaten down altogether.

"So, seen your buddy Mako lately?"

Every trace of amusement fled. "No."

"He do this to you?" He wasn't buying the denial. "Is he already out?"

"Don't care." But the tension in his frame said something else.

"Is he trying to make you steal again? Trying to scare you

Chapter Five

Despite the late night and busy day that had preceded it, Jilly still awoke with the birds, just as her mother always had. She adored her mother and wanted to be like her in almost every way…emphasis on *almost.* To be a bona fide night owl seemed so sophisticated, so worldly…but she could count on one hand the number of mornings she'd managed to sleep past six, even as a teenager.

Great for a rancher. Wholesome, all-American, disgustingly so.

Not one iota glamorous, or even interesting.

Oh, good grief, what was wrong with her? She seldom spent time navel-gazing. She was a person who acted, who was sure—of herself, of her opinions, of the next step and the next…

She stared out the window at the blessedly crisp fall morning that gave everyone hope that the endless summer would finally be over. She sipped her coffee and tried not to think about anything of substance.

Then she chuckled and shook her head. Her brain never seemed to shut off, and today was no different. Work, that was the answer to any kind of blues. Get off your tush and get busy.

She glanced at the clock, then considered. She could start

some soup, then she'd leave it in the slow cooker al. when she got home, the house would smell fanta. homey and welcoming, and she'd have a nourishing instead of a carton of yogurt or whatever she could together after a long day.

One more glance out into the faint light of morning.

Yes, her house would smell like a welcome home, but it would still just be her here, all by herself. She loved her little cottage and had never felt lonely here before. Maybe it was Dane's fault. She'd gotten used to having him stay with her, then he'd gone and fallen in love—and okay, she'd set him and Vanessa up to be together and was glad they were, but now the house felt empty. Would she ever have her own someone? What would he be like?

Her mind leaped to the man she'd met, Gabriel Coronado. What was his story? Had he been her rescuer? He was gorgeous, in a real man kind of way—not a pretty boy at all, but dark and…compelling.

But friendly? Approachable? No. Not her type at all.

Would anyone ever be?

Snap out of it, Jilly. If you're lonely, get that dog you've been wanting.

Resolutely, she turned from the window and started pulling ingredients from the refrigerator. This was just a passing phase, a reaction to the last of her brothers finding his true love. She was younger than all of them, and she had plenty of time. None of them had anticipated meeting the love of his life when he had. Each had been leading a productive existence, just as she was. Her time would come, and in the meantime, she had plans, lots of them.

She threw an apron over her tank and sleep shorts and began cooking.

f visiting the current jobsite nearly daily, ome was under construction.

hat she told herself as she drove over on her way ffice, despite having been there at the close of the ious day and already well aware of exactly what progress had been made.

This visit had nothing at all to do with any interest in the tall, dark and delicious new volunteer who'd saved their bacon the day before. He wasn't, after all, very forthcoming about himself. He could be anyone, a visitor to their city, a rich man slumming, an out of work laborer—though with those skills and such a formidable work ethic, to say nothing of that powerful body, being unemployed would make absolutely no sense—but, okay, the point was that he was a mystery, one just begging to be solved.

And he also might be the man who'd saved her.

She wouldn't push, she wouldn't pry. And if she could hear her brothers snickering inside her mind, well, they weren't here, were they? *You're relentless, Jilly*, they would say—and had. *Once you get something in your head, heaven help anyone who hopes to get it out.*

She stopped her car and mentally flicked her brothers away like so many drops of water from wet hands.

Teo looked up from where he was making notes in a little pad he carried in his front shirt pocket. "He's not coming."

"What?"

"That's why you're here, right? You didn't get the new guy's life story within the first hour, and you can't stand it. You're back for more."

"When did you start channeling my family?"

"You are an open book to me, little girl. Anyway, women just can't stand mystery in a man. Got to dig until it's all gone, along with every last scrap of magic."

"Teo! You're a romantic. I never knew."

The tips of his ears turned red, and he took off his cap, scratched his head and replaced the cap, settling the brim. "Lot about me you don't know."

"I know you're amazing," she said in perfect sincerity. "And that the day you showed up, a whole lot of people's lives got better, especially mine."

"Stop that." He scowled.

Yet she could see his pleasure. She nudged his arm with her shoulder. "Oh, suck it up. A few compliments won't kill you."

"Won't change the facts either. He's not coming. Wish to hell he would 'cause he's a find, but someone with those skills has a real job. Don't know why he showed up yesterday, but I'm sure glad he did. We're back caught up, and if nothing else happens, Lucia's gonna have her house in time for Halloween." He nodded toward the street. "Troops arriving. Got to get everybody squared away. Head on over to your office and start dialing for dollars, don't be hanging around and in my hair."

Jilly grinned. Teo was as crusty as he was irreplaceable. She adored him. "Love you, too, Teo," she said, blowing a kiss just to get his goat.

"Will you stop that?" He made a dismissing motion with his hand and headed for his workers, his ears and the back of his neck fiery red now.

She'd grown up with ornery old guys and she had a big soft spot for the breed. Nothing started her day—or yanked her out of the pity party she'd been fighting this morning—quite like a little mutual razzing with Teo. She waved to the workers, noting that Gabriel Coronado indeed was not among them, and turned back to her car.

Then she saw that same ancient, scarred dark blue pickup coming down the street with the very man in question inside it.

She glanced back at Teo, lifted her eyebrows and gave him a cocky smile as if to say *See?* She hesitated before grasping her door handle, ever so tempted to stay for a while.

You didn't get the new guy's life story within the first hour, and you can't stand it.

And what was so bad about that? Teo certainly wouldn't make the effort—guys never did. Besides, she still had that feeling about Gabriel Coronado, that he might very well have been the man who rescued her.

But he'd also chosen to disappear. Why? Was he wanted by the authorities? Surely not, or he was taking a terrible risk showing up in broad daylight. Maybe he just didn't like the limelight, but he still deserved her thanks. She could do so quietly, without a lot of fuss.

Okay, so quietly was not exactly her modus operandi. She could, though, if she wanted to.

But what did *he* want, her savior? What was he saying by his silence? By showing up here?

Women just can't stand mystery in a man. Got to dig until it's all gone, along with every last scrap of magic.

Mostly, Teo was exactly right—about her, anyway. She wasn't a fan of the unsolved. She liked to figure out exactly how things worked, what the puzzle pieces were, and put them all together. Make things happen with what she learned.

But maybe this once, a little mystery wouldn't be a bad thing. She'd thanked her rescuer, and she would do so again when she was certain of his identity, but whatever his reasons were for not revealing himself to her, didn't she owe him for keeping her from serious harm? What kind of repayment would it be if she forced herself on him, dragged him into a spotlight he didn't welcome?

She wasn't unfamiliar with men with shadows—her brother Rafe had nearly died in combat and spent a very long time recovering both physically and from the loss of his men. The horrific cases Alex handled when he was in the FBI, especially when he was a hostage negotiator, had marked him. Liam was generally more sunny like her, but when his former girlfriend had committed suicide, he'd struggled with blaming himself for not saving her, and most recently, Dane had lost his best friend and guide on a mountaintop. Falling in love with Vanessa had brought sunlight into his darkness, but he was still wrestling with his guilt, no matter that Dane himself had barely survived the mountain.

She had no idea what this man's story was or why he was so reserved, but the girl who'd thought sunshine and kisses could banish all clouds had grown up at least a little in these years of working with people caught in the grips of hardship.

Her family members would probably fall over in a dead faint to hear it, but she was going to leave this man alone.

For now, anyway.

She saw him emerge from his truck and she simply nodded and smiled.

He did the same. Minus the smile.

It was a start.

She got in her car and left to dial for dollars.

Gabriel halted with one hand on the open window frame. There she was again, the sunny strawberry blonde, a bright, fresh note in a day filled with misgivings.

She nodded and smiled.

Taken aback, he hesitated, then returned the greeting.

But he exhaled with relief when she simply got into her car and left. After a moment, he stirred and shut his truck door, then moved to the tool chest in the back and lifted his tool belt from inside.

Movement in the shadows caught his eye.

The boy was here. Hiding. Staring toward where Jilly had driven off. Gabriel stayed where he was, letting the boy decide his next move. He would come or he wouldn't.

Out of the corner of his eye, he spotted movement from the trees. Casually he strolled around the bed of his truck to give the boy a more sheltered spot to approach, then waited.

"Hey." The boy was dressed in the same clothes as yesterday.

"Hey." Gabriel nodded. "You ready?"

Freddie hesitated. "Miss Jilly coming back?"

"No idea. She wasn't dressed for construction, so maybe not."

"Good. I mean, she's okay and all, but…" The boy shrugged. "I'd rather just work."

"Your breakfast is in that bag on the passenger seat. Eat first."

Freddie didn't waste any time. While he practically inhaled the food, Gabriel busied himself gathering tools. "What did you do when you were here before?"

"Just picked up trash and stuff."

"Might be all you get to do today."

"You said you'd teach me."

"I will, but I'm not running the job. You might have to do both."

Freddie finished the last bite, drank the rest of the milk

Gabriel had brought, then put his trash in the sack. “Okay. What now?”

“Now we go talk to the boss man and see what he needs from us.” Gabriel kept his movements slow as he clapped one hand on the boy’s shoulder. Freddie tensed at the touch, but Gabriel kept his grip light and easy, and eventually the boy relaxed.

“Somebody did a damn fine job doctoring you.”

“Yeah, right. I was thinkin’ about suin’ the quack.”

“The quack doesn’t have any money.”

“Figures.”

“Okay, ready?”

“Yeah.”

“Yes, sir. Important job skill.”

A flick of suspicious dark eyes. “Yes, sir.”

“Good.” Gabriel removed his hand. “You get enough breakfast?”

“Yeah—yes, sir. The breakfast tacos were good.”

“Work hard, and lunch might be on me.”

A small curve of the boy’s mouth. “Yes, sir.”

Gabriel walked toward Teo. “Morning.”

The older man turned. “Didn’t know if you’d show.”

“Me, either.”

A brisk nod. “See you picked up a helper. Freddie, right?”

“Yea—yes, sir.”

“What do you need today?” Gabriel asked. “Repainting the kitchen?”

“Got folks less skilled than you who can do that. You ever hang cabinets?”

“A few.”

“Should be arriving anytime. Can I put you on that? You can start in the bathrooms while we’re painting in here. I can help or find someone, since it’s not a one-man job.”

"I've done it alone, but I have help right here." Gabriel turned to Freddie. "You ever used a nail gun before?"

"Really?" The boy's eyes went wide, then darkened. "No—but I could learn, I know I could."

"You'll be watching in the beginning, helping measure and hold while I nail first, but you pay close attention, and you'll get your chance." The boy was skinny and malnourished, but Gabriel knew how much strength desperation could provide.

"Sweet!"

"Let's get you in a tool belt first."

Skinny shoulders stiffened. "I don't have one."

"You can use my old one."

"I'll get it!" Freddie took off running toward Gabriel's truck.

"Where'd you turn him up?" Teo asked. "And why's he not in school?"

"I'm not a social worker."

Teo gave him a long, measuring look. "Doesn't matter. Jilly might as well be." He stuck out his hand. "Real glad to have you back."

Gabriel hesitated. "Only for today. Got work to get back to."

Teo kept his hand out there. "I'll take whatever I can get. You do good work."

Gabriel accepted the hand and shook. "I could say the same."

Chapter Six

Jilly read the paragraph again, then stared into space, fingers tapping on her desk. Grant applications were the bane of her existence. Oh, she could write well enough, but she was so much more persuasive in person.

Her phone rang, and she eagerly seized the distraction. "Foundations for Families, Jilly speaking."

"There you are, Sunshine," boomed her favorite voice in the world.

"Hi, Dad. How are you?"

"Missing my best girl."

"I miss you, too. How's Mom?"

"Still too good for me, but I'm counting on you to keep my secret."

Jilly smiled. The ongoing love affair between her parents was the rock-solid foundation of her life. After nearly forty years, the love between the elegant Celeste Sandoval Sullivan and her big, burly Hal burned steady and bright. "Wild horses couldn't drag it from me."

"Speaking of horses, young Robbie is training a yearling out of Rafe's Chieftain, and he's going to be every bit the horseman his father is."

"That's a high bar. I've never seen anyone whose touch with horses even came close to Rafe's." Jilly settled in for a good chat, smiling. Her father adored all his grandchildren, but little Roberto—not so little now at nine—had been his first, and their not being biologically related counted for nothing in Hal Sullivan's definition of family. He'd taken on her two eldest brothers as part of the package of marrying the widowed Celeste, and he loved Rafe and Alex as fiercely as if he'd been there from their conception.

"You should come see for yourself. It's been too long."

"I know." She sighed. "It's hard to get away. You'll be here in less than three weeks, though. I can't believe Dane the wanderer is getting married."

"We Sullivans may take our own sweet time, but when we fall, we fall hard. Anyone caught your eye yet, Sunshine?"

Her mind immediately drifted to the mysterious man who'd surprised her by showing up at the jobsite this morning. Immediately she straightened in her chair. Interest in a man was another topic sure to alert the bat-sensitive ears of the men in her family. "Not really."

"What about that lawyer fella Clarice told Diana about?"

Exactly her point. She'd dated Patrick twice, and the Sullivan jungle drums were already making them into a couple. Her privacy was a moot point when it came to the raft of brothers and sisters-in-law and their sisters and brothers and friends…every one of whom considered watching over Jilly a sacred duty.

"Dad…." she remonstrated.

"You have held my heart in your hand since the first moment I saw you, little mite of a thing you were after all those strapping boys. I won't apologize for caring about your happiness." She heard both the lack of remorse in his voice and the tiny note of hurt.

"No girl ever had a better father," she said, and it was true. If in his heart Hal Sullivan wanted her close by until the day he was forced to give her into the keeping of a man who'd damn well better treat her like a queen, he'd never tried to corral her into being some hothouse flower. She'd learned to ride and hunt and fish with him and her brothers, and he'd told her from her earliest memory that she was as smart as anyone and as capable. He'd encouraged her to reach out and grab what she wanted and not take any guff for her beliefs or who she was.

"Mom got the best man in the world, but sadly, there's only one of you. I know you wish I'd find my prince, but I don't see any reason to simply settle, not when I've seen what can be. You and Mom have set a tough example to follow, but I'd rather be alone the rest of my life than be with a man who's only suitable. I want a man who'll look at me the way you look at Mom, like she's a miracle."

"She is," he responded, "But don't make us into a fairytale. Lord knows we've had to smooth off a lot of rough edges on each other. Your mother is not exactly a shrinking violet, and it's possible I might have been a little hard-headed about a thing or two."

Might have. Jilly burst out laughing. Her dad was stone-hard stubborn, the proverbial bull in the china shop, a plain-spoken man with a clear vision of what should happen and plenty of will to manhandle it into reality. Her mother, on the other hand, was so smooth about her handling that most people didn't realize how thoroughly they'd been managed until later, if ever. They had probably fought more in the early years of their marriage, long before Jilly came into the family, but she'd never seen that. She did know, however, that they were both capable of a blazing row.

Followed by long disappearances into their bedroom which mortified the children when they emerged with bright smiles and embarrassing displays of affection.

"Love takes work, Sunshine. What you see between Celeste and me is years in the making. Happy marriages don't spring into being fully-formed."

"So how do you know?" she asked him. "When so many marriages end in divorce, how can you ever be sure you've picked the right person?"

Now it was her father who was laughing. "You don't, sweetheart. You listen to your heart, and you hope you're right, but that's where the work begins. You cling to that hope and you don't give up on it. You stick, even when you want to cut and run. You don't assume that every bad patch is a sign that you're wrong for each other. Couples give up too easily these days. Love is hard, but nothing worthwhile ever just falls into your lap. Love takes a lot of pure-dee stubbornness, honey. And sometimes only one of you has that sort of faith at any given point, so that one has to hold onto it for both of you until the storm passes. You can't throw in the towel, even when it seems like everything's coming apart."

Wow. Her parents' marriage seemed so ideal from the outside that she'd never seriously considered that they might have had more hurdles to deal with than simple spats. She didn't want to discourage her father's unusual candor, though, by probing, so she lightened the moment. "Well, I guess I've got that pure-dee stubbornness part down, at least." Hearing him talk, however, only made her more aware that she'd never truly had her heart touched by a man. "Maybe one day I'll meet someone worthy of that level of work."

Again, maddeningly, her rescuer sprang to mind. If Gabriel Coronado was indeed that man, he clearly had no interest in her, so why couldn't she forget him?

"That's what I'm telling you, sweetheart. You don't always know ahead of time. Love unfolds at its own pace. And sometimes the best person for you isn't the obvious choice.

I'm speaking of your mother, of course," he joked. "I was definitely already a prince when she met me—no, Celeste, you can't have the phone. I'm telling this story my way."

Jilly heard her mother's laughter in the background, the affection in it. "Tell Mom I can't wait to see her. I'm so glad you're staying with me."

"Well, Vanessa gives better room service in that honeymoon cottage of hers, I have to say."

Jilly grinned. "Yeah, but you love being my handyman, you know you do."

A gusty sigh. "A man has to take care of his little girl, at least until some ruffian comes along and tries to say he's worthy to take over."

"I don't need taking care of, Dad. I'm all grown up now."

"You will always be my little girl."

And however much she balked at the over-protectiveness, she cherished her father's love. "You'll always be my hero, Dad."

"Thank you, Sunshine." Hal cleared his throat. "Your mother is reminding me that you're at work, and I'd better let you go."

"I work plenty of extra hours, not to worry."

"See, that's the problem. All you do is work. You need to get out and play more—"

"Okay, bye, Dad. I hear my other line wanting to ring."

He chuckled. "All right, all right. See you soon, sweetheart. Get that to-do list ready for me."

"You're the best, Dad. Love to Mom."

"We love you, too."

Jilly hung up reluctantly, feeling the stab of homesickness. She glanced out the window and tried to resettle herself in urban Austin instead of the big old house in La Paloma that, like the constant wind of West Texas, always called to her.

But when she still couldn't resolve how to fix this section of the application, she closed the file on her laptop and began the process of closing the office. She'd work on this more tonight at home, but for now, she'd head over to the jobsite. She had invoices to discuss with Teo. Sure, she could simply call him and relay the information, but she'd stayed away and been a good little office drone for as long as she could stand it.

The staccato of the nail gun was under Gabriel's control today, so the sharp pops, too reminiscent of small arms fire, could be anticipated. Two volunteers conducted a desultory conversation while picking up trash and sweeping dust in compliance with Teo's rule that the premises be cleaned up at the end of every day, rather than leaving debris strewn everywhere until the end, as was common practice on most jobsites.

Teo himself was outside, talking landscaping with Lucia's father-in-law Alfredo. The old man seemed to be discussing which neighbors were volunteering cuttings from their gardens and how much his wife had loved her flowers, especially her irises.

Mama C had loved them, too. She had masses of them in both her front and back yards.

"Fifty and a half, right?" Freddie asked as he held the measuring tape against the wall, starting at floor level.

"That's right. How far is that from the ceiling? And don't use the tape measure. Do the math."

"Oh, maaan. Why you keep doing that?"

Gabriel stifled a grin. "Because you don't think math matters."

Freddie cast him a slant-eyed look of disapproval. "I know you gonna ask me why I ain't in school," he muttered. "I can see it comin'."

"You're reading my mind now?"

"Don't know who could," the boy muttered, then looked off into space, scowling ferociously, but it didn't take him long. "Forty-five and half inches."

The kid was smarter than he let on, Gabriel was convinced. Ahmed had been smart, too, despite the total lack of formal education.

But he didn't want to think about Ahmed. He focused on Freddie. "That wasn't so hard, now was it?"

Freddie marked the spot with the pencil he'd put behind his ear, imitating Gabriel. "So I already know how to do that. Don't need school. Can I use the nail gun again?" His eager gaze shifted when it caught on something outside. "Oh, shit."

"Hey—watch your mouth." Gabriel turned and saw Jilly emerge from her car.

"Look, I gotta go. Be seein' you." Freddie wheeled for the back door.

Gabriel snagged his shoulder. "We're not done here."

"But—"

"You said you liked her."

The boy stared at the ground and all but shuffled his feet. "I do, but—" A twitch of his shoulder. "She got hurt 'cause I left."

"So you're going to run away again? A man faces the consequences of his decisions."

The boy's face was a study in misery.

"You don't think she'll forgive you?" Gabriel didn't know her at all, but a blind man could see what she was like. The boy had little positive experience with adults, however, from what few details Gabriel had unearthed about the harsh reality of Freddie's life. "C'mon, you know she will." But that wasn't the point, was it? "Man up and tell her."

Freddie's head rose. "Tell her what?"

"Whatever you're feeling."

A small snort. "That's girl talk."

It really was. Or worse, shrink talk. "Look, you don't have to cry or get all flowery. Just…hell, I don't know. Tell her you're sorry for what Mako did or—Screw it." He returned to the work. "Measure the cut for the stringer so we can get done." He hadn't signed on to be a counselor. Some days he only talked to the cat, if he spoke at all.

The boy walked to the pile of one by twos, shoulders stiff with hurt.

Damn it. Gabriel shut his eyes and grasped for one more shred of patience at the end of a long day filled with way too much human contact.

Once he'd been good at this. Hadn't *Mama C* called him her Pied Piper because of the way kids flocked to him?

"Hi, Freddie."

Gabriel whirled, braced to defend. He, who'd once had the best ears on his team, hadn't even heard her approach.

"I'm sorry. I didn't mean…"

Their eyes met, hers a sweetly concerned blue that crept in under his guard. He tore his gaze away. "Freddie. Someone's here to talk to you."

The boy approached, lumber in hand, and laid the piece on top of the base cabinet they'd already installed. "Hey," he greeted Jilly. "I'm measuring this before we cut it." He held up the tape in his other hand.

"I see that." She flicked a glance at Gabriel, then returned her attention to the boy. "What happened to you, Freddie? Who hurt you?"

"Nobody." A little shrug. "Just a fight."

She hesitated. "Ah. I have four brothers. I don't get why guys fight, but I know it happens." Freddie seemed as surprised at her acceptance as Gabriel was. She grinned. "How does the other guy look?"

Freddie wilted a little, exchanged a quick glance with Gabriel, then found his bravado. "I did me some damage."

"Fighting's no solution, you know that, right?"

Okay, here was the do-gooder he expected.

Freddie's eyes darted over to Gabriel. Gabriel shrugged. *Play it however you want* was his message.

"Yeah—uh, yes, ma'am."

"Good. Are you okay to be working?"

Yep. Do-gooder.

The kid was clearly affronted. "I'm fine."

"All right."

Gabriel wasn't sure he believed her easy acceptance, but it was none of his business. Best thing that could happen to him was for Jilly to take the boy under her wing. The system failed a lot of people, but it didn't fail everyone. Maybe Freddie would be the exception.

"Is Beto here, too?" she asked.

"Uh-uh…" His gaze slid to Gabriel. "I mean, no, ma'am."

"I see. So you're helping Mr. Coronado?" Her gaze at Gabriel held speculation before she focused again on the boy. "Freddie?"

"Yeah—uh, yes, ma'am. That is, he's teaching me about carpentry and stuff." His face screwed up in a frown, and he spoke in a rush. "Um, I'm sorry. Mako, he one bad motherf—uh, dude. I shoulda stayed with you," he mumbled, eyes locked on the wood clenched in his hand.

"Oh, Freddie," she said, moving to place a hand on his shoulder. Gabriel waited for her to gush or something, but she didn't. "I'm glad you left. Everything turned out okay. I'm really happy you're safe. Thank you for coming to help out today. Does Beto know you were there with Mako?"

"You didn't tell Ms. Marin?"

"Of course not." She glanced over at Gabriel. "You told Mr. Coronado about it?"

"He guessed. I came back the next night to see was the place okay now. He, uh, he caught me and we, um, we talked."

Her look at Gabriel was difficult to decipher. "You were here the night after?"

Just as you were, Gabriel almost said. *And shouldn't have been.* He only shrugged. "I was out running."

Her gaze caught on his, and she worried at that plump lower lip for a second before turning back to the boy.

He was not at all pleased to find himself reacting to the sight of her teeth pressing against a far too lush mouth that generated images he did not welcome.

Crap. Why did this fierce, nosy little blonde, of all people, manage to remind him for the first time since he'd returned that he was male and had once had a very strong sexual appetite?

"So you came here after school today?" she asked.

A panicked look sprang into the boy's eyes.

Apparently she saw it, too. "Freddie, you know we appreciate your help, and I'm happy that you're learning from Mr. Coronado, but we don't want the truant officer coming down on us, or other authorities, as a matter of fact. You aren't old enough to quit school, and you're too smart to do that, anyway, right?"

Gabriel could feel as well as see the boy's fear. "We're working on it," he said. Now why the hell had he stepped in?

Her head rose, her chin jutting. "Mr. Coronado—"

"Freddie, I need my other nail punch. It's in my toolbox. Go get it, so we can finish."

The boy dashed off, and Gabriel shifted to keep the boy in sight, in case Freddie took a notion to disappear because of the interrogation. "Don't do that," he ordered her over his shoulder.

"Excuse me?"

The snotty tone was nails on a chalkboard. He whirled on her. "You push him too hard with rules, and you'll force him right back into the arms of guys like Mako. Or do you not get that he's on his own, Miss Goody Two-Shoes?"

She recoiled. "What? You have a lot of nerve—hey!" she said when he turned away again. "Don't ignore me."

"I'm not. I'm watching to see if he comes back or runs."

She followed the direction of his gaze. He wondered if she could tell that Freddie was deliberating whether to bring the punch Gabriel didn't actually need or to take off.

Gabriel nodded at him reassuringly. And prepared to chase the kid.

Oh, yeah. He'd sure learned his lesson in Iraq, hadn't he?

"Do you think he's homeless?" she asked quietly.

"He says not, but…"

"I can get him into a shelter. I'll go make some calls right now."

He clamped his hand on her arm. "Leave it. Are you that naïve? He'll run the first chance he gets, and we'll never see him again."

Blue eyes narrowed. "I can't just leave him out on the streets."

Gabriel sighed. "I've got it covered."

"He's staying with you?"

"Not exactly."

"Then I have to—"

"Have you ever tried to tame anything wild?" he interrupted.

"Have I what?"

At last Freddie held up the tool Gabriel had requested and began to walk back toward the house.

"Not now," he told her, *sotto voce.* "Promise me you'll leave him alone for now."

"I can't do that."

He locked his eyes on hers. "Give me a week."

"To do what? Get him back in school? Find him a home?"

"To show him there's someone in the world he can trust." *Heaven help him. And me.*

She leaned in, whispering furiously. "He can trust me. I have a lot of experience."

"Not in any world he understands. I bet you have two parents who adore each other and siblings who are close."

"What?" She blinked. "So?"

"Knew it." Freddie was nearly to them. "Later," he muttered to her. "You said you were grateful for my help on the house. I'm asking for one lousy week in return."

She stared at him, mouth open. Then she spotted the boy, too. "One week," she practically spat. "But if you lose him…"

Gabriel only shook his head and went to meet Freddie partway. "That's the one. Now tell Ms. Sullivan—"

"Jilly," she said, mouth tight. "Everyone calls me Jilly."

"Tell her goodbye. We've got one last cabinet to hang before we can quit."

"But he's just a boy and that's a heavy—" she began.

Gabriel whipped around and glared at her. "Goodbye, Ms. Sullivan." He gave her his back. "Okay," he said to Freddie, who was glancing between them. "Measure the board. Remember, measure twice…"

"Cut once," Freddie finished. "Got it." He looked around Gabriel. "See ya, Miss Jilly."

"Oh, you can count on that." Irritation rang in every syllable.

Gabriel could almost feel the darts of disapproval she was aiming into his back.

"You ready?" he said to Freddie, ignoring her.

"I get to use the nail gun, right?"

Gabriel found himself grinning. "Right."

"Yesss!" Freddie danced ahead, everything else forgotten.

Chapter Seven

"You trying to run off my best volunteer?" Teo ambled up behind her, then got a gander at her expression. "Whoa. You mad, girl? I've never seen you angry."

Because she seldom allowed anger the upper hand. She was of the opinion that cheerfulness was a habit that made the world a better place, but that man… "What do you know about him?"

"The boy or Gabriel?"

"Mr. Coronado."

"Wow, he sure put a burr under your saddle, didn't he? Mr. Coronado, huh? What happened?"

"That child is homeless."

Teo frowned. "And?"

"He's also not in school, and he's malnourished. I bet you can see his ribs under that shirt."

"He had breakfast, I know that much, because Gabriel brought him some. Also bought the boy lunch today. He's good with him. Real patient, teaching him skills but expecting him to work hard, too. And he makes the boy clean up his language and say *sir* and *ma'am*."

"That's stopgap at best. Freddie needs a safe place to stay and a family to care for him."

"We all do, but the kid's skittish. He hung back in the

bushes behind the house this morning until Gabriel got here. Says something about both of them that he's stayed here all day and worked hard."

"He feels guilty."

"Why?"

"He was one of the thieves who tore up the house."

Teo's eyes narrowed. "When Beto's his friend?"

"I think he's scared of the other guy, the one who—" She bit her lip. No one but the officers and her savior knew what had really happened that night. "The one who orchestrated the theft."

"Why's the kid not in jail, too?"

"He can be saved. I made him leave before the police arrived."

Teo closed his eyes for a second. "*Madre de Dios*...you sent him away, and he left you here alone with a guy who's in jail now?" He appeared ready to charge over and give Freddie an earful.

"Don't, Teo. He needs help, not a tongue-lashing. Anyway, he already apologized."

"Wait a minute. Let me get this straight. There were two guys here, late at night, and you were with them before the cops arrived? Alone?" He loomed over her. "We never got to finish this conversation, I'm realizing. Please tell me you stayed inside your car while you called 9-1-1."

"A man arrived and took control of the situation before the cops got here."

"A man? Who was it?"

She couldn't help glancing toward the house. The man. "I didn't get his name. He left once the cops arrived."

Teo followed her gaze. "You saying you think it was Gabriel? Can't you tell?"

"It was dark, and that man had a full beard and a cap

pulled down over his face."

"Easy enough to find out." Teo took a step.

"No, Teo. I don't think… That man wasn't eager to take credit. And Gabriel isn't exactly talkative, either."

"Gabriel, huh? So you might forgive him, after all?"

She sighed. "He accused me of being naïve. Said I couldn't possibly understand Freddie's life because my family loves me too much." She glanced over at Teo and shrugged. "I'm not as innocent as he seems to think. I've dealt with a lot of people whose lives are in crisis."

"You have, and you've helped a whole bunch of them. No telling how many people you've gotten jobs for or helped work out their Social Security or found housing for them. You don't have to apologize for an accident of birth. Seems to me that loving family gave you a real good foundation for spreading love around to those who need it."

She ducked her head, touched by his words. "Thank you. Just because I'm cheerful doesn't mean I can't see that the world is a troubled place."

"Your Dad's nickname is appropriate. You are a ray of sunshine for a whole lot of folks."

"Wow, Mr. Grumpy. Better watch out or other people will realize that you're a softie."

Teo snorted. "About as soft as that hard head of yours. Said you were cheerful, didn't say you were easy to deal with. Don't get too high on yourself."

Cheer restored, Jilly pressed a kiss to his cheek, simply because she knew it would fluster him.

Just then her phone rang.

"Good thing," Teo muttered. "Get on with you now. Don't need a bunch of foolishness on my jobsite."

Jilly pressed the button to answer and moved to a quieter spot, grinning over Teo's discomfiture. When she heard who the caller was, she whirled and did a little happy dance at Teo, pumping her fist while trying to keep her composure on the phone.

The second the call ended, she raced across the ground and threw herself into Teo's arms. "We got the that last grant I applied for in the spring—the entire amount I asked for! We can build two houses at once, for a change! The Fosters and the Delgados both move to the front of the line!" She grabbed Teo and danced him in a circle, laughing, thrilled that two families who'd lost everything in last summer's wildfires would get a second chance.

But soon Teo slowed the dance, his expression troubled.

"What is it?" she asked.

"I was going to talk to you. My wife has her heart set on doing some traveling. I wouldn't be able to run these two jobs at the same time, anyway. The lots for those families are nowhere close to each other, and with most of our help being unskilled volunteers, I have to be onsite most of the time."

Jilly's delight fizzled. It wasn't as though she hadn't known Teo couldn't keep going forever, but…

"I'm sure sorry, Jilly. I've been trying to figure out how to tell you, but…"

She squeezed his shoulder. "Of course you need to slow down. You work as hard as a man half your age. Don't feel bad about it, Teo, just help me figure out who…" She saw his eyes drift toward the man loading up his old blue pickup. "Gabriel? You want him to run one of them, is that what you're thinking?"

"He's either worked construction for a living or done a lot of it. He knows his stuff."

"You think he'd accept? It's a full-time job, and we can't pay him much."

"No idea. I wasn't sure he'd be here for a second day."

"Oh." She gnawed her lip. "We could ask, though, right?"

Teo observed him and pondered. "The man is not exactly an open book. Something weighs on him, but he's not a talker." He turned to her. "How soon were you wanting to start those jobs?"

"We won't get the funds for probably at least two weeks, and you know how much planning goes into setting up the schedule and ordering the materials, far better than I do."

He removed his cap, scratched his head and replaced the cap. "Let's see how things go for a few days. If Gabriel continues to show up, that'll tell us something. And the wife will understand if we have to wait. She's not much for traveling in winter, anyway."

"Family comes first, Teo. We'll figure this out." She grimaced. "But I'd better see if I can increase our chances that he'll return by apologizing. I probably was a little high-handed in my reaction, though I don't like leaving things hanging with Freddie."

Have you ever tried to tame anything wild?

She remembered Rafe's endless patience with injured animals and his dog, Lobo. While she would jump in too quickly and too often scare them off.

In some ways, Gabriel reminded her of her eldest brother, the silent depths, the haunted shadows, the stealth with which he moved and the power. Something about him called to her. Kept him on her mind.

And the similarity struck her. Could it be that he was former military like Rafe? That would explain his intense reaction when she'd surprised him earlier.

A lot to consider, especially for someone more skilled in action and conversation than contemplation.

Maybe Freddie wasn't the only wild thing that needed tender care.

"Okay, gotta book, man." Freddie gave a casual wave over his shoulder.

Gabriel resisted the urge to ask him where he'd go. "You all set?" he asked instead.

Freddie glanced back, all teenage bravado. "Yeah, sure." He flashed a grin. "I mean yes, sir."

Gabriel chuckled. "You did good work today."

The boy's smile widened. "A natural with a nail gun—pop, pop." He mimed the triggering motion, reminding Gabriel all too readily of boys with deadly weapons caught in wars of all kinds. Of small, skinny Ahmed with an automatic rifle he'd scavenged. The weapon had been more than half his height. Gabriel had first tried to confiscated it, then settled for teaching the boy how to operate it safely.

Ahmed might still be alive if he were unarmed.

Gabriel had trained young men in several countries to defend themselves and their homes, and he'd been good at it, but teaching this one ways to get through the world without violence felt better. "Maybe I'll see you tomorrow."

"Maybe." Freddie shrugged and kept walking.

"Freddie, wait!" Jilly called, hurrying across the ground.

The boy's shoulders hunched.

"I'm not going to ask about school, I promise," she teased, drawing up even with Gabriel.

Freddie finally faced her.

"I got a little crazy this morning and made this big pot of stew that's been cooking all day, but now I realize it's about ten times as much as I can eat. I could use some help with it. Could I interest you?"

Well. She wasn't only determined, she was cagey. Dangling food in front of a teenage boy…he had to hand it to her. She didn't give up easily. And that would be one more step in shifting the burden to her. She lived for the stuff, he could tell.

"I dunno…" Freddie glanced over at him.

"Oh. Well, of course Mr. Coronado is welcome, too." Wide blue eyes turned on him.

No. Not happening. "I don't—"

Freddie spoke over him. "I guess I could, if Gabriel's going."

He jittered with his need to get away from all of them. He'd already gotten too involved. He craved silence. And solitude.

If he accepted, there'd be more talking. No way this woman would simply eat and be done. He'd done more talking today than he had in a long time.

But he could be sure the boy would eat if he said yes.

Hell. "I could probably eat."

"So glad I could twist your arm."

Cheeky, too. No telling what else was wrapped up in that curvy little package.

"Okay!" she said brightly. "Freddie, would you like to ride with me?"

The boy hesitated.

"That's all right. You and, um, Gabriel can follow me over. It's not far."

Gabriel now, was it? She got her way, so now the frost vanished?

The boy would eat, he reminded himself. Resigned that solitude would have to wait, he headed for his truck.

She was right, she didn't live far. He wasn't sure what he'd expected, given that she drove a sporty but not expensive car and wore young, hip clothes suited to her age, which he'd guess at mid-to-late twenties. A condo, he'd assumed, or an apartment, one of the trendy ones now dotting SoCo.

But no, she lived in a house, a little cottage as old as Mama C's house. An overgrown vacant lot was across the street. The neighborhood was being gentrified here and there, but the homes around her were mostly older and modest like hers.

The covered front porch ran the width of the cottage, and on it hung a wicker porch swing amply cushioned by bright pillows. Plants spilled from an assortment of colorful pots. The front door swung wide to reveal a cheery, vibrant interior, the living room filled with a comfortable instead of stylish sofa and a scattering of cozy chairs.

Every inch of the place said *Welcome.*

"I'm glad you came," she said to Freddie. "If you'd like to wash up, there's a bathroom right down the hall."

Freddie glanced at him, and Gabriel nodded.

Then he was alone with her. He hadn't made small talk in a very long time.

"Nice place," he managed.

"Thank you."

"You always invite strangers home?"

"You're not strangers."

"Next thing to it."

"I like making new friends." Blithely ignoring his warning, she led the way into the kitchen.

He lingered in the living room. Something did smell amazing.

You didn't used to be an asshole, Gabriel.

A sharp exhale. He shook his head, then followed. "What can I do to help?" He moved to the sink and washed his hands. "Sorry we're both so sweaty."

She pulled a baguette toward her and began slicing. "I have a close personal acquaintance with sweat. My parents were big on their kids helping out around the ranch."

"You grew up on a ranch?" Freddie asked as he entered, eyes round.

"I sure did."

"With horses and cows and stuff?"

"And chickens and dogs and cats."

"Wow. So you can, like, ride?"

"I even have my own saddle. Here, would you set out these napkins, Freddie? Gabriel, there's iced tea in the fridge and glasses in the cabinet to the right of it, if you'd pour us drinks. Freddie, is iced tea okay with you? I have milk and water."

"Milk is for kids."

"Milk is for strong bones and protein to build muscles. My grown brothers, each of whom is as big as Gabriel here, all drank milk when they were your age—lots of it."

Freddie wasn't convinced. "From your own cow?"

Jilly grinned. "Yep. I have four brothers. She was a busy cow."

Freddie laughed. "So do you know how to milk one?"

"Sure. You want lessons?"

Gabriel watched her with Freddie, noted how she brightened the mood. How she patiently answered the flood of other questions that poured from the boy. She had a knack with people. She didn't treat Freddie as a charity case but simply acted as though they belonged here. Just a normal family dinner.

From the way the kid soaked up the experience, Gabriel doubted the boy had had many such times in his young life, if any.

He hadn't had anything like it in a long time himself. A part of him he'd thought dead unfurled and stretched toward the sunshine that was so much a part of her.

The food tasted as good as it smelled, and the split lip didn't seem to slow Freddie down as he devoured two bowls of stew, several slices of bread and two glasses of milk, chattering between bites. His table manners were nearly non-existent, but Jilly didn't chide him for talking with his mouth full or leaving his napkin on the table instead of putting it in his lap.

Gabriel had to admire that. Maybe she understood the boy better than he'd given her credit for.

She was damn sure a good cook. Food had only been fuel for a long time, but tonight he found himself unexpectedly hungry.

"Would you care for another bowl?" she asked.

"We haven't cleaned you out yet?"

She smiled. "I think I could scrape a spoonful or two off the bottom."

Freddie patted his belly. "I'm so full I might pop. It was real good, Miss Jilly."

"I'm glad." She cocked her head. "But does that mean you couldn't find room for a little ice cream?"

The boy's eyes went wide. "Ice cream?"

"Blue Bell. I even have two kinds, cookies 'n' cream and vanilla. And I'm pretty sure I have some chocolate syrup to go with it."

"Sweet!"

"We clean up first," Gabriel said to Freddie, rising from his chair. "The work will make you some room."

"Okay!" Freddie all but leaped from the table, grabbing his bowl and Jilly's, juggling them as he headed for the sink. There was no sign of the sulky, skittish teen. Even Freddie wasn't proof against the magic of the refuge she'd created.

Neither, it seemed, was he. He could feel deep pockets of tension inside him easing.

She started to rise, but he shook his head. "You cooked. We'll clean."

Her eyes widened. "Oh, I couldn't…"

He bent closer so only she could hear. "Consider it a payback that you didn't badger him about school or where he lives."

Her sweet lips curved. "It was my brother who tamed the wild animals, but I watched." Her blue eyes were warm and soft, a refuge of their own.

A bolt of yearning ambushed him, so swift and unexpected that he had to turn away.

He wanted to kiss her. Grab hold and hang on. Drink in her vibrant joy, her ease with the world, her faith in human nature. The sunshine that flowed from her in such abundance.

What would it be like to have those eyes, that smile, on you every day?

And she was looking back, her pupils wide and dark with awareness of him. Electricity sparked the air around them.

Don't even go there. She was so young, so innocent. He was a thousand years older, in more ways than years. Gabriel retreated quickly, made his way blindly to the sink. Focused on washing dishes before foolhardy yearning could get the better of wisdom. Before his newly-aware body could follow up on the impulse to get closer to her.

But when washing dishes didn't help, desperation hit. "We should go as soon as we finish here," he said abruptly.

"What about ice cream?" The kid looked devastated.

"I'll get you some on the way." To where? What the hell was he doing with this boy?

"Don't need you anyhow. I can get home fine by myself."

"Freddie," Jilly began. "You shouldn't be out alone at night. Why don't you sleep here, and Mr. Coronado can go on."

The daggers shooting in his direction made no bones of her displeasure. "No," he said flatly to the boy. "You're not staying here." How did he know the boy wouldn't steal her blind or let that Mako creep in or… "Absolutely not."

"It's my house," she objected. "You have no say in my guests."

He merely cocked one eyebrow in her direction. *Because you defend yourself so well on your own?* he started to point out.

But she hadn't said anything about the first night, and no way was he blowing the whistle on himself.

She opened her mouth to protest again, and it was pretty clear that she would not give up until the boy was staying here.

Which was exactly what he wanted, right? For the kid to be someone else's problem?

Damn it. Damn it.

He exhaled in a gust. "I'll wait, then give you a ride home." To the home he'd bet didn't exist, but at least it would keep Jilly from her foolhardy notion. He huffed out his defeat. "Go ahead and have your ice cream."

"Don't want none now." Freddie pushed toward the door. "I'm outta here." He raced for the front.

"Freddie!" Jilly started after him.

Gabriel grabbed her arm, then dropped it immediately. "I'll handle it."

"Because you're doing such a great job? Leave him to me. I couldn't possible do worse than you."

"If you take one step toward that door, I'll—"

"You'll what?" Her chin stuck up in the air.

"I'll find out who it was you didn't want knowing about

the other night, and I'll call them." So much for self-protection.

Her eyes popped wide. "You! It was you. I knew it!" Then she sobered. "Why didn't you stay? I never got to really thank you."

"I don't want thanks. I don't want anything. Just leave me the hell alone. All of you." And with that, he stormed out the door.

He made his way out to the street with long strides, scanning for the kid.

But Freddie was long gone.

Chapter Eight

"Jilly?" April Stevens, an intern working on her master's degree in social work at the University of Texas, stood in the doorway of Jilly's broom-closet-sized office. "There's someone here to see you." April's cheeks were flushed, her eyes bright.

Jilly couldn't imagine who would visit and cause that sort of reaction. "I'll be right there. I just have to input a couple more items for the new budget projections." She bent to her task again, though her heart wasn't in it. She had her hands full not racing to the jobsite first thing this morning to see if Gabriel was there. If he'd seen Freddie.

Not that he hadn't been very clear that her interest wasn't welcome.

"If budget projections take precedence over me—" a cheerful baritone broke into her musings. "—I've definitely lost my touch."

She looked up. "Go away, Sean," she responded, but she was already smiling. "Not all of us are jetting around the country with America's Sweetheart. Some of us have to work for a living." She punched in one last figure, then rounded her desk at top speed and threw herself into his arms. "I wondered if all that time you've been logging in the gossip magazines had made you too good for the little people."

He tweaked her nose. "You are still a giant pain in the ass, you know that?"

She socked her fifth—or was that sixth, behind Saint?—big brother in the arm. Then she gasped. "Oh, Sean, I'm so sorry. Did I hurt you?"

He rolled his eyes. "Like that could ever happen, midget." But he smiled fondly. "I've been out of the hospital for nearly five months, Jilly."

But she couldn't forget that he'd nearly died saving Annabelle's life. She'd been there for the vigil at the hospital. "How could I forget? Your rehab was the longest six years of my life."

"Six weeks, brat."

"Felt a lot longer." He and Annabelle had parted ways, and Jilly had been his entertainment committee. Sean was not a cheerful patient, especially with the broken heart he'd been sporting.

She spied April lingering behind them, attempting to appear busy, and decided to take pity on her. "April Stevens, have you met Sean Fitzgerald, former supercop, now globe-trotting glamour boy?"

Sean snorted. "Hello, April." He extended a hand, and a flustered April finally found hers to shake. "If you get tired of working for the slave-driver here, come see me at the Meryem Foundation. I'm much nicer than Jilly."

Jilly laughed. "Prettier, too."

He darted her a glare. "Cut that out." He'd been called Pretty Boy and Romeo by his fellow cops, and both were sources of intense frustration to him.

Which was why, of course, she had to get in a dig now and again. Even if she'd once had a teeny crush on him herself—she wasn't blind, after all, to how gorgeous he was, all tall and lean and golden-haired—it had been completely one-sided. Sean had never treated her as anything but a kid sister to tease mercilessly, and she returned the favor as often as possible.

"Well, I, uh…" April stammered. "I mean, thank you and all, but…"

"Keep your hands off my help, Studmuffin. Though," she said to April, "He does pay better, I'm sure."

"Since you don't pay me at all."

"But I'm a dream to work with, right?"

Sean snickered.

"She really is," earnest April said to Sean. "And what we're doing here is so important. I mean, not that what you're doing, fighting human trafficking and helping the victims of violence and all, isn't really important, too."

Sean and Annabelle had formed a foundation to deal with victims' rights after Sean had spent years in law enforcement seeing the toll violent crime cost the victims. No guilty verdict could ever fix the damage done, and after his time first working Vice, then on an inter-agency violent crimes task force known as VICTAF, he'd seen firsthand that it was women and children who were harmed most. He'd confessed to Jilly during his recovery period after the shooting that he was burned out. The switch to heading the Meryem Foundation, named after one of the victims in the case that had nearly gotten him and Annabelle killed, had re-energized him. Though Jilly missed seeing him as often due to his frequent travels to speak and raise awareness, she admired the zeal he brought to his cause.

"Thanks, April. I appreciate it."

Another blush. April seemed frozen in place.

She'd have to get Sean out of here to bring April out of her fan-girl coma. "So what brings you here, stranger?"

"I have a couple of things I wanted to run by you. Got

time for a cup of coffee? I'm buying."

She hesitated. She really needed to get those budget projections finished to see if there was a way in the world they could afford to pay Gabriel Coronado to come onboard. Although after last night's awkwardness, she knew she had her work cut out for her to convince him.

"I know you're busy. I won't take long." Sean seemed unusually serious. Mostly they bantered with each other.

"Sure. Just let me close down the spreadsheet." She returned to her desk and did so, then grabbed her purse. "April, if Teo returns my call about the building permits for the Delgado and Foster homes, would you tell him I'm hoping to file the applications tomorrow?"

"Will do." But she was still gawking at Sean.

"Bye, April," he said and took her hand, which had her blushing again. "Thank you for letting me borrow Jilly—and don't forget that job offer."

"I won't—I mean, I really couldn't, I'm barely started on grad school and—" She broke off. "That is, thank you. It's just…" Her gaze cut to Jilly.

Sean grinned. "I understand. She's lucky to have you on her team."

"Oh, gee, well, thanks, but I—" A pause. "Um, would you, um, could you tell your, uh, Ms. Quinn that I think she's just wonderful?"

"I absolutely will. And I couldn't agree more." Sean opened the door for Jilly to precede him.

"But—I mean, you're wonderful, too," April called after him.

He started to turn back to answer her, but Jilly stayed him with a hand on his arm.

"Leave the poor girl alone, would you?"

"Hey, I was being nice!"

"I know…that's the problem." Jilly sighed extravagantly. "April's been a little…sheltered. Home schooled, raised out in the country…she's sweet and the best help I ever had, but she's not ready for you, Pretty Boy."

"You know I hate that name."

"Deal with it, Romeo."

Sean shook his head and picked up the pace.

"So what's up?"

"Let's get our coffee first." He opened the door to the coffee shop. Once inside, she looked for a table while he went to order. They had their routine down.

After a few minutes, he set her drink on the table, then took his seat and studied her.

"What?"

"So…I happened to pay a visit to some of my buddies at APD…"

Oh, drat. She focused on her coffee and waited.

"Interesting story I heard about this little blonde who managed to get herself knocked around and wouldn't press charges on the perp."

"Big mouth," she muttered. Could no one keep a confidence? "I'm sorry for her. She's all right, I hope?" She lifted guileless eyes to him.

"Cut the crap, Jilly. Are you okay?" He looked honestly worried.

"I'm fine. Nothing happened."

Concern flared into blazing anger. Sean didn't get mad easily, but when he did…watch out. "Bullshit. Do you know what could have happened to you? What in the hell were you doing out there at night alone? And why in the name of all that's holy wouldn't you press charges?" He held up a hand. "Never mind. I bet I can guess. *Why, officer, he's just a boy, and he deserves a second chance*," he said in a falsetto.

"I—"

"I'm not done. Look, everybody appreciates your optimistic view of human nature, but not when it puts your life in danger. That was the stupidest thing you've ever done. Do you realize what could have happened to you?"

"It didn't."

"I said I'm not done."

She rose. "If you're just going to yell at me, I have work to do. Thanks for the coffee. No thanks for the lecture." She grabbed her cup.

"Sit down. I'm not through."

"Too bad. I am."

They were beginning to attract attention.

Sean exhaled and pinched the bridge of his nose. "All right. I'm through yelling."

"You're still mad."

"Of course I am. It's nothing to what your brothers are going to say when I tell them."

"Don't you dare," she said bitterly.

"If it was such a good idea, why are you hiding what happened?"

"Look…" She bit back her own harsh words and sat down. "I'm okay. There was a man who helped me." She frowned. "And I got my own blows in, I promise you."

"Jilly, you—" He halted, shook his head. "Listen, nobody doubts your courage, but why in the hell didn't you stay in your car? And why on earth didn't you press charges? That guy tested positive for crack—you know what a crackhead can do when he's high?"

"It wasn't—I wasn't being stupid, Sean. I'm over there all the time. The neighbors are great, and they look out for each other."

"So that was one of them who helped you?"

She glanced away. "Not exactly."

"Want to explain that?"

"No."

"I go back to my original premise—why did you get out of the car?"

"I...okay," she admitted. "I shouldn't have. I wasn't thinking. I really do feel safe over there." Or she had.

She would again. She'd make sure of it. "But there was this boy. I know him."

"You know the perp?"

"Not—not really. This is a boy who was being forced to participate. I think he's homeless, and he's not a bad kid. I'm trying to help him."

"Of course you are. So, what, you said, *Okay, homeless boy, I know you're really a nice person so I'm just going to give you some money and take you to the shelter and—*"

"Sean." She ground her teeth. "If you're going to ridicule me, I'm going back to work."

He closed his eyes. Exhaled loudly. Again. "All right. I'm listening."

"It's just...I've got a lot invested in this particular house. This family. They're...special. I saw a broken window, and I just...reacted."

His jaw clenched, but he didn't speak.

"And yes, it was dumb and I won't do it again, I swear. But I just got roughed up a little, that's all."

"Who was this guy? The one who helped?"

"I'm not sure."

"Why not?"

"Because he sort of...disappeared. When the cops came."

"*Sort of* disappeared?"

"I was talking to the officer, then I turned around and he was...gone." *And maybe I know who he is, but no way am I saying anything*. Sean would be investigating Gabriel, next thing she knew.

She got mad all over again that the officer had squealed on her.

"I know that look. You're lucky Saint hasn't heard about it yet. He still might."

Jilly groaned. "I am so eternally sick of everybody treating me like I'm ten."

"Then stop acting like it." He held up a hand. "Okay. Not lecturing." His gaze softened. "You're really okay? No nightmares? No flashbacks?"

"None." But she couldn't look at him and lie.

"You can come to me, you know. I've been there."

"So I can be treated to another lecture?"

"Jilly, you're the light of all our lives. You're important to a whole lot of people. We worry."

"I can take care of myself."

He looked at her askance.

"I can," she insisted.

"If that guy hadn't shown up…" he reminded her.

She blew out a breath. "So who are you calling first? Dad? Alex? Who?"

He studied her. "I'm not telling anyone if—" He held up a hand as she smiled. "*If* you promise never to do something so stupid again. I mean it, Jilly. I'll babysit you myself if I have to."

Jilly was torn between gratitude and anger. Did none of them understand how humiliating it was to be treated as though she had fluff for brains? Granted, that night things had gone wrong, but she'd been living by herself in the city ever since college, and she'd had her own apartment her junior and senior years. She wasn't a stupid woman—and she was a woman, not a child—but good luck getting any of them to believe that. Her mother was the only person in her whole family who gave her credit for being an adult.

But she saw the worry in his eyes, and she knew, too, that what he said was true. However unfair the treatment felt at times, she understood that she did occupy a special place in her family, that she was cherished.

Being cherished sometimes felt more like being suffocated, however. She was so blasted tired of having to struggle for autonomy. She headed an organization, for Pete's sake, and she did a good job of it.

"I can see that head of steam building."

Her head whipped up. "It's not funny, Sean."

He sighed. "I know. Believe me, if I never heard the names Pretty Boy and Romeo again, I'd be one happy man." He took her hand. "But there's love behind that, too, just as everyone's concern for you is motivated by love. You're irreplaceable, Jilly. Your dad had it right—you are our sunshine."

But I'm tired of being everyone's sunny girl.

She didn't say it, though. He was right that no one meant anything but the best for her. "I just wonder when I'll ever be seen as an adult."

He sat up straight. "Well, I might be able to help you with that. I didn't just come to chew you out—actually, I didn't intend that at all, but once the guys at the department told me…" He held up a hand. "Forget that. Over and done. I know you're a smart woman, and I'm trusting you to be careful. I mean that."

She settled a little. "Thank you."

"Actually, you being smart is part of what brought me here."

She cocked her head.

"I want to offer you a job."

Jilly blinked. "A…job?"

"Yeah, and you'd actually get paid more than peanuts for a change. I want you to be the Executive Director of the Meryem Foundation."

"The Executive Director?" she echoed. "Me?"

"Can you think of anyone better?" He held up a finger. "One, you're a born organizer—also known as bossy." He grinned when she spluttered. "Two—" Another finger held up. "Your compassion is part of the reason for the lecture we're going to forget about. Three, I respect you and what you've accomplished and I'd like to turn that formidable energy toward my cause. Four—"

"Wait. Back up to the *I respect you* part. Seriously?"

"Why wouldn't I? You're transforming a whole neighborhood, one house at a time, one family at a time, most of it through sheer will."

"But—" She fell silent. He looked absolutely sincere. "You think we could work together?" They were best friends, but he was still a big brother by inclination if not by birth, and she liked the autonomy she had now.

"Sure." He shrugged. "You just do everything my way, and we're golden." The twinkle in his eyes gave him away.

"Yeah, that's gonna happen." But her mind was already spinning off in a thousand directions. "Isn't the office in L.A.?"

"We set one up there, yes, because it's a great place to raise money, given Annabelle's connections, but that can just as easily be a satellite. I don't want to live in L.A. full-time, and neither does Annabelle. She has to spend time there, so I will, too, but she's fallen in love with Austin. The reality is that in this mobile computing world, you could work from here as easily as anywhere else—though if you'd like a fresh start, L.A. is there for you to conquer."

A fresh start. Being somewhere that she was taken on her own merits, not as someone's kid sister. And L.A.…wow.

Then she remembered the Marins and the Fosters and the Delgados. Who would take care of them if she left? "Oh, Sean, I don't know…how soon do you have to decide? I really can't—this isn't a good time. We're about to start two more houses."

"At the risk of making you feel even more indispensable than you already may…you're the one I want for the job, Jilly. Don't say no yet. We're only starting out, and I'd rather have you onboard yesterday, but I can wait—for a while at least. Not forever, but…until the end of the year maybe. I'll manage that long if I need to."

Then he named a salary figure that had her eyes widening. "That's too much overhead, Sean."

"What did I tell you? Bossy, bossy." He shook his head, but he was grinning. "Annabelle seems intent on beggaring herself so that I'll quit complaining about her luxurious lifestyle. She's set aside a fund for overhead, so no donations will be used to pay for any of that. We want those to be spent on behalf of the victims only. Salve your conscience, Sunshine?"

Jilly stared off into the distance, trying to absorb how much her life would change—had changed—in the last hour. She didn't know what her answer would be, but she'd certainly not awakened expecting anything like this to happen today.

For sure not after last night's disaster. Her thoughts drifted back to Freddie, shoveling in soup like he hadn't eaten in weeks. The brusque, somber man who'd insisted on cleaning her kitchen.

Then threatened to out her to her family. *Well, too late for that threat, Gabriel…*

He was her savior, the man who'd rescued her when Mako had been willing to do worse than he had.

Then he'd vanished. What was his story?

And how could she leave now, when Freddie was out there somewhere and this mysterious man had such haunted eyes and then there were Teo and her families…

"Oh, Sean…." she sighed eloquently. "I'm incredibly flattered, as well as interested, but—"

"No buts right now. I get it. You've poured your heart and soul into what you're doing now. You're one big walking heart, and every person you help has tendrils of that heart that stay connected to them from that moment on." He placed a hand on hers. "Maybe I'll have to take no for an answer down the road, but I'm not accepting it yet. Just…think about it. You know how to reach me if you have questions." He rose. "I know you've got work to do and so do I, so I won't keep you. But the Meryems of the world, who are bought and sold like cattle, who are treated like garbage and live short miserable lives before they die…they need you, too, Jilly. I'm not giving up easily." He bent and kissed her cheek. "Bye now."

Jilly walked out with him until they parted as he went in a different direction toward his car.

Then she walked right past her office door, lost in thought, and didn't realize it for another block.

Chapter Nine

"Neither of them showed up?" Jilly listened to Teo when he'd finally returned her call late in the afternoon. "Oh, Teo, I'm so sorry." She sighed. "It's my fault."

"Yours? How?"

Her mind was a jumble, trying to sort out her feelings about Sean's job offer, about this organization that she loved, about how alone Freddie might be…and, okay, about the man who'd saved her but seemed bent on avoiding her now. "Gabriel and I don't see eye to eye on what to do about Freddie." That was about as succinct as she could make it.

"Girl, you cannot save the whole world."

"I'm not trying to."

"Yeah, right." He snorted. "It's just as well that Freddie's not here. Beto is really upset."

"I'll come talk to him. Freddie is a mixed-up kid, Teo. He wasn't there that night of his free will." Besides, Beto might know where to look for Freddie.

"I'm assuming I can't stop you."

"Why would you want to?"

"Tell me you need to take on one more battle."

She pinched the bridge of her nose. Not really but… She sat up straight. "I'm fine, except for having no idea what to do to help you ease your load. Gabriel has no right to take it out on you because we had a disagreement."

"Whoa, girl, taking this a little personal? He never made any promises. We don't know what else he's got going on in his life."

True. She thought of the haunted look of him, the unease in dealing with others. Her suspicions that he was former military.

He was a good man, that much was obvious. One who drew her more than was probably wise. But he was also a very unwilling one, sort of…rusty at dealing with people. That he wanted to be left alone couldn't be more clear.

She needed to talk to Rafe. He'd understand. Maybe he'd help her understand, too.

But he'd also want to know the background of their acquaintance.

"You still there? We done?"

She yanked her attention back to the conversation. "I'm coming by. I want to talk to Beto. See you in a few minutes, okay?"

"Can I stop you?"

She grinned. "What do you think?"

A gusty sigh. "You need a cape and a mask, Crusader."

Jilly was chuckling as she said goodbye.

Beto's build was similar to Freddie's, yet where Freddie's face wore the pinched look of someone who seldom had enough to eat, Beto's face had the rounded contours of someone who not only had enough food but enough love. Lucia worked hard and had many expenses to deal with, but her children never went hungry.

Jilly wondered why she'd never before realized that Freddie was not naturally lean as a stray cat, why she hadn't paid enough attention to ever consider that the boy might be homeless. If anything, she'd barely noticed him in her zeal to help the Marins—not until she'd caught him stealing from them.

Now she'd witnessed Freddie eating as though food was a luxury and understood that it likely was. If he'd go to school more often, he'd be able to get breakfast and lunch, at least…

Good grief, Jilly. There would be paperwork involved. The boy clearly operated under the radar, that much was clear from his terror of the shelter.

She recalled some figures she'd learned from Clarice, whose practice focused on abused women and teens, while Saint had done a lot of work with gang members. They'd even gotten themselves licensed as foster parents as a result of the heartache they'd witnessed. They had two girls with them right now, in addition to their own two children.

Homeless teens, both runaways and the abandoned, were prey to so much. The numbers were staggering: 1.5 million teens homeless at any given time, 25,000 of them coming out of foster care each year due to passing the age limit; 10,000 of those added to the homeless ranks. Besides all the terrors waiting out there—sexual predators, prostitution, substance abuse, mental illness—simply obtaining enough food was an enormous challenge all by itself. Jilly thought of how Dane and Liam could plow through double and triple meals when they were teens. They'd been walking stomachs, she'd heard her mother say on more than one occasion.

She had to find Freddie. Had to convince him to let her help. The look on his face before he'd fled last night broke her heart.

Are you that naïve? He'll run the first chance he gets, and we'll never see him again.

And look how well you did, Gabriel. I gave you your way, and you scared him off.

The thought of never seeing the boy again, of having no idea if he was safe or even alive…

Jilly counted the blocks left until she could find Beto, and when she made it to the house, she practically ran.

"Hey, Miss Jilly," greeted Beto's sister Lili. "Come see my bedroom—it's painted now!"

Urgency was a hive of bees beneath her skin, but Jilly forced herself to follow the shy girl instead. *These moments are why you do this work*, she reminded herself.

But now that Freddie's plight had her focusing on homeless children, she was mentally beginning to frame a proposal for Annabelle and Sean. Even if she didn't take the job, the victims their foundation was trying to help often had their beginnings as orphans and runaways.

"Look!" Lili twirled in the center of the room. "My bed will go there, and Mr. Teo says he can build me a desk for over there."

Jilly listened, spending precious minutes discussing Lili's room with her, how Lucia had promised they would make curtains to match the bedspread Lili was saving for, shelving Teo had promised to help Lili make by herself.

"Beto will share with the other boys, right?"

Lili shook her head. "*Mami* says we should both have our own rooms until we graduate. *Abuelo* has volunteered to share with Joey until I graduate, and baby Marisa will sleep in *Mami's* room." It was so like Lucia to give up her own privacy so that her children could have some.

"Is Beto here?" Though Jilly knew he was. "Maybe he'd like to show me his room." That way she could talk to him in private.

"You never know with my brother, but I'll ask." She left the room.

Beto arrived alone, his forehead wrinkled. "Miss Jilly? You asked for me?"

Jilly smiled. "Let's go in your room. Show me around, okay?"

"It's just a room. Not that big, either." But pride was in his gaze.

"So have you thought about how you'll decorate it?"

Beto shrugged. "I got some posters." He frowned. "But *Mami* doesn't want me putting holes in the brand new walls."

She laughed. "Sorry—not making fun of you. It made me think about my brother Liam's first dorm room." At Beto's curious glance, she continued. "They weren't supposed to put holes in the walls, but Liam was a real geek, and he rigged up this elaborate system using fishing wire and pulleys. Most of the guys on his floor had a couple of posters taped up, and those kept falling to the floor when the tape came loose. Liam's room looked like a museum exhibit—okay, that's completely wrong. A museum of messiness, maybe. But as far as the walls were concerned, he could display whatever he wanted."

Beto grinned. "I still can't believe your brother is Liam Sullivan. Wicked cool. He wasn't really a geek, right?"

"He absolutely was. He was slow to mature and always had his nose in a book. To me, he's still just that pain in the rear who read my diary or threatened my dates when I was old enough to go out." Not much had changed on that last point.

Beto laughed. "Yeah, but he's crazy famous and rich."

"Would you like to meet him next time he's in town?" She seldom made such an offer because Liam treasured his privacy, but Beto was beginning to give Lucia some problems, and Liam was a good influence. A word from him might go a long way.

"Sweet!"

Here was her opening. "Maybe Freddie could come, too."

Beto's brows snapped together. "No freaking way."

"Why not?"

His head whipped to hers. "You know what he did. He'd better stay away from me and mine."

"Beto," she began carefully. "Do you know where he hangs out?"

"Why? You gonna get the cops on him? You should. My mom is killing herself to make this house happen, and that *cabron* breaks in and steals—"

"It wasn't his idea. He was scared of Mako."

"Mako's crazy scary, but still… Freddie was supposed to be my friend."

"He's done a lot of work on this house," she reminded him. "And yesterday he spent all day here working."

"Don't care. Gonna kick his tail when I see him."

"Where would you look?" she tried to ask casually. "Do you know where he lives?"

"You gonna turn him in?"

"No, Beto, I'm not." She decided on candor. "I'm concerned about him. I don't think he has a place to live. It's dangerous out there alone."

"Freddie takes care of himself. Damien, too."

"Who's Damien?"

"Freddie's little brother. Sometimes Damien's mama leaves him all alone. He's only six."

Jilly was speechless. "She's not Freddie's mother?"

"No, his mama died, but Freddie does okay, most of the time."

"Against a guy like Mako?"

Beto no longer seemed quite so unconcerned.

"Where would I look for him? He needs help, Beto, and if he has a six-year-old out there with him, then that's even more dangerous."

"He takes care of Damien. Won't let no harm come to him."

"He's a boy. He needs shelter and food and someone to watch over him."

"You gonna do that?" Beto asked. "Because he won't go to any shelter, Miss Jilly. He got—" Beto looked away. "Something happened to him when he was in one."

Oh, dear mercy. Jilly's eyes filled. "Please help me find him. I swear I'll figure out a way to keep him safe—to keep both of them safe—but first I have to locate him." And keep him away from people like Mako.

"I don't know…" Beto's gaze searched hers. "You don't understand, Miss Jilly. The system doesn't work for people like us."

She gestured to the house around them. "I'm not the system, Beto, and I do make things work for people I care about."

A short nod. "You do that, all right." Still he pondered for a minute, then exhaled. "I might know a couple of places for you to look."

"I'm listening." She touched his arm. "Thank you, Beto."

"Don't thank me. I'm still gonna kick his butt when I see him. You tell him that."

Where should she begin? Beto had told her where Damien's mother lived, so that was probably the obvious first step.

Freddie was cagey even with his friend, so Beto didn't know much. He mentioned an abandoned house not far from their school where he'd met Freddie once. There was also a convenience store several blocks from the Marins' new house where the boys hung out—though Beto, not so much, he admitted ruefully, since his mother kept a tight rein on him. She might be a working mom, but boy, did she have a network, he said.

Jilly had to grin. Her own mother had the ears of a bat, plus the small town she'd grown up in was filled with friends and family of both the Sullivans and Sandovals. In addition, Rafe and Alex's grandmother, Abuelita, was worshipped by one and all. There wasn't a soul in the surrounding area she hadn't helped or healed at one time or another.

At that moment, she very much wished she could see Abuelita again. The woman was about to turn ninety-four, but though her body had slowed and her eyesight dimmed, her mind was as agile as ever. She wasn't Jilly's blood grandmother, but she was definitely the grandmother of her heart. She was the single most comforting presence Jilly had ever known. The little stucco house in which she still lived alone—refusing to move in with Rafe and Diana, who were close by and visited every day—had provided shelter for many, many people, their bodies, their minds and their souls.

Gabriel could use some time with Abuelita, she thought, too.

She had to stop thinking about him, however much she wanted to get to know him better. He'd been very clear with her last night. *I don't want thanks. I don't want anything. Just leave me the hell alone. All of you.*

She'd give him some space for now, but she wouldn't—couldn't—abandon Freddie. Not only taking care of himself but a six-year-old? Something had to be done.

She pulled up to the apartment building where Beto had directed her. Apartment 213. She scanned for the numbers on the doors, but some were missing and others damaged.

At last she found one on the second floor with the number 3 at the end of a broken tag and knocked.

No answer.

She knocked again, feeling foolish that she didn't know the woman's name thus could not call it out.

"What you want?" said a voice down the walkway. "Who you lookin' for?" A woman of indeterminate age, weary and worn and slovenly, stood there glaring.

"I'm looking for Freddie Miller."

"He ain't here."

"Do you know where he is?"

"No, and I don't care. He nothin' but trouble."

"Are you..." What did she call this woman? "Are you Damien's mother?"

"Damien who?" But the furtive look in her eyes gave her away.

"I'm not with the authorities," Jilly reassured her. "I'm only a...friend of Freddie's. I'd like to talk to him."

"Said I don't know where he is and don't care."

"Then may I speak to Damien, please?"

"No." Antagonism prickled from her, sharp as porcupine quills. "Who the hell are you?"

It was difficult to know how to deal with someone so suspicious. Did she reassure the woman again or threaten her? What would get Jilly the answers she sought?

"Look, I'm not here to cause any problems. Freddie has friends who are...worried about him. We simply want to know he's all right."

"Ain't seen him. Don't want to. Get out."

The woman was taller than Jilly, but stringy. Jilly visualized what her mother would do, a woman who kept five large males in place anytime she wanted to. She took a step closer. "I'm not the authorities, but I know plenty of them. I am concerned about Damien and Freddie. Do I need to get Child Protective Services involved? Neither is of age, and there are those who would be happy to start monitoring their welfare."

"What you know about anything, white girl? You ain't been in need your whole life. You don't come here telling me how to take care of my boy. You get your nose the hell out of my business." Fear and the jitters that probably came from drug use had her wild-eyed.

"Where. Is. Damien?" Jilly's tone was quiet but firm.

"With his dad. Be back in a bit." But she wouldn't meet Jilly's eyes.

I am going to rescue these children from you, Jilly thought but didn't say out loud. No telling where the woman would run to or what would happen to Damien if she did.

"Here is my card," she said, passing the paper over to the woman. "I would appreciate a call if you see Freddie, and I would like to speak with Damien as soon as he returns."

She didn't like the look of this, and—Gabriel Coronado be damned—she was not turning her head one second longer. "Are we clear?" she asked the woman.

The woman's mouth pursed, but her eyes darted around. She was likely too high to remember anything. "We clear," she said, then turned on her heel and returned the way she'd come.

Tearing the card into pieces and tossing them into the air.

That went well, Jilly thought, and started dialing the phone. Gabriel might be right and Freddie would hate her, but she knew people in the child welfare system and knew that while very much overworked, they genuinely tried to do the best by their charges. Also, Jilly was a CASA volunteer, trained as a child advocate, so she could see about getting herself appointed to their case in order to watch over the two boys.

But first, someone had to find them.

"Hi, Selma," she said to the person on the other end. "I have two kids I'm concerned about."

And night was on its way.

She could barely stand the thought of Freddie out there alone.

Gabriel stood in *Mama C's* kitchen and tried to visualize it with the speckled formica removed from the counters, the yellowed linoleum scraped up from the floors, the decrepit stove, ancient refrigerator, aluminum table and chairs all replaced by shiny new furnishings.

He could knock out that wall to the living room, build a bar with cabinets below. The house would open up. Sunshine would pour through a new, larger window over the sink.

Sunshine could pour into his life.

Hey, Sunshine, good to see you. Teo's greeting was apt.

Jilly was indeed pure sunshine.

As long as she stayed away from him.

That was you? I never got to say thank you.

I don't want thanks. I don't want anything. Just leave me the hell alone. All of you. Why had he been so rough on her? She didn't deserve it. Goodness spilled from her every pore.

Not that she didn't have a temper. Oh yeah. Woman definitely thought her way was best. Bossy as hell. Nosy. Pushed too hard. Asked too much.

Go away.

Even when he wasn't near her, he couldn't seem to forget

her. Might as well have returned to the job today.

And why didn't you? You know they need your help.

Because he was tired of being pushed, that's all. Boxed in by commitments and obligations and worries…

No more.

Gabriel Asim, Ahmed had called him—Arabic for protector—because they'd first met when Gabriel had dispatched two older kids who were beating the boy up over food he'd stolen for himself and his sister. Some protector he'd been. He'd gotten involved and others had taken offense, even though the children were orphans. They'd have been better off if he'd left them alone.

He had no business getting involved with all these people. No matter how good it had felt to have a simple goal, like hanging a set of cabinets.

Like teaching a boy.

Don't need your help.

Freddie was probably right about Gabriel, but he did need someone's help. Never mind that Gabriel's gut said Jilly was coming on too strong, that Freddie would flee rather than be taken to a shelter or put in foster care.

Damien got no food that night.

How often did he find himself in charge of his younger brother? Where could they hide?

As darkness fell, Gabriel thought of two boys alone. Winter was coming.

Damn it. Might as well admit that he was going out to look for them.

One glance back at *Mama C's*, and Gabriel realized that the place was old but he'd made it sound enough for someone to occupy. Cosmetics weren't important. *Mama C* and what she'd taught him about compassion was.

All right, Freddie. He left the house and returned to the

garage to change into his running shoes.

He'd start at the convenience store, asking questions.

He'd been hanging around the convenience store so long that the clerk was probably ready to call the cops. Okay, no…not given how many others loitered here.

So far, no luck. He'd talked to the clerk, asked several customers, but no one remembered Freddie. He had no extraordinary features to identify him, nothing to make him stand out from any of twenty other skinny kids Gabriel had seen come in and out since he'd arrived tonight.

Gabriel had started working his way through the parking lot, but that was a dicey proposition. Though his hair was longer now and his work clothes were scruffy, he was big, and his Special Forces training plus his experiences in the hellhole of the Middle East had marked him as someone not to screw with. Usually he didn't mind—appreciated that it made people give him distance—but right now his bearing seemed to scream *cop* to those gathered just beyond the lights doing drug deals and who knew what else.

He'd learned a lot about allaying suspicion in his various postings, though, so he approached quietly, hands in plain sight, his manner as low-key and non-threatening as he could make it.

It didn't really help, however. Either none of these losers floating around the edges knew Freddie or they were lying…but regardless, they weren't talking.

Until he mentioned Mako, that is. The name generated two reactions: stone silence and furtive looks or belligerence.

"What you want with Mako?" one cocky kid—all of

eighteen maybe—demanded.

"Maybe I owe him some money," Gabriel replied. That usually brought lowlifes out of the woodwork.

"For what?" the kid scanned him, staring at the multitude of scars on his legs. "You after some Cotton?"

One of the street names for the painkiller oxycontin, he knew, as well as why the kid made that assumption. In the beginning, Gabriel had hated for people to look at his scars, but now he didn't even flinch. He was alive, he had both legs, he was back to running. His legs might not be pretty, but they served him well.

So Mako was a drug dealer, in addition to being a thief.

"Got some dings in the sand pit." He shrugged. It was hardly his first time undercover, though never in this country.

The kid and his friend flicked glances back at the damage. "Some kinda shit, huh, man? That had to suck."

Punks. They might think their lives were rough, but here they stood with earbuds playing hater rap so loud he could hear the music, with their skivvies hanging out over their jeans, posturing as though they were somebody when good men were dying or coming back without arms and legs and little kids were killed over—

Stop. He could not go there. A negligent lift of his shoulder. "Your boy Mako could help?"

"Maybe. He just got out of lockup yesterday. He not real happy right now."

"Yeah," his buddy snickered. "But maybe he find the white girl who wants to save him. She sweet, he say. Cherry pie ripe. Then he be in a better mood."

It was all Gabriel could do not to grab both of them by the throat. To send a message to Mako to leave Jilly the hell alone.

But he'd already warned her to be more careful, and she'd

promised. She wasn't a fool, however impulsive she might be or how much a romantic.

He wasn't here as her bodyguard, he was here to find Freddie. Maybe if the boy didn't have to fear Mako, he'd be more visible.

"So if I want to see if Mako can fix me up, how do I contact him?"

One of them sneered. "You don't. He find you. Assumin' you ain't a cop."

"I'm not."

"Don't know if I believe that."

"Doesn't matter what you believe. I can go somewhere else, just as easy." He started to turn away to keep the bluff going.

"Hey, now. Tell me what you need and I can get it for you."

"And have you cut it and raise the price, too? Uh-uh. I'll just go somewhere else."

The two looked at each other. "So where can he find you?"

"Here is as good as anyplace." Just then a familiar vehicle pulled into the parking lot.

No. Way.

But indeed, a familiar head of strawberry blond hair emerged, coupled with—holy hell, where did she get those legs? She wore one of those lady suits with the short, close-fitting jacket and the even shorter tight skirt and sky-high heels…with about a mile and a half of legs he would never have expected from someone that small.

A piercing whistle from one of the idiots beside him. "Da-yum! I'd like me a piece of that."

Gabriel barely restrained the fist already forming at his side. "So you'd rather stare at some chick than make your friend some money that you might get a piece of?"

At last the two returned their attention to him. "Be at the park over on Quinn. Ten tomorrow night."

"Got it." Amateurs and punks, looking to be important. He turned away and let them go while he watched Jilly inside, talking earnestly to the clerk as every male eye inside the place and out was glued to her. Holding onto his temper, reminding himself that at least she wasn't out in the shadows of the parking lot talking to creeps like the two he'd just met, Gabriel forced himself to walk slowly inside.

But when she nodded at the clerk and handed over her card, he closed the distance between them and spoke from behind her as she headed for the next person she saw.

"What the hell are you doing here?" he all but growled.

Chapter Ten

Jilly nearly jumped out of her skin. She whirled so fast she lost her balance.

He steadied her. *Gabriel.* But no Gabriel she'd seen before.

"Are you all right?" she asked.

"Outside." He gripped her upper arm, his jaw clenched so tightly she thought he might break it. "Now."

"Let go of me. What's wrong with you?"

He closed his eyes. "Get in your car and get out of here."

"Are you in trouble, Gabriel?"

"Jilly." His voice was impossibly deep and rough. "You have to go." He glanced out the window. Cursed and stepped back behind a row of shelves, pulling her with him.

"People are starting to look," she hissed. "Tell me what's wrong."

"For the love of—" His eyes bored into hers. "You have to leave. You can't be seen with me."

"I'm not leaving you if you're in trouble. Do you want me to call the cops?"

"No!" He exhaled. "Listen, just…okay, look—get in your car and drive to the barbecue place down the street. Go inside and wait for me."

"Why?"

"Do you see those two in the hoodies?" he pointed.

"They're friends of Mako's. They're wondering if you—" He shook his head. "I'm not going to say it. Just please, Jilly, do as I ask. I'll be there in a few minutes."

"I don't want to leave you. They might hurt you."

He snorted. "Babe, I could wipe up the floor with them and not break a sweat. Not bragging, just…I could, okay? I have the training and the experience, too. I'm trying to get information from them is all, and beating the crap out of them won't accomplish that."

"Information on Freddie?"

He rolled his eyes the way her brothers did when they were praying for patience. "Yes. But the longer I stay in here, the more likely it is that they see us together. You don't want to be talking to those punks, I promise you. And you sure don't want them getting their hands on you."

She glanced back at the two he'd indicated. She knew more about self-defense than he might imagine, but she hadn't done so well the other night, had she? Plus they had a clear size advantage, and she had on these stupid heels.

And Gabriel looked really worried. "All right. But if you're not there in ten minutes, I'm calling Saint."

"Who's—" he shook his head. "Never mind. I'd rather you just went home."

"No way. I know the people who own the barbecue joint. I'll be fine there."

"Stay around people. And mention your boyfriend who's joining you so nobody bothers you, all right?"

He was so intense, so clearly worried.

"All right." She started for the door, then turned back. "Ten minutes," she said.

A quick nod as his eyes switched to staring out the front window.

She thought about calling Saint anyway. She still would if

Gabriel didn't meet her deadline.

But if he could find out anything about Freddie…

Jilly got in her car, newly aware that she might not be as anonymous as she would have assumed, should she have even thought about it.

She locked the doors as she always did. Cops in the family were good for some things. Two minutes later, she was pulling into what she considered to be one of Austin's best-kept secrets, Ray's BBQ. As she opened the door, she realized she was starving, then she wondered if Gabriel had eaten. Well, even if he had, he'd be wise to partake of the ambrosia Ray cooked up in his big pit out back.

"Jilly!" greeted Fayrene, Ray's wife of forty-odd years. The woman looked behind her. "You here alone?"

Jilly answered Fayrene's hug with one of her own. "Someone's joining me. He got held up." She hadn't taken the time to explain to Gabriel that she knew this place well. Anyway, she couldn't use the word *boyfriend* with Fayrene. The woman would start planning a bridal shower on the spot.

"How about a booth?"

"Sounds great." Jilly came here fairly often, and when she was alone, she just sat at the counter so she could visit with Fayrene and with Ray when he had a second. Since Gabriel was more than a little wound up, though, the privacy of a booth might be preferable.

He'd better not yell at her, though. She wasn't doing one thing dangerous, going into a well-lit convenience store asking about Freddie.

She sat facing the door.

"Sweet tea?" Fayrene asked. "I know you don't need a menu."

"Half and half," she answered. "And leave one menu. My friend's never been here."

"Would that be a *he* friend or a *she* friend?"

"Not that you're nosy."

Fayrene's smile was unrepentant. "A person has to get her entertainment where she can."

Jilly laughed. "Well, I'm going to disappoint you. He's just someone I work with." Sort of.

The door opened, and Gabriel walked in.

Jilly watched as he scanned the room looking for her, then moved in her direction. She hadn't had a chance to notice that he was in running clothes, all sweaty and muscled and—

"Sweetpea, if that's your coworker, you should be burning the midnight oil. Mm-mm…"

Then he got near enough that she saw how terribly scarred his legs were.

"Oh, honey," Fayrene murmured. "You treat him nice, you hear?"

"He will not welcome sympathy," she whispered furiously.

"He won't get it either. Those are some damn fine legs."

They were, all lean and muscled and powerful.

Then he arrived.

"Hi there," Fayrene said. "I'm Fayrene. Jilly here says you might need a menu, but if you come in often enough, like her, you won't for long. What can I get you to drink?"

"I'm eating," Jilly said to him. "I haven't had supper, and if you're smart, you won't leave here without eating, either. Best barbecue that will ever cross your lips." She turned to Fayrene. "This is Gabriel, by the way. Gabriel Coronado."

"Pleased to meet you. You new around here?"

He shook his head. "I grew up not far away."

Fayrene cocked her head. "You wouldn't be Carmen's grandson, now would you?"

Jilly couldn't decipher the welter of emotions that crossed his face. "Did you know her?" he asked.

"Sugar, I wouldn't be here without that woman. This place wouldn't exist. You order everything you want because this meal is on the house."

He seemed startled. "No, I—"

"Your money's no good here. Several years ago we had a bad fire that started in the kitchen. We didn't have insurance and couldn't afford to replace all the appliances. The barbecue pit was okay, but if we couldn't make any money, we couldn't rebuild. Carmen let us use her kitchen to cook the rest of what we sell, every single day for four months, while we put this place back together. She even rounded up some folks to contribute labor." Fayrene threw her arms around a very startled Gabriel and gave him a huge hug. "Wait until I tell Ray. Lord, I miss Carmen. She worried over you while you were in Iraq, kept her rosary with her all the time, praying practically every second." She bustled off, rushing to tell Ray.

But Gabriel didn't look pleased.

Instead he seemed miserable.

"What is it?"

He shook his head. "I can't be here."

"Sit down." Now she was the one barking out orders. "That is one of the nicest women on the planet. Don't you dare walk out on her."

He sighed and started to lower himself to the bench, but just then Fayrene returned, Ray in tow.

"Son, I am mighty glad to meet the grandson Carmen was so proud of." Ray grasped Gabriel's hand and gave it a hearty shake, then pulled him into a back-slapping hug. "You come from the finest stock on God's green earth. You eat here every day if you want to, and it's on us. We owe your grandmother a debt we could never repay."

"Thank you, sir." Jilly could see him mentally squirming at the attention.

"So it's good to see you walking around. Carmen was worried sick about you after the helicopter crash. Said the doctors were afraid you'd never walk again, but look at you." Fayrene turned to Jilly and gave her a big wink before bringing her focus back to him. "Mighty glad to see you on your feet. You staying at Carmen's place? Well, your place now, I guess."

Just then the bell in the kitchen dinged, and Ray swore. "Got to get back to work. You remember what I said, though, son. You are welcome here anytime, and it's on the house. This place would be long gone if not for Carmen."

More people arrived, and Fayrene, too, had to leave as soon as Gabriel gave her his order.

But he looked so uncomfortable that Jilly didn't know what to say to him, and he wouldn't look at her.

When he finally did, all he said was, "I don't want to talk about it."

Jilly's eyebrows rose, but she'd understood from the beginning that he was a very private man, so she guessed she shouldn't be surprised.

And she did have some experience with men with shadows. Her own family was rife with them.

She'd been right, she paused a second to absorb. Apparently Gabriel had a great deal in common with Rafe. She'd cut him some slack. "So did you find out anything about Freddie?"

Relief was in his gaze as he looked up. "Not enough. If I had a picture to show around, that would help, but his description could be anyone." He scowled. "Mako, though…you should have pressed charges. That is not just some mixed-up kid. I'm meeting with him tomorrow to discuss buying drugs."

"What? You can't be serious about doing that."

"Of course I'm not, but I need to meet this guy and put the fear of God into him about Freddie."

"Gabriel, you can't meet with a drug dealer. You could get hurt!"

"I've been in far more dangerous situations. I'll be fine."

"But you've already—" *Been badly hurt*, she wanted to say.

"The scars aren't from a punk like Mako," he said grimly. "So tell me what you've found out. And—" he closed his eyes for a second "—I don't know if I want to know where else you've been."

"I found Damien's mother. Gabriel, she doesn't just neglect Freddie, she hates him. And where they live...I know you don't want me to, but I've put in a call to Child Protective Services. Those children have to be better cared for."

"Don't be—" He didn't finish. Instead, he exhaled and rubbed the bridge of his nose. Then started again. "Was it really bad enough for the authorities to need to charge in and yank the younger one out of there? What I mean is, surely there's some kind of procedure, right? Unless the child is in imminent danger?"

"You're right, of course, it's just—" She looked into his eyes. "Children shouldn't have to live with someone who doesn't care about them."

Pain swept over his face. "Believe me, I know that."

"But your grandmother..." She was confused.

"*Mama C* was the best thing that ever happened to me." He stared at his hands. "My mother...not so much." His head rose. "But you have no idea how much worse kids have it in other parts of the world."

"You mean in a war zone? Like what you saw?"

He shut down. "We were talking about Freddie and his

brother. Those boys would wind up separated, you know that, right?" Without waiting for her answer, he pressed on. "My take is that Freddie is all the stability his brother has. Being parted won't do either of them any good."

"So you're asking me to do nothing?"

"Of course not. I asked you to give me some time."

"And he ran away from you."

Just then the other waitress arrived with their tea. "Ray said to tell you he's making up a plate for you special," she said to Gabriel.

Gabriel seemed flustered, an odd state for such a formidable man. "Thanks."

"Why does that bother you so much?" she asked after the woman left. "Clearly Ray and Fayrene want to do it."

"Their debt is to *Mama C*, not to me." Each word was a bullet. "I haven't earned it."

She placed her hand on his and he jolted a little, as though unused to being touched. "Let them," she urged. "I know it's not easy to accept favors, but it would make them so happy. They're two of the best people I know. Please, Gabriel."

He was still clearly uneasy, but at least he nodded. "All right." His hand beneath hers relaxed a little, and she was sorry when he removed it.

She wanted to touch him again. Be touched by him.

Have you ever tried to tame anything wild?

That could apply to him every bit as much as to Freddie.

Patience.

She gathered her thoughts. "Thank you. And I'm sorry. For what I said earlier, I mean. Freddie's skittish. You've been good to him, and it wasn't your fault that he ran away."

"It definitely was. But my reaction that night had nothing to do with him." He flicked her a glance she couldn't decipher.

"Do I want to know what you mean by that?"

"Probably not." For a moment their gazes locked, his dark eyes soft and full of secrets, but he volunteered nothing more.

Just then their plates arrived, and she was too starved to do anything but eat.

She wasn't wrong. The food was phenomenal. He hadn't realized how tired he was of his own cooking, though to be fair, even if he had been a gourmet chef, this meal would still be off the charts.

He'd cleared half his plate before she sighed happily, and he noticed she'd plowed through hers, too, though he had no idea where she'd put it. She ate like a trucker, small as she was.

"So…paradise, right?"

He nodded as he finished a mouthful. "Definitely." He pointed at her nearly spotless plate. "It's a wonder you don't weight three hundred pounds."

"With four older brothers, you learn not to fool around when food is on the table."

"You definitely work it off."

Her head tilted. "Would that be a compliment, Mr. Coronado?"

"I doubt I'm the first man to tell you you're beautiful."

Her eyes widened and locked on his. For a moment he thought she might be feeling the same zing of attraction.

Just then Fayrene came by, and he yanked his attention from Jilly, doing his best to ignore his discomfort over Fayrene's charity and focus on thanking her. From the way the woman's eyes sparkled and her cheeks turned pink with pleasure, he thought he might have succeeded.

Once they were alone again, Jilly cleared her throat. "So..." she said casually. "I'd probably be right in guessing you'd want to come along to the abandoned house Beto told me Freddie sleeps in sometimes."

He couldn't help smiling. She was a real piece of work. "Did that hurt much?"

"What?"

"Asking for help?"

"I wasn't asking for help. I could go there just fine on my own." She made a face at him. "And no, I wouldn't go this late by myself, *Dad*."

He only lifted an eyebrow—and not only because he felt not the slightest bit paternal toward her. "Thank you." He decided on the most diplomatic answer. "Seriously. I want to find him, too—both of them."

"Would you like dessert?" Fayrene asked, arriving to clear their plates.

"I don't know where I'd put it." He patted the belly that felt uncomfortably tight. "Though if it's anything like the rest of the meal, that's a crying shame."

"It is," Jilly said. "The banana pudding is to die for."

"You want some, hon? You could share it."

Jilly shook her head. "We have to be going, Fayrene." She dug into her purse, but Fayrene waved her off. "Nope, on the house, both of you."

"Him, I understand, but—" Jilly protested.

"Honey, in your own way, you remind me of his grandmother. You've done a lot for this part of town. Let me use this as just a little of the thank you that you deserve."

"But—"

Gabriel cleared his throat, and her cheeks reddened. *I know it's not easy to accept favors...*

Her glance said *Touché*. "Thank you, Fayrene. That's very sweet."

"And you, young man, we expect to see you back here often." Fayrene grabbed him in a hug before he could react. "I am so very glad to know you're safe. Carmen is smiling from heaven."

If only she knew how little he deserved that. Feeling like a fraud, he patted the older woman's back, then stepped away. "Thank you again. The food is amazing."

Business demanded that Fayrene not linger, and Gabriel gratefully escaped.

"Where's your truck?" Jilly asked when they were outside.

"I was on my run," he said.

"I'll drive."

He eyed her small car dubiously.

"All the men in my family are as big as you. Just watch your knees, and you'll make it." She grinned. "Not without a lot of grousing, if you're anything like them, but…you'll survive."

He did.

But just barely.

Holy crap, he thought as Jilly pulled up in front of a house that, if it wasn't already a crack house, would become one sooner or later. "You were seriously going to come here by yourself?"

Even Ms. *I Know What I'm Doing* seemed a little unnerved. "I…" She shook her head. "I've never been on this street before." She pointed behind them. "Just over on the next block or two, it's fine. A poor neighborhood, sure, but…normal." Her gaze whipped to his. "I wouldn't have gone in."

He only lifted one eyebrow.

Hard to tell in the faint light from the dash, but he thought she might be blushing.

"Well, you're here with me now, aren't you?"

She would have gone in. He knew it, and so did she.

Because she didn't give up on people.

"I wish I knew what you were thinking," she muttered. "Or maybe not."

Her disgruntled tone made him smile. He started to reach out, to brush her cheek with one finger and see if it was as soft as it looked.

Her head began to turn at the motion, and he quickly returned to his senses. *Not here, not now.*

Not ever.

"I have a flashlight on my keychain and a new, bigger one in the glove box," she said.

"The glove box that won't open because my knees are jammed up against it?"

She grinned. "That's the one. I should get a giant shoe horn to scoop you big guys out."

"Or a car larger than a matchbox." Cautiously, he began to extricate himself from the tin can deathtrap she was driving.

"I'm sorry." But she was laughing, and her laughter made him smile.

"Ow! Hey, no laughing 'til I'm out of here."

"Not laughing," she said, the fingers of one hand over her mouth. But her eyes were sparkling, and he wanted to cradle her head in his hand and bring that laughing mouth to his.

Instead he unfolded himself from the seat and stood. "So you're not perfect after all. Even a little mean streak, maybe."

"Have you been talking to my brothers?" She grinned. "Trust me, none of them think I'm remotely perfect." Deep affection was in every syllable. If he were one of her brothers, he'd lock her away from the world to protect that big heart from getting damaged by all the forces that didn't care about laughter and sunshine, that thrived on hate.

"So should I have worn black?" she asked. "Like a cat burglar or a ninja assassin?"

"I'm pretty sure anyone who's in the vicinity knows we're here." *Don't look at those legs, don't imagine your hands around that waist, don't*—"Be careful where you step. Or better yet, wait here and let me look first. Those heels could get you killed."

"And you think that's going to work. I was not raised to be a shrinking violet."

"I sorta got that already, but you have no idea what shape that structure's in."

"I'll be careful." She paused and sighed. "Would you like to take the lead? Would that make you feel better?"

I'll feel better when you're tucked in your bed, sound asleep. But that wasn't a good image for his concentration, either. "It would." He took the proffered flashlight and turned. "Stay right next to me." He wished for a weapon as he had not in a very long time. "And do exactly what I tell you." He looked back at her, surprised to discover that apparently she was taking him seriously. She nodded her agreement, big eyes solemn now.

He led the way, scanning their surroundings constantly, using every skill he'd ever learned to be sure he was in position to protect her.

Chapter Eleven

Freddie had definitely been here—or someone had. Inside a closet was stashed a threadbare blanket, a ratty quilt, and two dented cans of beans that had probably come from the dumpster. Up in the corner of a high shelf was a torn backpack containing one pair of jeans and two t-shirts, one of them a shirt that she'd seen Freddie wearing.

But what killed her was the worn toothbrush and nearly-gone tube of toothpaste.

Oh, Freddie… Jilly's heart broke for the child who'd had to grow up much too soon. Who, even though he had to struggle constantly simply to survive, still tried to make himself presentable.

She backed out of the closet and turned away so Gabriel wouldn't see her tears. She must have made some sound, though, because a large hand clasped her shoulder and turned her into him. "I'm sorry. It's just that…I've had so much in my life, and some children have such a hard time…it's so unfair."

His arm slid around her back, and she accepted the comfort of settling against his broad chest.

"Life isn't fair," he murmured. "But Freddie's a strong kid. He'll make it."

She lifted her head. "Will he? We can't know that."

"You'd be surprised what kids can survive." Something in his voice resonated with sorrow and pain. She very much wanted to ask about it, but she didn't want to disturb their fragile peace, so she didn't push.

His big palm cradled the back of her head as his strong arm held her close. "But we'll find him. We'll help him." His gaze locked on hers. "We won't give up."

We. A very powerful word to someone who was used to making her own way, to calling the shots, to fighting all attempts to make her obedient and cautious and…protected from the world.

He was so much better a man than he seemed to believe. "Gabriel," she whispered. *Kiss me*, she started to say but had the sense that he would never take that first step.

So she took it for both of them. Rose to her toes and laid her mouth on his.

He tried to resist; she felt it. Sensed him layering more chains on any urges he might feel.

But she also felt the shudder that ran through him as her tongue traced the contours of his lips. He was a hard man, a wounded one…but he had a beautiful mouth meant for kissing.

She wrapped her arms around his muscled torso and held on tight.

Until his chains broke.

Gabriel had lost his mind, that's all he could figure with what little brainpower he had left, as he succumbed to the yearning Jilly had brought to life inside him since their first meeting. She was sweet, she was light and life and joy…she was a scorching-hot kisser. And the curves he felt against him…

Sweet hell. Need roared through him like someone had opened a blast furnace door.

She whimpered and tightened her grip.

He froze. Realized how far gone he was and let go of her. Stepped back, hands out. "I'm sorry."

She stood there, chest heaving, her eyes huge and luminous in the moonlight. "What?"

He turned away. He couldn't look at her. His body was raging. He was much too close to losing control.

"He's not here," he said brusquely. "And this is no place for someone like you. Let's go." Actually, he'd have her let him out as soon as they were back inside a safer perimeter. He wasn't worried about himself, and he could sure as hell use the run home to blast away whatever insanity had taken hold of him.

But he wouldn't leave her, not out here. As a matter of fact, he'd insist that they drive to her house where he could see her safely inside first.

Then he would take the long route home. Burn out his brain and the lust that was even now clamoring for relief.

And no, it wasn't that simple. Lust was an easy answer, but it wasn't the whole picture. This valiant little creature made him ache. Made his heart yearn, the heart he'd thought lost and cold. Dead—and good riddance.

"Go?" she echoed.

"It's late. I've had a long day," he forced himself to say casually, though the sleepless night before had little to do with why he needed to call an end to time spent with her. The night to come would be worse. That kiss—hell, so many impressions of her he would never, ever forget—would keep him awake for hours. But she was too kind not to go along with his request.

Or at least that's what he'd thought, but when he had regained possession of himself enough, he faced her, expecting—well, he wasn't sure what he'd expected.

But not what awaited him.

"I'm not leaving," she said, chin jutting.

Actually, why was he surprised? "No way."

"You go right ahead, but it's not that late. He might still show up."

"He won't."

"You don't know that."

"I do. Kids are more resourceful than you realize, when survival's at stake." He felt a sharp stab of guilt at just how thoroughly he knew that.

"Why does that upset you?"

Something must have shown on his face. "It doesn't. The only thing that upsets me is that you're being purposely dense. I know you're not stupid, so sheer stubbornness is the only explanation."

She stared at him, and he was grateful for whatever cover the shadows gave him. "I said let's go," he repeated.

Damned if she didn't cross her arms over her chest, all but daring him to make her.

He couldn't help it. He chuckled. "I feel sorry for your brothers. You must have been hell on wheels as a little sister."

Temper vied with her general good nature. "With four of them and only one of me, I had to be strong to keep from getting run over."

"Strong. Uh-huh. I bet that's the term they used." One good thing—the battle of wills, coupled with the humor, had put a temporary cap on his near-violent need to bury himself inside her.

Something to be grateful for. Now if he could only manage to get her the hell out of this dump. Ordering her, however, was clearly not going to work, however sensible his intention was.

"Jilly…" He exhaled in a gust. "Look, I've had experience with this."

"I thought you said your grandmother kept you when your mother left. Am I wrong? Were you on the streets?" Her compassion kicked into high gear.

"No. It wasn't me. I was lucky. But where I've been…"

"In Iraq?"

He wished she hadn't been present to hear what Ray and Fayrene had said earlier, but he had enough experience with her now to understand that she didn't forget anything. "Yeah. A lot of kids were orphaned, and they had to fend for themselves. There were so many—too many to help as much as they needed. And the extremists didn't want us anywhere near the children, so the kids—" He snapped himself back from that abyss. "Anyway, kids like Freddie don't make it this long without being cagey. He's probably out there right now waiting for us to leave."

Her eyes went wide. "Then we need to stand outside and let him see it's us."

He sighed. At least she'd been distracted from asking him for details. "I doubt it will work, but all right." He stepped in front of her as she made her way toward the front door. "But I go outside, not you."

She was all set to object, but he overrode her. "That's the deal, Jilly, take it or leave it. You stay behind the door, and you don't say a word. I'm trained for fighting. You're not."

"You're unarmed. And you can't stop a bullet, Superman."

"Don't push me," he warned. "These houses seem empty, but we can't assume anything. Do you have any paper in your purse?"

She didn't blink. "Yes."

"Then write him a note and leave it rolled up in his blankets." It might send Freddie running, but it might not, and writing it would keep her out of the way while he scanned the surroundings again.

"What do I say?"

That she would even ask surprised him. "I don't know. He's sure not going to show himself if he thinks you're taking him to the authorities."

She pondered a minute. "I'll tell him I'm worried about you. That I need his help."

He frowned. "No."

"You're the one he relates to. He wouldn't have taken off the other night except that he thought you were going to ditch him. You're his father figure, Gabriel."

"Don't say that!" He didn't want that, not ever again.

"You really don't want anyone getting close to you, do you?"

He turned on one heel. "Write your note. I'll be outside. Do not come out until I say so."

He put distance between them as fast as he could.

She had a lot to think about. Too many reactions of her own to filter through. So when Gabriel gave her the green light, then used his body to shield hers, she didn't fight him. She didn't even argue when he asked her to drive to her place.

She was on the money about his need for privacy and distance, though, she was positive.

She was definitely going to call Rafe. The hour was late, but he was a night owl, and he was one time zone earlier in the far reaches of West Texas. She couldn't wait; she felt like she was stomping around in jackboots with Gabriel, and she didn't want to do any damage.

Not that he'd let her close enough to do so…except for those brief, staggering moments when he'd all but consumed her. When they'd been so wrapped up in each other that she could have been anywhere—Austin, Paris…Paradise…

Lordy. The man could kiss. No, he was nothing like the man she'd have picked for herself, someone normal, easy to read, someone who was charming and fun and on a solid career path—wait, she'd dated that guy already. Several of them.

Even she could see the humor in that.

This man was worlds away from any of them, all shadows and mysteries and sorrows…and he fascinated her. *Admit it, girlfriend. Teo wasn't wrong. He's a mystery you are dying to solve.*

Whether he wants you to or not. Which he clearly doesn't.

"I'll wait for you to get inside," he said, interrupting what she realized had been a silent ride.

"I'm fine here. This neighborhood is safe." She swiveled to face him, parked in front of her house just in case she could convince him to change his mind and let her take him home.

He just looked at her.

She sighed. "All right, all right, but this is silly. You said you didn't live that far away. It's no trouble at all for me to take you there."

"I like this time of night. It's when I most often run."

Well. She should probably be grateful he shared that factoid about himself. Heaven knows he guarded them as though they were diamonds.

Give it up, Jilly. He's not budging.

A smart person cut her losses and moved on to the next

goal. "Okay, so what about tomorrow?"

"What about it?" She could practically see the shutters slamming.

"If Freddie gets my note, how will he find you? Does he know where you live?" *Since I'm not allowed to?*

"Jilly…" His voice was surprisingly gentle. "He may never show up."

"And you're just going to leave it at that? Abandon him? Well, I'm not going to, I assure—"

The hand on her forearm halted her outrage. He was not someone who touched easily…and the feel of his skin on hers was something she wouldn't forget in this lifetime.

"I'm not giving up."

"Oh, no—you still have that meeting with Mako, don't you?" How had she forgotten? "You need backup. I could come with you."

He swore and twisted awkwardly in the small front seat, gripping her shoulder with all the vehemence on his face. "You. Will. Not. Interfere. Is that clear?"

If his eyes hadn't been as worried as his words were determined, she might have lost her temper.

Before she could speak, he continued. "I have experiences you cannot imagine. I am trained. I've killed people, Jilly." Then, as if regretting his candor, he subsided, though he didn't let her go yet. "I'm not going to walk into a situation I can't handle. It's a fact-finding mission, that's all. We've found Freddie's hiding place, so I may not need to show up at all." He pushed into her space. "But you will not get involved in this. If you think you have to involve Child Protective Services for Damien, then fine, but I'm betting they won't do anything about Freddie because he's not that woman's child. Freddie's on his own, and if he gets pushed too hard, we may lose him altogether."

That *we* again. She couldn't accuse him of being high-handed because he was clearly very concerned about both the boy and her. She wasn't foolish and wouldn't deliberately put herself in harm's way—at least not unless the circumstances called for it. She had to admit that the feeling of being on a team with this strong and capable man, however complicated he might be, was a good one.

"All right." She nodded, and she could feel the tension in him ease.

But when he backed away altogether, she was sorry. Even if the night had been plenty intense and she needed some time to absorb all that had changed.

"I'm going to do some checking into the options for Damien tomorrow, so we can assess the burden of proof for CPS to get involved and figure out our next step." She could see unspoken words spring to his lips, probably words like *I'll take care of this* or *it's not my problem* or maybe just *leave me alone.*

But he said none of them. Only nodded.

Then unfolded himself from her car and got out.

But he didn't move from the spot until she'd pulled into her driveway and gone inside.

She went to the front window and waved to him.

He didn't smile, didn't do anything but give her a half-wave and take off running.

She pressed her hand to the window and watched until he was out of sight.

"Rafe? Did I wake you?"

"Jilly? What's wrong?"

"Everything's fine."

"You forget that I own a clock. Everyone's okay down there?"

"As far as I know. How are all of you? How's Abuelita?"

"She misses you, but she's doing as well as anyone can expect for a woman her age."

"I miss her, too."

"What troubles you, Bright Eyes?" Rafe was a formidable healer—not only of bodies but of spirits—and part of it was the deep vein of intuition in him. He'd taken over for his grandmother as *curandero*, but he had additional medical training through the military that made him a godsend for many. Right now his deep voice, as soothing and patient as ever, made her want to climb into his lap and weep.

"I'm all right, really, it's just that there's this man—"

Her other brothers would have been jumping in, snapping off *What man? Who is this guy?* and barking out orders to be careful.

But Rafe only listened.

"It's not…we're not—Rafe, he's been in Iraq. He has terrible scars, and not all of them are physical, I don't think. But he's all closed in and doesn't want to talk about himself or get involved with anyone, yet he's kind, I'm positive, and he's reached out to this troubled boy and…" She sighed. "I don't know how to handle him."

"He doesn't want to be managed, honey." Her brother's voice held fond amusement. "Do you remember Lobo when he first showed up?"

"Yes." Lobo was a German shepherd, severely injured and a stray, who'd come to Rafe when her brother was recovering from nearly dying on a mission. The two had healed together, and they were still inseparable. "Why?" Though she shouldn't ask. Rafe was a serious man who never said anything frivolously.

"You were young."

"I was headed off to college."

"My point exactly." Already grown when she was born, Rafe could have ignored her altogether or treated her like a nuisance when she arrived in the family, but he never had. "He was terrified of people, and he would bite and snap at everyone but me and Abuelita."

"Sort of like you," she noted with a small smile.

"Very much like me. I wanted to be left alone, not only to heal my body but because my spirit was so troubled and I was so ashamed."

"Ashamed? Of what? You were a hero. You won medals."

"My team didn't survive. What is a piece of metal compared to a life lost? Why wasn't it me who died? How could I be certain I'd done everything possible to save them? It was my fault they were in that place to be ambushed, Jilly. They came with me out of personal loyalty on a mission of mercy that was my priority, not theirs." He fell silent again. "It's not easy to rejoin the living when you feel that way. It's like all the pain and shame and guilt you feel is on the outside of your skin, and even allowing yourself laughter or letting yourself enjoy the world others take for granted is acid poured on bleeding skin. It's the nature of those who care for you to reach out to you, but sometimes letting go of your guilt feels like you're betraying those who can never laugh with friends again or hold a loved one or…" That he still felt echoes of that pain was evident in his tone.

"But you have nothing to feel guilty for."

"I pray you're never in the position to understand how wrong you are or how logic means nothing to someone in that dark place."

"I am so sorry. I never knew…"

"I didn't want you to. And no one can, truly, except another who's walked that path."

"But it's better now, right?"

"Most days. But you never forget. It's a part of you. At best, you reach an uneasy peace. When a life is lost and you play a role in that loss, however unintentional, a scar is left."

"But you forgive yourself, don't you?"

"To a degree. You accept that however much you regret it, you cannot change what happened. You can only seek to make up for it somehow."

"Is that why you stayed in La Paloma?"

"It's one reason."

"Rafe, I love you." Her eyes burned and her heart ached with it. "And I admire you so much. Even more than I did before."

"You're part of what brought me back from that dark place, Bright Eyes. Your love is a formidable power."

"I don't do anything as important as you do, saving lives."

"I disagree. And you make lives better simply by being who you are."

"Hardheaded and bossy?"

He chuckled. "The love of my life could meet that description, too, but there's much more to both of you."

"Tell Dane that. Or Liam."

"The smart brothers understand your value." He meant himself and Alex, her other much-older half-brother who had also been so gentle with her from birth.

They shared a laugh.

"So what can I do for Gabriel?"

"That's his name?"

"Gabriel Coronado."

"Alex or Saint could find out more about him if you asked."

No way. Not even if she weren't hiding her incident from them. "But that would be wrong, wouldn't it? He needs to tell me himself."

"You're not so young."

"Thank you. But I need to do *something*."

"Are you attracted to him, Bright Eyes?"

"Are you going to tell the others?"

"Not right now."

"That's honest." But a big step for one of her guardians. "If it's any consolation, he's as bad as the rest of you about trying to protect me."

"I like him already."

"I think you really would. He reminds me of you in some ways. That's a compliment, by the way."

"And one I appreciate." He paused. "To answer your question, you can help him most by being perhaps a little less *you* than normal. That's not a complaint, but you do tend to be, shall we say, a little driven? Push him, but not too hard. Be his friend. Give him space but not too much. It's a hard place he is in, and a dark one. Your light is bright, but sometimes the light you crave is the light you can't allow yourself to enjoy. Does that make any sense?"

"Sort of—I mean, yes, but…"

"Listen to your heart—listen carefully, Jilly. Not to your head. Logic and will are assets you have in abundance, but this situation calls for patience, above all."

"Never my strong suit."

"Maybe not, but your heart is as big as the world. He's a lucky man, this…friend."

"You know you don't want to hear that I find him outrageously sexy."

She could almost hear his brotherly wince. "Not really. But I know you'll be careful."

His fingers were undoubtedly crossed. She laughed. "You do not. You're already itching to dial the phone and tell Alex and Saint and Dane to keep an eye on me."

"I am…but I won't. At least not as long as you check in with me regularly and ease my mind."

"Blackmail? That's all kinds of wrong." But she was grinning.

"Jilly," he said, his voice completely serious. "There is nothing I wouldn't do to protect you. Every one of us feels the same. You are our treasure."

"I know that. Sometimes I even appreciate it."

"I'm not kidding. Call me soon."

Or. But he left the threat unspoken. "I will. Love to Diana and the kids, and please give Abuelita a hug for me and tell her I'll come for a visit as soon as I can. I wish she was going to be at the wedding. Travel is hard for her, I know. I just—I really do miss her…and I miss you, big brother."

"I'm always here for you, Bright Eyes."

"I know that. And thank you for the advice."

"Sweet dreams, little sister."

"I love you, Rafe."

"*Te amo*," he replied in kind.

Jilly disconnected. Glanced over at the window through which she'd last seen Gabriel.

And stared into the darkness for a long time.

Gabriel covered ground faster than ever before, as if putting distance between himself and Jilly would help.

He'd never forget the feel of her. The fire in her kiss. She made him ache, damn it, and not only for that sweet body beneath the lady suit. She was a warm hearth on a cold night, the ray of light in a dark dawn.

But even if he were in any condition to be with someone, it wouldn't be her. Couldn't be. For so many reasons.

She'd wear him out, for one, and his grim thought turned to a short huff of laughter. The woman was relentless. He wondered what on earth it would take to make her give up on something she wanted...but he actually didn't want to know. Didn't want to see that sparkle dimmed. Didn't want any of his shadows to block out her sunny view of the world.

So how the hell did he put distance between them?

Find Freddie first. Make sure the kid was okay, even if that meant that Jilly's belief in the system would win out. The boy needed someone, and he could sure as hell do worse than have the fearfully intense Miss Sunshine claim him as her cause, whatever Gabriel had initially thought.

As he covered the blocks, his rhythm and breathing steady, he tried to figure out his next step.

"Hey now!" A whistle announced the car pulling up beside him. "Where's the hot *chica*?"

Mako's boys, from the convenience store earlier. Great. Just what he wanted.

He halted because he was too close to his place and didn't want them knowing where he lived.

"Watch your mouth," he responded.

The car jammed to a stop. "What you say to me, *cabron*?" The passenger, sleeve tattoos down both arms, jumped out. Flicked open a switchblade.

Gabriel registered the weapon but didn't react to the threat. "I said watch your mouth. Where's your boss?"

"If you talkin' about Mako, he not my boss. He ain't gonna see you anyway."

"Why? He's too busy using little boys to help him with

petty theft?" Gabriel sneered. Suddenly a good fight sounded like just the thing to burn off some of what was boiling inside him.

"Don't you be callin' me boy."

"I meant the kid—what's his name? Freddie or something?" Gabriel kept his voice dismissive. "Why isn't he with you?"

"Freddie, he ain't gonna be trouble for no one pretty soon."

The second kid, the one with a soul patch, snickered.

"Yeah? Why's that?" Carefully he kept his tone casual.

"Cause Freddie got in Mako's face over the *chica*. Mako mess him up good."

Gabriel's gut clenched. "Where is he now?"

"Dunno. Don't care," said Tattoo.

"Thass right. Why we should care?" said his sidekick, now out of the car and rounding the hood.

Gabriel grabbed Tattoo and disarmed him in one lightning move, then held the punk's own knife at his throat.

Soul Patch's eyes bugged out. "What the hell?"

"Tell. Me." Gabriel held Tattoo still and stared into Soul Patch's eyes. "Where is the boy?"

"I don't know. What's wrong with you?"

"You want me to drop him and come after you?"

The punk swiveled his eyes back and forth between their faces, not so full of himself now. He braced to run back to the car.

"Try it. I'll be on you before you make it."

The kid looked ready to wet his pants, all bravado fled. "I don't know. Last I saw he was across from the school, trying to get up off the ground."

"And you just left him."

"He ain't my friend. He just some kid who got a big

mouth."

Gabriel let Tattoo go. He fell to the ground gasping. "What about you?" Gabriel said to him. "Where is Freddie?"

"Don't…know. You…crazy."

Gabriel pulled him up by his collar and glared at Soul Patch. "You tell Mako I'm watching him. And if he ever lays a hand on that boy again, he will answer to me." He shook Tattoo. "You hear that? Same goes for you and your buddies. Stay away from Freddie. I'll be watching all of you."

"Mako ain't gonna like that," Soul Patch warned.

"Mako is a punk. I'm not scared of him." He leaned into the Soul Patch's face and let Tattoo go. "But you'd better be afraid of me. Now get the hell out of here."

He watched as they scrambled up and left, tires squealing.

Then he took off himself, headed home for his truck.

He had to find Freddie.

Chapter Twelve

Gabriel had tried the school grounds first, but they were abandoned. He hadn't wasted a lot of time searching for signs of the attack to track Freddie, though that would be his next step if Freddie wasn't in the abandoned house nearby.

Though it was only a couple of streets away, he drove, even if it was a risk that Freddie would hear and escape out the back into the dense vegetation when he heard a vehicle pull up. Maybe the boy would recognize Gabriel's truck, but he might not even look.

On the other hand, he might be hurt too badly to run, and if so, Gabriel would need his truck nearby to be able to take Freddie for medical help. Not that he couldn't carry the boy for miles, if need be—the kid weighed maybe a hundred pounds, and Gabriel had shouldered wounded comrades weighing twice that, carrying them over rough terrain in brutal heat.

Blood...the dead weight of the chopper pilot's body as Gabriel tried to rise on legs that wouldn't hold—

No. He blinked hard. Shoved the image down deep.

Fists clenched, he emerged from the truck, scanning the deep shadows both for threats and for any sense that Freddie was nearby. When he reached the house, he walked around the entire structure before entering at the back.

Once inside he stood very still, listening both with his ears and the extra sense he'd honed over years of living in a hostile environment where you couldn't be sure which direction threats would come from…only that they would.

He'd hoped to leave that world behind, but what was the old saying? *Life is what happens while you're busy making plans?*

Too many night patrols, too many adrenaline spikes. And never, ever, a deep and restful sleep. The sky could suddenly flare into day, the world going utterly still in that heavy pause like the world holding its breath, then…

Shattering explosions. Shouts from the terrified. Screams of the injured.

Groans of the dying…

No! No—Sayidah…Ahmed…blood, so much blood, parts of…

Gabriel bent double. Sank to his knees, hands clapped to his ears, feeling himself pulled into that place, that dark, airless tunnel—

Chest heaving, he shook like a fever victim, uncontrollable shivers that—

Stop. For the love of—Stop. Gabriel rocked, hands gripping his hair, head moving side to side as he gasped for air. *No more. No…more.*

Then he heard it. The sound that was…real. That was…here.

Slowly he began to crawl out of that place, the Gabriel that was left of him, the one he'd hidden from *Mama C*, from…everyone.

Long, slow pulls of air dragged from the depths of him…*slow*….

Another sound, this time a sob.

Like an old man, Gabriel painstakingly rose to his feet, stumbling back into this place, this time. "Freddie?" He moved toward the sound, and every step brought him more into the present, helped him find solid ground, push away the wraiths who haunted his dreams.

He halted, listened hard.

Nothing.

After a moment, he resumed searching, going first to the closet where they'd uncovered Freddie's pitiful stash of belongings.

Which were undisturbed.

Forehead wrinkled, Gabriel glanced around him, tried to pinpoint the source of the sounds he'd heard. "Freddie, it's Gabriel. I want to help you. Speak up so I can find you."

Maybe there had been a noise, or maybe his mind was playing tricks. Gabriel picked up the pace, going from room to room, opening closets and peering into shadows with the aid of his flashlight.

There was no basement and only a square opening for the attic with nothing to climb on to get up there. But his spidey sense was telling him that he wasn't alone.

He reentered the kitchen, and his gaze arrowed to the sink. With quick steps he reached the cabinet doors beneath and opened them. Only darkness greeted him.

Except—

At the back of the adjoining cabinet, which was open to the area under the sink, he spotted the tip of a sneaker. "Freddie," he said quietly. "How badly are you hurt?"

Then he heard the shallow pants, smelled the coppery tang of blood.

That smell…

Gabriel clenched his fists and fought to remain present, though a low buzz was rising inside his head.

No. "I'm here, son. I'll take care of you. Just hold on."

Gabriel cursed himself for refusing to join the modern age and get a cell phone. Because of that, Freddie's survival was up to him. He was all the kid had right now.

God help him.

"Okay." Gabriel moved into place in front of the adjoining cabinet doors and opened them.

Freddie lay there in an impossibly shallow space that would be hell to get him out of, his eyes glazed over with pain, his face sweaty and abnormally pale.

"You're gonna be okay, Freddie." he said because that's what you say, even to guys who are missing half their bodies, to keep them from going into shock. Or giving up. He scanned the space, puzzling his way through how to extract the boy with the least amount of movement when he had no idea how badly injured Freddie was.

He got down on his belly and reached into the cabinet, running his hands over the boy's legs and chest, pausing to estimate his heart rate and feel Freddie's forehead. His fingers came away slick with blood.

A small, battered body…

His mind started to slip again, but ruthlessly he held on.

A head wound, but how bad? No way to be sure—even mild cuts to the scalp bled like crazy. Freddie's heart rate was rapid but even, and Gabriel grabbed onto that reassurance while Freddie whimpered nearly everywhere Gabriel touched.

"Look at me," he told the boy. "I have to get you out of here, but I'll be as gentle as I can. We'll take it slow, and you need to tell me if it hurts too badly. Relax as much as you can while I try to slide you out, okay? Can you do that, Freddie? Can you hear me?"

"What…happened?" Freddie's breath was short, harsh gasps.

"Sh-h. Don't talk unless you have to." Loss of memory? Also not good, but that the boy was talking made Gabriel's concern ease a fraction. "Okay, here we go. I'm sorry it's going to hurt, but I have to get you out so I can help you."

"Who are you?"

Oh, hell. Really not a good sign. Classic symptom of either closed head injury or lack of oxygen. "It's me, Gabriel."

Freddie clutched at his arm. "What happened?"

"You've been hurt, Freddie, but you're not alone anymore. I'm here now. You don't have to be afraid. I'm not going to let anyone hurt you."

The brown eyes were stark with pain and fear. Gabriel didn't want to care. Bad things happened that he couldn't prevent. This kid couldn't know just how little faith he should have in Gabriel.

But right now, he was all the boy had.

"You are going to be fine," he said. "We'll take it slowly, and you tell me to stop whenever you need to, all right?" Gabriel didn't wait for an answer. If this kid's lung was collapsed as his gasping indicated, that, along with the confusion, meant it was critical that he be seen immediately.

With one arm he lifted Freddie a couple of inches, using his other hand to brace the boy's upper body. Freddie groaned but remained as still as possible.

"You're doing good," Gabriel soothed as he let one arm protect the boy's body from hitting any of the wood. He drew Freddie out with the other hand as smoothly and gently as the close quarters would allow.

Sweat rolled into Gabriel's eyes, and Freddie's face had gone tight with pain, but inch by inch, he got first the upper body, then the lower out of the cabinet, easing him to the floor on his back, so Gabriel could examine him better.

Immediately, Freddie cried out in pain and curled up on the filthy floor, tears rolling down his cheeks, his breathing hoarse, shallow pants. Gabriel did a quick scan of his extremities and checked his heart rate again while listening to his breathing, examining his pupils and their reaction to the light.

When he touched the boy's belly, the boy cried out again. Curled in a tighter ball.

Crap. Internal bleeding.

Freddie coughed, and he writhed in pain. "What happened?"

A second cough, this time with blood. Freddie began crying in earnest.

Damn it. The limited medical training every Special Forces team member got wasn't enough. But keeping Freddie calm was essential. "Sh-h," Gabriel said as he stripped off his shirt to press against the boy's head, tying it in a rough knot at the front. "Freddie, you have to stay as calm as you can, all right?" Why the hell couldn't he be in this situation with his pack full of supplies? Or a damn cell phone to call for proper handling? How long would an ambulance take to get here if he could?

Moot point. He couldn't call. Freddie's survival was up to him right now.

Then, at long last, the tunnel receded completely. As he'd always done in times of crisis before, Gabriel's world narrowed to the needs of the moment, his mind deadly calm and cold.

He had no gurney, no medical kit. There was only him. His body that hadn't been seriously tested since it had been broken to pieces.

Didn't matter. This boy was not going to die on his watch. No one else was, ever again.

"Freddie, I have to go to my truck."

Desperate, frightened eyes stared into his.

"You'll be fine. I'll be back real quick. I'm going to make you a bed from your blanket and quilt, okay?" He wished he had a backboard or something, anything to keep the boy's movement to a minimum. "Freddie?"

"What happened? Who are you?"

He'd seen this before, the confusion, the asking of questions again and again. You still had to answer them, especially when there was need for the patient to be calm. Though everything in him shouted for haste, he answered once more. "It's Gabriel, Freddie. You've been hurt, but you're going to be all right. I'm going to get your blanket and your quilt, all right?"

A tiny nod.

"No one's going to get past me. You're safe."

Hopeless eyes looked into his, and Gabriel couldn't blame the kid. When had Freddie ever had anyone to count on?

"You're going to be okay," he repeated. "Be back in a second."

He made record time assembling a pallet in the bed of his pickup. If he'd had a new truck with a second seat, he wouldn't have to put the boy back here, but there was no way Freddie could sit up, and fastening a seat belt around him was out of the question.

He returned to find Freddie silently crying as much as his gasping breath would let him. He crouched beside the boy and put a hand on his shoulder. "It's me, Gabriel. You're safe." He bent and scooped the boy into his arms as gingerly as possible, but he could see the agony on the boy's face. Every step seemed to take an hour as he tried not to jostle him, but crossing unsteady ground with only the moon to light the way made the task nearly impossible. He couldn't hold the flashlight, though—he needed both hands to hold Freddie without squeezing him more than absolutely necessary.

When he laid the boy down on his side, Freddie screamed, then went limp, no doubt passed out from the pain. It was a mixed blessing. Unconsciousness was not what you wanted when a head injury was involved, but the fifteen minutes or so it would take to get to the trauma center wasn't likely to be an easy trip. Gabriel did a quick second check for pupil response, and it wasn't great, but no worse than before.

He used what he had in the bed of the truck to block around Freddie and secure him the best he could manage.

"Freddie," he said, leaning over the pickup bed, talking to ease them both, even if only one of them was listening. You never really knew what people would hear at times like this, and a soothing voice could help. "Stay with me. You are going to be fine." *I promise* would have been a stronger reassurance.

But Gabriel knew only too well the limits of promises he'd made in the past.

He climbed into the truck and started the engine, windows down, listening hard for sounds from the back.

Hold on, Freddie. You have to hold on.

"Hello?" Jilly croaked into the phone when the ringing woke her.

"It's Gabriel."

Gabriel? She glanced at the clock. Three a.m.

"I didn't want to call you, but—"

"Are you in trouble?" She sat up quickly and flicked on the lamp.

"No. It's Freddie." His tone was ominous.

Her breath seized. "You found him?"

"Yeah. After Mako and his boys beat the hell out of him. I'm at Mercy Hospital with him."

Oh, Freddie… "How bad is it?"

"Bad. Don't know the extent of his injuries yet, but a

concussion at a minimum, probably cracked or broken ribs, possible internal bleeding." He sounded weary and…hollow. His voice was nearly a monotone.

"Are you all right, Gabriel?"

"Yeah."

He didn't sound fine. "I'll be there as soon as I get dressed."

"Not asking that."

"Doesn't matter. I'm coming anyway." She was already slipping on jeans and searching for a shirt. "Why would you call if you didn't—oh, no! He's going to be okay, right?"

"Hope so." But he still sounded…off.

"Gabriel, thank you. For finding him, I mean. And for taking care of him."

"Yeah." He exhaled. "Called because the nurses have already contacted Child Protective Services. Damn it," he muttered, the first real sign of life in his voice. "I promised."

"Promised what?"

"That he'd be safe. Knew better." The depth of Gabriel's despair didn't match with the situation.

"He will be safe with foster parents," she reassured him. "I've met quite a few of them. People don't get involved with that program if they don't care about kids, and they're screened. He'll be fine, Gabriel."

"Nobody's safe," she thought she heard him say.

Just what had he seen in Iraq? She thought of Rafe's advice. *Push him, but not too hard. Be his friend. Give him space but not too much.*

Instinct told her this wasn't the right time. Being physically present might help, however. "I'm on my way," she said. "Are you in the ER waiting room?"

"Yeah." He sounded exhausted and discouraged.

"Have the police shown up yet?"

"No."

"There's someone I can call. He'll help us. Don't leave, Gabriel, please, just…wait for me."

She disconnected as she headed for her chest of drawers, grabbing the first t-shirt she could find—but then she hesitated. If she was going to have to fight for Freddie, she'd better look a little more professional. Though it made her uneasy to take the time when Gabriel sounded strange and had a habit of vanishing, she paused long enough to change into slacks and a top, grabbing a snappy jacket to cover it. A slick of lipstick, a quick brushing of her hair, and she looked more like a woman than the teenager she was too often mistaken for. Sensible pumps on her feet, and she was already dialing as she walked to her car, apology on her lips as the phone rang.

"Valdez," answered the deep, sleepy voice.

"Saint, it's Jilly. I'm really sorry to wake you, but I need help."

"Where are you?" He sounded instantly awake. "Are you safe?"

"I am, but someone I care about isn't. A boy, and it may be both gang and drug-related."

Saint Valdez was an Austin police detective and member of VICTAF, an interagency violent crimes task force. He had a special spot in his heart for kids and a great deal of experience with gangs.

And he was almost family, married to her dear friend Clarice, the sister of Rafe's wife Diana.

"What's going on?"

"Freddie's fifteen. He's at Mercy, badly beaten. He's…a kid I know. From one of the Foundation houses." Jilly resisted an inner sigh. There was no way Saint wasn't going to put the pieces together eventually and know all about her incident.

And he would spread the word in the family. She so did not want to have the discussion that would ensue.

But Freddie was in need, and she was clearly fine now, so maybe Saint would only lecture her and not bring the rest of the family into it.

Uh-huh. Sure thing.

"You know who beat him up?"

"Gabriel said it was a guy named Mako and his boys."

"Gabriel?"

Yep…going to get complicated, all right. "He's a…friend."

"Okay." But she could hear both a smile and a cocked eyebrow in Saint's voice. "So give me details."

"I don't have any. I'm headed to the hospital now."

"Stay home. I'll call you when I know more."

"I'm already on my way. And…they need me."

"They?"

Jilly sighed. "It's a long story."

"I've got nothing else to do while I'm driving over. Bye, babe," she heard him say. And heard Clarice's sleepy answer. As a cop's wife, Clarice was no doubt accustomed to late night calls.

But then Jilly heard the unmistakable sound of kissing. "I love you," Saint said softly to his wife.

"Love you, too. Be safe." Clarice's voice was faint.

"Always." A few moments of silence, the sound of a door opening and closing. "Okay, kid. Spill. Who's this Gabriel, and what are you doing involved with a kid with gang problems?" He paused. "As if I can't guess, Ms. Bleeding Heart."

"Saint, can we keep this between us? Please?"

"A mystery man, a kid you call me out in the middle of the night for, and you're asking me to lie to the family that adores you? I don't think so."

"I'm not in any trouble. There's—it's just..." She exhaled in frustration. "Saint, Freddie needs your help. Please can we just start there? I'm fine, and I'm not in any danger. This is just about a homeless kid I'm trying to help."

"Freddie's homeless? What's his last name?"

"It's Miller."

"Any priors?"

"I don't think so."

"In a gang?"

"Not that I know of."

"So how come this gang attacked him?"

"I'm not sure. Gabriel might know. He's the one who found Freddie hurt."

"Where?"

"I don't know that, either. Gabriel just called me from the hospital. I didn't ask, I just—"

"Jumped out of bed and raced toward the gunfire. Jilly to the rescue—no surprise there."

"There's no gunfire."

"You know what I mean."

"I'm not an idiot, Saint. I'm a grown woman in charge of a whole organization, I support myself, I—"

"Okay, okay...you're right. I'm sounding like one of your brothers, aren't I?"

"You are. Please, could you just be my friend tonight?"

"You didn't call because I'm a cop?"

She had to smile. "Well...yeah. But you're my friend, too."

"Okay, *friend*, next question: who is this Gabriel? And who is he to you?"

For one of the few times in her life, Jilly didn't have a ready answer.

"I'm not sure," she said slowly, realizing it was true. That somehow Gabriel wasn't just one of her clients or one of, as her family called them, her charity cases. Even before that kiss that had rocked her to her toes, he'd had a hold on her, though he clearly didn't return the sentiment. He didn't want to be involved with people, he'd made that clear without saying a word.

But he'd said *we. We'll find him. We'll help him. We won't give up.*

Then he'd gone after Freddie until he'd found him.

And…he'd called her. When he needed someone, he'd called *her.*

"You still there?" Saint asked. "I'm five minutes away from the hospital."

"I'm parking across the street. See you inside?"

"Absolutely." Saint disconnected.

Jilly did the same. Got out of her car and locked it, then quickly crossed the street and the circle drive that led to the front door, veering to the right to head for the waiting room just across the lobby.

And there he was, still in his running clothes.

With blood smeared all over him. Though she didn't think it was his, her heart stuttered.

"Gabriel," she said.

He turned, and for a second she thought his eyes held gladness.

Who is he to you?

I'm not sure.

She wasn't.

But whoever he was, he was becoming more important all the time.

She smiled and walked toward him.

He started to reach for her, but he quickly stepped back,

his expression shutting down. "I'm filthy."

"I couldn't care less." She placed her hand on his muscled forearm. "Unless the blood's yours. It's not, right?"

He was staring down at her hand, which looked so small and so pale on his bronzed skin. Slowly his eyes met hers, dull and lifeless. "All Freddie's."

Her stomach clenched, but she didn't let herself react. He looked exhausted, and from more than the late hour. His weariness seemed as much of the soul as the body. "Why don't we sit down?" She took his hand and moved toward a set of chairs in the corner.

Astonishingly, he followed. And with no argument.

Once there, he sank heavily into a chair and let his head fall back against the wall.

But incredibly, he didn't pull his hand from hers.

"Thank you" seemed the best way to begin. "For finding him." She bit her lower lip. "He's going to make it, right?"

"One lung was collapsed. Pretty sure there was internal bleeding from the way he couldn't lie flat. His head bled like crazy, but head wounds always do. But he's confused, and there are some other signs that might mean either a closed head injury or lack of oxygen from the lung—damn it!" He launched himself from the chair and began to pace.

Jilly was set to follow when she heard her name called and turned to spot Saint headed toward her.

"Hey, kiddo." He pulled her into a quick hug. "That him?"

"Yes. Gabriel?"

Gabriel turned at the sound of her voice. When he spotted Saint beside her, he closed down again.

She crossed to him, Saint in tow. "Gabriel Coronado, this is Saint Valdez. He's a detective but also a member of the family." *So you can trust him*, she tried to convey with her eyes.

"Good to meet you," Saint said as they shook hands.

"Same here." But the caution didn't disappear.

"Listen," Saint said. "I can get you some scrubs so you can change out of those. They're used to us asking."

Gabriel's gaze shifted to hers. "No need." He tore his gaze away. "But thanks."

"It won't take a sec." Saint got the attention of a clerk and had a rapid discussion before he returned. "Let's go in here and talk." Saint pointed to a room next door meant for doctors to talk to family members.

Gabriel went in first but didn't take a seat. Instead he walked to the far wall and leaned against it, still and waiting.

An orderly arrived with a scrub top. Saint thanked him, then shut the door before handing the top to Gabriel.

"Thanks." His face a mask, Gabriel donned the shirt.

"I'm not gonna ask how you got involved with Jilly," Saint began. "She already warned me off. Plus she's little, but she's snake-mean."

Jilly stuck out her tongue at him.

Saint chuckled. Gabriel hardly reacted. Nonetheless, she appreciated Saint trying to take down the tension a notch.

Even if the improvement was barely noticeable.

Then Saint got down to business. "So what can you tell me about who attacked the boy?"

First Gabriel glanced toward the closed door. "Will they come look for us in here? Because Freddie's been in there awhile."

Saint glanced at Jilly, who really didn't want to leave. Gabriel was a big man, even a little taller than Saint, but foolishly or not, she felt protective of Gabriel.

Saint only lifted an eyebrow. "Jilly? Would you let them know where we are?"

She was being sent to her room, and Gabriel would receive dire warnings about how many people stood in line to inflict punishment if he hurt her.

Oh, lordy. That one kiss would not likely be repeated.

The story of her life.

"I'll go," she conceded. "But if you issue one threat, Saint, I'll—"

The first eyebrow was joined by the second, as in *you and whose army?*

"Remember those overprotective brothers we discussed?" she asked Gabriel. "Well, here's one of my honorary big brothers." She inflected the word *honorary* with all the sarcasm she could layer on. "Don't believe one word he says about me." She turned to Saint. "And he'd better be right here when I get back, you hear me?"

Saint grinned and turned to Gabriel. "See? Don't assume she's as sweet as she looks."

To her astonishment, Gabriel actually smiled faintly. "I've had my taste of her temper already. Several times."

"I'm not listening," she sang as she walked from the room with one finger in each ear.

"Okay, she's gone, so before she gets back, a) consider yourself warned, anyway, and b) what the hell are you doing getting her involved in something like this?"

The detective's voice seemed to be coming from a great distance down the tunnel where nothing touched him, nothing was…real.

With effort Gabriel responded, striving for normal. "Can anyone stop her when her mind is made up?"

The detective didn't seem to notice the disconnect. His

eyes warmed, and he nodded. "Too true. Okay, warnings over, though I promise I will kick your ass, even if I might have to stand in line." He paused. "What branch of the military?"

The guy was a detective, after all. Gabriel shouldn't be surprised he could tell. "Army. Special Forces."

Saint glanced at his legs. "That where you were torn all to hell?" But not a trace of pity in the statement.

Which made it easier to respond. "Yeah. Chopper crash outside Mosul."

"Thank you for your service." Said with such quiet sincerity, it might have been the most welcome expression of the sentiment Gabriel had ever heard.

The tunnel receded a little, and he nodded. "I appreciate that."

"She's amazing, you know, and not as invulnerable as she comes across. But scrappy, more than the rest of us wish sometimes."

"I don't want her involved, but she already was before I came along." The other man's forehead wrinkled. "She didn't tell you, huh?"

Alarm leaped into Saint's eyes. "Tell me what?"

Gabriel hesitated. "She's gonna be pissed."

"Then she shouldn't be holding out on us. What happened?"

Gabriel began to explain about the theft and her encounter with Freddie and Mako, and with every word, every memory, he edged closer to the light and out of the tunnel. He tried to describe how he'd found her as unemotionally as possible for Saint's sake, but the man had been a cop a long time. He could read between the lines. The muscle jumping in his jaw was evidence of that.

"On behalf of the family, thank you for stepping in to save her."

"Didn't say I did."

"You didn't have to. Okay, so this Mako—height, weight, build, anything you've got. His sidekicks, too."

Gabriel gave him as complete a description as he could remember. He was all the way out of the tunnel now, anger a growing buzz in his head. "But if I find him first…"

"Not a good idea to say that to a cop."

"Yeah." Gabriel didn't care who knew. Freddie's cries rose to a roar in his head, a howling, murderous wind of all the death he'd seen, the children he didn't save. *Ahmed and Sayidah at play with the rest of the kids who'd sought him out, gunned down by zealots who considered them tainted by their association with him…*

Once more he fought the tunnel. "He's the one who nearly killed Freddie—him and a couple of other punks. He wants to posture like he's some kind of badass dealer, but that's all he is, a punk."

"A punk who isn't in jail, why?"

"Jilly wouldn't press charges."

Fury flared in the other man's eyes. A few ripe words escaped his lips. "I swear I am going to lock that girl in a closet somewhere." Saint's eyes shifted to his. "But like the kicking your ass thing, I'll have to stand in line. She may find herself back in West Texas before sundown."

"I most certainly will not," Jilly said from the doorway, and if Gabriel had thought Saint's eyes were bright with anger, they were cool compared to hers as they shifted to him. "What? You couldn't wait to squeal on me? What did you tell him?" She marched right over and stabbed her finger into Gabriel's chest. "You had no right."

"And you have no sense, if you think letting someone like Mako go free is anything but stupid," Saint said. "Did it occur to you that the boy wouldn't have been beaten within an inch of his life if you hadn't been playing Pollyanna?"

Jilly gasped and recoiled as if he'd struck her.

The roaring in his head died in the face of her devastation. "He could have gotten out on bail already," Gabriel said, glaring at Saint. "You know he could have." He turned Jilly toward him. "It's not your fault."

Her eyes were filled with horror, her face gone bloodless. "It *is* my fault. I never thought…oh, Freddie…" Tears spilled over her lashes.

She looked so stricken. For an insane instant, Gabriel wanted to take her into his arms, but she should not be turning to him.

"Jilly, I'm sorry," Saint said. "You just…you scare the hell out of me sometimes."

"But you were right," she said, voice shaking. Then resolutely she straightened and sniffed back her tears. "I have to live with that." She brushed at her eyes. "I was going to tell you that the nurse says they're taking Freddie into surgery. The CT scan showed that his spleen needs to be taken out and his liver is badly bruised. They've re-inflated his lung, but he's also got a concussion and swelling in the brain. They're guessing two hours before he's out of surgery."

"What about the social workers?" Gabriel asked.

"I can't call anyone I know until morning."

Saint looked at them both. "I can. Tell me what you want, Jilly, and I'll make it happen."

"I want to be his foster parent," she said.

"No," Gabriel said instantly.

"No," Saint said at the same moment.

When Gabriel looked at him, he knew that *it's not safe* was their shared understanding. There could be further repercussions of the attack, and she should be nowhere near the boy.

"You asked what I wanted, Saint," she said quietly but

firmly. "I want to take care of that boy. You've been a foster parent. You can help me get approved."

The two had a staring contest.

At last, Saint exhaled. "I'll see what I can do," he said, jaw clenched. "As soon as I put out a bulletin on Mako." He left the room.

"Jilly..." Gabriel began.

She stepped away, her eyes snapping as she looked up at him. "You had no right to tell him about that night."

"He'd have found out soon enough."

"I thought you were my friend. I thought—never mind." She turned on her heel and headed for the door.

"I can't be anyone's friend," he warned her.

But she was already gone.

In place of the roaring fury, fatigue invaded him down to the bone. Left him desperate to go somewhere quiet and dark, to just lie down. To not think.

But he couldn't do that. Not yet.

First he was going to change out of these clothes.

Then he was going after that little bastard Mako.

Once out the door, however, he spotted her in front of a glass wall, staring into the darkness, standing vigil for a boy she barely knew. She held herself motionless, her posture lacking her normal bounce, that lively cheer and boundless interest in the world around her gone missing altogether. In the glass, he could see that her eyes no longer sparkled, that they were sad and...despairing.

He had no business going to her. He had nothing to offer.

But he couldn't leave her.

"Jilly…I'm sorry. It's just…this can't end well. I don't want to hurt you," he said as he approached. "But I'm no good for you."

She didn't turn, only met his gaze in the glass before her. A rueful smile curved her lips. "What, you think one kiss, and I'm gone? Just…head over heels because I'm so foolish. Because I don't understand reality."

At last her eyes sparked, and he welcomed her anger. *Get mad—that's good. Just don't let me damage you.*

"I'll have you know I'm not a dainty virgin, nor am I some fainthearted miss who needs a big, strong man to lean on." Her voice picked up steam, and he welcomed the blast of heat. "I was raised by a gutsy woman who took the tough blows life handed her and made something good out of them." Her eyes locked on his. "Is it so wrong to want to believe in the good? Why does everyone immediately equate that with naiveté? Of course I know evil exists, but can't good people overcome that if they just hold true to what they believe?"

He'd never been that much an optimist, but *Mama C* had lived exactly in the manner that Jilly was describing. Had he failed others because he didn't believe fully?

"Jilly," he began.

At the same time she spoke. "Looking on the bright side doesn't mean I'm a fool, and I—"

"I think you're brave as hell," he interrupted. "And I wish I could be good for you." His chest felt tight, and his head was buzzing. He had to look away. "I'm not that man anymore." *If I ever was.*

"Why not?" she asked softly. "What happened to you over there, Gabriel?"

Despite the rising angry buzz that felt like bees under his skin, a part of him wanted to answer, he was surprised to discover.

Just then the automatic doors swished open, and a family crowded in, some crying, some soothing, and he realized how very much *not* alone they were.

He couldn't explain, anyway, not in any terms she could comprehend. She might not be naïve, but her world did not, thank God, include the carnage he'd experienced.

"Gabriel…" She turned toward him. Pressed her small, soft hand to his cheek.

For an instant, the buzzing stopped, and in that instant, he wanted many things—to spirit her away to some refuge where the world would not interfere, to be the man she thought he was, to—

He gripped her arms. Brought her closer.

Kissed her with all the longings he couldn't voice, all the wishes trapped inside him, all the yearnings he dared not speak. He held onto her as the only thing that kept him from sliding into that empty, echoing place where he was alone with only the cries, only the slow-motion destruction he could never, ever stop.

She tightened her grasp on him, and for a moment he had hope. Felt the balm of her cool fingers in his hair, the benediction of her kiss a blessing of hope and faith and peace.

And for those moments when there was nothing but the two of them, he found a place inside himself that he'd forgotten, a tiny seed of hope, pure and untouched, that answered to the sunshine in her as a seedling seeks the warm surface, the light that will sustain it.

Jilly kissed him and held him, and he clasped her tightly as if he would never let her go—

Then someone screamed pure anguish, and he knew that sound, knew that terrible clarity when you understand that your world is forever changed.

He broke the kiss and stared at Jilly, but he was seeing other young tender faces—dying, screaming in pain as he tried to save them—

"It never stops," he said, breaking away to save her from it. "I can't—I'm sorry," was all he could manage as the roaring came back and smothered the sound of her voice as she reached out for him.

He saw his name on her lips, but she was too lovely, too sweet.

He backed away, stumbling into a group, their shouts faint echoes in his head as he found his feet and escaped out the door.

Jilly tried to follow, but by the time she got through the crowd, he had vanished into the night. Still she ran out the front doors, scanning the surroundings, but there was no sign of him.

It never stops.

Rafe's words came back. *Acid poured on bleeding skin…it's not easy to rejoin the living.*

What happened to you over there, Gabriel?

I wanted to be left alone, not only to heal my body but because my spirit was so troubled and I was so ashamed.

Gabriel needed help she didn't know how to give.

Even if he would ask her.

Which he wouldn't.

She still hadn't moved, though humanity swirled around her. She watched the darkness long after he was gone, and her heart went with him. A good man, far better than he let himself believe.

She wanted to be there as he found his way to the sunlight. Wanted to be the one opening the window of his prison cell to let in fresh, clean air.

But how could she when he didn't trust her? Head hanging, she walked back inside.

"Excuse me," said a voice off to her side. "You're here for Freddie Miller?"

Jilly whirled to face the nurse she'd spoken with before. "Yes. How is he?"

"He's still in surgery, but he's stable. It will probably be at least another hour." The nurse glanced around at the room that was suddenly bursting at the seams. "I could write down your phone number and call you if you'd like to go home and wait."

So she could be surrounded by the lonely quiet, by her unsettled thoughts? "No, but thank you. I'll wait."

Gabriel drove on autopilot, his thoughts coming too fast, battering him with all he didn't want to feel, didn't want to remember…and when fragments of Jilly arose, he batted them away, shoved and swore and cursed. It was wrong to remember her when he was like this, to be with her when rage rode him hard, when even the sound of conversation was an agony beneath his skin.

Only barely did he manage to make himself take the turn home instead of heading straight for the convenience store and Mako.

But he had enough sanity left to know that showing up covered in blood would be inviting attention he didn't need.

He quickly shed the clothes and rifled through his meager

wardrobe, wishing for the first time for his camos and their myriad pockets. He'd refused to ever carry another pistol, but he'd kept the Gerber knife that fit so smoothly into his hand from long years of practice. Grimly he assembled a small set of supplies—rope, his Leatherman tool which would fold into a pocket, and the telescoping billy club he kept by his cot.

Five minutes later, he was back in his truck, clad this time in dark clothing and boots. As he'd readied himself, his mind had throttled back to a low, steady hum, all banked fury ready to explode when he found them.

What the hell are you doing? a small voice sounding suspiciously like Jilly asked.

But he wasn't answering questions. He was taking care of business. When he reached the store, he scanned the lot for any sign of Mako.

Nothing.

Then Tattoo pulled up.

Gabriel jammed his transmission to Park and slammed out of his truck, covering the ground between them in seconds.

Soul Patch jumped from the passenger seat and backed away. "You leave us alone, man." He turned and ran.

Gabriel dragged Tattoo from the front seat and escorted him around the corner. The punk whimpered when Gabriel's Leatherman appeared in his hand, the blade locked in place and ready, out of sight of anyone but the two of them.

"You can't do nothin' out here, man. You be in jail fast."

"You don't make threats, you hear me?" Gabriel growled, getting right in the kid's face, his knifepoint pricking the boy's side. "I've got a message for Mako," Gabriel said loud enough for others to hear. "He so much as looks at that boy again, and he will have to climb up a long way to get to hell. Same goes for the woman. Tell Mako he's a coward for attacking women and kids. If he wants to show how tough he is, bring it on. You got that? You little boys are nothing more than pussies, preying on the weak." He let Tattoo go, and the kid scrambled to open the car door.

"You got that?" Gabriel looked around to be sure others heard and would spread the word. "Mako wants to show he's more than a boy playing gangsta, you tell him to come find me. The cops have your descriptions, all three of you, but that's not who you need to be worrying about. You tell him that." He glared down at the kid fumbling for the keys. "And you and your gutless friend remember I'm watching you, too."

The kid gunned the engine and backed out, not even waiting for his sidekick. Face pale, eyes wild, he took off, tires squealing.

From behind Gabriel, a new voice spoke. "Mako ain't gonna like that."

"Tough," Gabriel said, turning. "Mako's a piece of shit. My bet is he runs and hides."

"Mako, he mean. Crazy, too. Sorta like you."

Gabriel smiled without a trace of humor. He felt crazy. And drained to his bones.

"Good," he said. "We'll meet. See who wins the crown for crazy." Satisfied that his message would spread, he walked back to his truck, every step a challenge, not that he let it show.

Somehow he drove home—it wasn't home, though. He didn't belong anywhere on this earth.

He emptied his pockets and tumbled onto his cot.

And prayed to fall into the chasm of sleep.

Chapter Thirteen

Saint returned and sat with Jilly while she waited.

"Where's Gabriel?"

She couldn't look at him. "He…had to leave." *Please don't ask me any more.*

He watched her for a moment but thankfully didn't ask. "Okay, so, you know being this kid's foster parent is a crazy idea, right?"

She laughed softly. "Maybe." But somehow it felt right. No, she'd never been a parent, but Freddie touched something in her. "He's got a little brother."

"Oh hell, no. Jilly, you can't just take on two kids. You need somebody to take care of, we'll loan you ours. Clarice and I could use a little, ahem, vacation." He waggled his eyebrows suggestively.

That did make her laugh. "I know it sounds crazy, but…I need to do this, Saint. That poor kid has been trying to take care of a half-brother when he has no parents himself. He's living in this abandoned house, and best I can tell, all he owns in the world is a blanket, a quilt and a couple of changes of clothes, yet he's been taking care of his little brother when the boy's mother disappears. She's horrible, Saint. She doesn't deserve to be anyone's mother."

"Jilly…" He touched her hand. "There are other people

to take care of children like this."

"I know..." she sighed. "But...Freddie's different. I've never even met the brother, but..."

"Honey, the world is better off because your heart is so huge, but you cannot take on every lost cause you encounter. You're already doing a very important job. Most people would find that enough."

"Sean offered me a job." She hadn't told a soul. "With the foundation he and Annabelle set up."

"Really. You gonna take it?"

"I don't know. I love what I do...but then I see kids like Freddie, and I think about what life holds for him on the street." She looked at Saint. "The only thing that would make him more of a victim would be if he was female. What Sean's doing is important."

Saint nodded. "It is."

Jilly shook her head. "I can't believe he didn't squeal on me."

"Who?"

"Sean. He knew...someone in the department told him about my...incident."

"He knew and didn't tell me?"

"Trust me, he made all kinds of threats about what would happen if I ever put myself in that position again. But all I did was drive by the house under construction. I do that all the time. I like to see the progress every day. I had no idea anything like that would happen. It's not a bad neighborhood, I swear."

"This kid was stealing from you, from the Foundation and the family. And you want him in your house?"

"He was desperate, Saint. And he came back to help." She shook her head. "I have no idea how Gabriel convinced him, but suddenly, there they both were." She smiled. "Teo and I are hoping Gabriel will agree to take Teo's place, so Teo can travel with this wife."

"What's his story, Gabriel? He's former military, you know."

She nodded. "I talked to Rafe about him. He's…troubled."

"How much do you know about PTSD? Post-traumatic stress syndrome? Those scars of his didn't come from a tea party."

"I just learned that he's been in Iraq. Apparently he nearly died."

"Chopper crash," Saint acknowledged.

She looked at him "I didn't know."

"He's a bad bet, sweetheart. Some guys never make it all the way back."

She thought about how strange Gabriel had been tonight, about those times when he'd seemed like someone she'd never met. How troubled he was, yet…that kiss…the sense she had of belonging. Not that he welcomed it, no, but…there was the oddest feeling of a puzzle piece that finally fit.

"He's got problems, that's for sure. I'm wondering if he went through something like Rafe did. Rafe told me more than he's ever shared before, when I called him earlier tonight." She glanced at her watch and realized it was probably dawn outside. "Last night, I should say." She slumped in her chair, exhausted.

"You should go home," Saint said.

"No, but you definitely ought to. Clarice probably wants to strangle me for dragging you out. Really, Saint, go ahead. I'll be fine."

"Nope, not until you're ready to leave." He grinned. "I'm your surrogate big brother right now."

She rolled her eyes. "Like I need any more." She bent her head to his shoulder. "You're the best, Saint. Thank you."

He leaned his head against the top of hers. "No problem, Sunshine."

Uh-oh. "Please tell me you're not going to call Dad as soon as you leave here."

"I was thinking Alex. Or Dane. Since they're here in town and can help me keep an eye on you."

Oh, man… "What would I have to promise to seal your lips?"

Saint chuckled and sat up. "Honey, your promises mean jack diddley. Oh, you'll have the best of intentions, but then some lost soul will cross your path and—bam! Instant change of course. *Okay*," he said in a falsetto, "*No, I didn't mean to adopt this entire family and all their relatives, but I just…they need me.*"

She smiled, even as chagrin overtook her. "I'm not that bad."

"Of course you are. It's what we all love about you, even as we're losing all our hair." He slicked his hair back from his forehead and pointed. "See this? My hairline was an inch lower just yesterday. At this rate, I'll be bald by Sunday."

She giggled. "Wonder if Clarice thinks bald guys are hot?"

"Anything I do is hot, Sunshine. Surely you know that."

She swatted playfully at him, and he rose. "The EMTs are good about sharing coffee with cops. Want some? My addiction's kicking in."

"Love some."

"Cream and sugar, right?"

"Right. You are a god among men."

A quick slash of grin in that handsome face. "All the women think so." He walked off, leaving Jilly grinning.

Then a doctor halted in the far doorway. "Freddie Miller?" he said. She'd noticed that families were summoned by the patient's name.

She stood up. "Over here." She began walking toward him.

"That's one very lucky young man. A little longer delay before he got here, and we wouldn't be having this conversation. He'd be in the morgue."

Thank you, Gabriel. Not for the first time since he'd left, she found herself wondering where Gabriel was and what he was dong. "How is he? Will he be all right?"

"Eventually," the doctor nodded. "But it's going to be a few days, at least, before we know the full extent of his injuries."

"Can I see him?"

"After he's out of recovery, probably another hour. He won't be conscious, however."

"Is that bad?"

"We're sedating him heavily. He suffered multiple blows to the head, and that causes swelling in the brain."

She bit her lip. "That sounds scary."

"There are worries about the extent of the neurological damage, but we can't assess that until he wakes up. His lung has been re-inflated, and we had to remove his spleen. His kidneys are bruised and will bear watching. He would have a better chance of recovering, were he not already malnourished. Who are you to him, Ms.—"

"Sullivan. Jilly Sullivan. He's…a friend. But I'm hoping to get custody of him. He has no parents and has been living on the streets."

"Do you have other children?" He looked doubtful.

"No, I'm single, but—"

"This is probably gang-related, you know. Sure you want to take this on?"

"I'm sure."

"CPS will be arriving later, I imagine."

"I know. As soon as their office opens, I'll be there. I'm a CASA volunteer already. That should help in qualifying me for foster parent."

The doctor shook his head. "Well, God bless you." He held out a hand to shake hers. "You're an optimist, clearly, and the world could use more like you. He's a lucky young man on many counts."

She shook hands. "Thank you, Dr. Evans, for saving his life."

"The man who brought him in here did that," he said. "But you're welcome." He glanced around. "Where is he, by the way?"

"I…don't know."

"A good Samaritan, eh? We need more of those, too."

He wouldn't call himself that, she suspected. "I agree."

"Well, just wait here, and the nurse will come get you when you can see the boy."

"I will. Thank you again."

The doctor nodded and left.

Jilly sank to her chair.

And released the tears she'd been bottling up for hours.

Saint returned, bearing not only coffee but pastries he'd cadged from the nurses.

"If Clarice ever gets tired of you, I get dibs," she said around a mouthful of a sugary treat that was surely the best thing to hit her mouth since Ray's barbecue.

Which led once more to thoughts of Gabriel. Where was he? She couldn't even contact him to let him know Freddie had come out of surgery.

Would she ever see Gabriel again?

"The women are lined up in droves," Saint said, dragging her back to the moment. "But I'll pencil you in at the top of the list, kiddo."

So. Gabriel was not someone she could count on, and she needed to accept that. She took another bracing sip of coffee. But she was lucky. Even if her family and friends doubted her sanity, they would support her. Freddie would have uncles galore, all the father figures he could possibly need.

"You worrying over the boy or Gabriel?" At her surprised look, Saint shrugged. "My detective badge didn't come in Cracker Jacks, you know. This guy really gets to you, doesn't he? Seems to go both ways, though."

Her heart skipped. "Not really. He's…I don't think so."

"I saw the way he looked at you, the sound of his voice when he talked about you."

She couldn't let herself go there. "While he was squealing on me, you mean?"

"He's right, and you know it. You should never have gotten out of that car. You're damned lucky he was around."

"Enough of the lecture, please. I get it."

"So why the hell didn't you press charges?"

Misery swam through her. "Freddie would be okay right now if I had. I am so sorry. I just thought…"

Saint rested his elbows on his knees as he spoke to her intently. "Sunshine, your faith in human nature is a gift to a whole lot of people. Don't beat yourself up. You were trying to live your beliefs."

"But you don't share them."

"Honey, I've been a cop a long time. I don't trust anybody." He shrugged. "Okay, some people. Clarice and her family, your family, but…you know what I mean. I've seen the dark side of human nature too often. But get it out of your head that this attack was your fault. The life Freddie's living, it's a miracle something like this hasn't happened sooner. And Gabriel's right—Mako could have made bail by now, even if you had pressed charges."

"Why did he attack Freddie?"

"No idea." Saint averted his gaze but not quickly enough.

"Oh, no. You think it could have involved me?"

Saint didn't answer but stood up. "Look, I need to make some calls. I'll be right over there when they come get you, okay?"

"You don't have to keep waiting with me."

"It's my case now. I need to interview the victim."

"Uh-huh." That was probably true, but she knew he'd be staying anyway. She also didn't believe his hasty denial that somehow she was involved in the attack.

But just as he was walking away, the nurse appeared. "Freddie Miller?"

"Over here." Jilly rose and scanned for Saint, but he'd heard and was nearly to her.

They followed the nurse into Freddie's room.

Gabriel shoved away from the corner where he'd concealed himself in the midst of the busy hospital lobby. He hadn't been able to sleep, so he'd returned, but now he'd seen what he needed to see: Jilly wasn't alone. Saint had waited with her. He'd watched the doctor speak to her, caught the mingled joy and worry on her beautiful face after the news.

Freddie had to be hanging in there. *Good job, kid. You're a survivor.*

He thought about leaving then, but he'd already driven around for awhile, hoping he and Mako would cross paths sooner rather than later. No such luck, and after the hours had spooled out, fatigue had crept in, banishing everything else.

He was drained, but if he went back now, with Jilly looking so vulnerable and scared, he'd still never sleep. He had some half-assed notion of escorting her home, though he'd never let her spot him. Watching over her was one thing; responding to her, trying to match that boundless optimism…caring about her?

There wasn't enough left of him for that. The whole business with Freddie had shaken him. Maybe he'd managed to find the kid, to get him help, yeah…but no one could know how truly close a thing it had been.

He hadn't had flashbacks like that in months. Hadn't been ripped apart by inexplicable fury or found himself falling down that long dark tunnel.

The best thing he could do for any of them was to go back to what had worked before: to keep himself apart. To focus on one minute after the next. To stay busy, working so hard that exhaustion would buy him a few hours' sleep.

He should leave now, take himself away from any chance of encountering any of them. He would…once he saw Jilly safely home.

Jilly barely stifled her gasp when she saw Freddie. He looked so small and helpless in that bed, hooked to tubes, surrounded by machines.

"He's seriously fifteen?" Saint asked.

"Very undernourished," she responded.

"Man." Saint looked at the nurse. "Any idea when the sedation will be discontinued?"

The nurse shook her head. "No. It's being done to reduce the brain's workload. It also keeps him from fighting the breathing tube. A ventilator is doing the work for him to further decrease the demands on his body. That will allow the brain to focus on healing and give time for the swelling to subside. He bore evidence of multiple blows to the head, and with a closed head injury, there's no room for the brain to expand. There's a sensor to monitor the intracranial pressure, so we can tell when the swelling decreases." She looked at Jilly. "You're welcome to stay, but he's in good hands, and it will probably be a few days before the pressure decreases enough to take him off the sedation. I hear you're applying for custody. I could take your phone number and call you with updates if you need to be taking care of paperwork. There is, however, going to be a limit to what we can tell you if you're not family, I'm afraid."

Jilly's instinct was to stay right here, to grab Freddie's hand and hold on, to will him to wake up. "Won't it help him to know I'm here?"

"It might, but he's not going to wake up until we think it's safe for him."

"Sunshine, it'll give you time for the other things you need to be doing for him right now."

Her throat was a cold, hard lump. Speaking around it was difficult. She glanced at Saint through a sheen of tears.

He put an arm around her shoulders. "All the equipment makes it look scarier. He's stable, right?" he asked the nurse.

"Absolutely. And though he's malnourished, we're feeding him through a tube, so he's getting nutrients, probably more than he's used to. In ICU, we have at most two patients each, and we never leave them unattended. I promise you he's in the best hands possible."

Jilly mustered a smile and brushed at her wet cheeks. "Thank you. It's just…how can people do this to children? Simply abandon them?"

"I know," the nurse responded. "We see a lot of heartbreak in here. But he's not a number to me, I swear to you. And he won't be to any nurse who follows me. Give me your contact information, and I'll put it in the front of his chart. I'll share with you as much as I possibly can while you work on the other end."

"Okay." Jilly cleared her throat and moved out of Saint's hold, approaching the bed. "Freddie," she said, covering the boy's hand with hers. "I'm so sorry you got hurt—" Her voice broke, but she tried again. "Gabriel saved you, and I'm here now. You're not alone. You're never going to be alone again," she said fiercely. "You're going to be fine. You have wonderful people watching over you, and I'll be back as soon as I can, okay?"

His head was bandaged, so she couldn't brush his hair. She settled for laying her hand on his forehead and murmuring a prayer over him. Then she bent and kissed his cheek. "You'll be okay, Freddie. No one's ever going to hurt you again, I swear it." One more kiss, and she stepped back, covering her mouth with her fingers while she composed herself.

Then she turned. "Okay. First, contact information. Then I want to know who to talk to at CPS, Saint, to cut through the red tape." She walked out of the cubicle and rattled off her phone numbers to the nurse, thanked her profusely and left with Saint.

It took a little time to convince him she could get herself home okay, but at last he left, promising to let her call her family when she had things sorted out a little better.

She found a quiet corner and called Teo, filling him in, and leaving a message for April that she wouldn't be in today, with instructions for a meeting to be rescheduled.

Then her phone rang with the promised call from Saint's contact at CPS. Somehow she managed not to sound as desperate as she felt or as strung out from lack of sleep. She found a scrap of paper in her purse and made notes about what she needed to gather up for them to consider her for foster parent status. The woman expressed doubts about a single woman taking a teenage boy into her home, so Jilly didn't bring up Damien just then, apologizing silently to the little boy and hoping her earlier call to them would result in some action to safeguard him.

She'd get to Damien as soon as she could. Maybe Gabriel—

Gabriel roared back, front and center, as he'd been most of the night.

Where was he? Was he all right?

Why wasn't he here?

The woman came back on the phone, and Jilly had to put Gabriel aside, in order to take care of the boy Gabriel had rescued just in the nick of time.

As if he'd conjured Jilly, she'd reappeared, heading his way. Quickly he'd slipped to the side near the double doors that led to the ER but where he could still see her face.

She was hugging Saint, telling him goodbye. Shaking her head as he clearly offered to see her home, holding up her cell phone as if to say she had business to take care of.

Saint gave in. Nodded and hugged her, then ruffled her

hair…which probably drove her nuts.

But she smiled, and this was a real one. Her eyes were clear if tired, and the pinched look of anxiety she'd worn for the last few hours was gone.

Now she looked determined as she punched in numbers.

It was his turn to smile. Heaven help whoever was on the other end. His bet was on Jilly. Whatever she wanted from the person she was calling, that person didn't stand a chance.

He saw the security guard look at him suspiciously, so he grabbed some brochures and bent his head to peruse them, keeping an eye on Jilly over the top of them. She engaged in a fervent conversation, head shaking, hands gesturing, every cell of her focused on her goal.

Yep, his bet was on her.

When at last she disconnected and looked, if not smug, certainly satisfied, he found himself smiling again.

Attagirl. But she wasn't a girl, he knew only too well. She was a woman, an extraordinary one. She had a fire in her for saving the world, and the world, like her caller, didn't stand a chance.

Look out, world.

She made two more quick calls, then left, making another one as she walked.

He lingered, still keeping her in sight, then followed.

She had to be completely exhausted, but still her step was sure, that red-gold hair bouncing as if she hadn't spent hours under tremendous strain.

She was a miracle, all right.

Just not for him. *Save yourself for that lucky as hell kid up there,* he silently cautioned. *And forget me.*

But all the way to her place, he found himself remembering the precious moments when sunshine had filled his arms and crept into his cold, dead heart.

He watched until she was safely inside, more tempted than he'd been by anything in years to cut off his engine and knock on her door. She'd let him in, he knew it. She might hold him in those arms again.

It would be heaven for him.

But it would be the worst thing that could happen to her.

Gabriel put his truck in gear and left.

Chapter Fourteen

Jilly lay on her mattress trying to summon the energy to rise. She'd only intended to nap a little, but from the drool stain on her comforter, she'd gone down hard.

Impressive, she congratulated herself. *Sometimes it's a good thing you live alone.*

She lifted her head to catch a glimpse of her alarm clock.

And bolted up straight. Seven o'clock? In the *evening?* Shadows filled her room and spread through the house. She staggered from the bed and bemoaned the fact that this was not morning, when she'd have had the coffeemaker all set to go.

It probably wasn't smart to be drinking coffee this late, anyway, given that she had a whole lot to do tomorrow and couldn't afford to be wide-eyed tonight.

Shower, she thought sluggishly. *Now.* One word sentences were all she felt capable of at the moment. Once under the spray, she moaned aloud. She felt like she'd taken a beating yesterday.

Her eyes flew open. *Freddie. Gabriel.* She took the quickest shower on record and raced for her phone, dialing the direct number in ICU she'd been given. After conversing with the night nurse, who was about to take over, she felt a little easier. A little.

Freddie was still stable. Nothing had changed, except the pressure inside his skull had gone down, if only a little. Saint had been by to see him once, about an hour ago.

Good man.

But no other visitors.

She made a mental note to take something up there for the nursing staff. She'd learned from Diana that the night staff seldom got goodies such as those brought to the day shift by patients' families.

She dressed hurriedly, this time in comfortable jeans, and though she was starving, she only took long enough to eat a carton of yogurt while staring out the window over her kitchen sink.

The encroaching night made her think of the hours she'd spent with Gabriel, searching for Freddie. *Where are you, Gabriel? Are you all right? Are you alone?* She feared he probably was, and yes, Rafe had spoken of the months when his own most fervent desire was to be left alone to heal. But he'd also admitted that those who loved him had helped bring him back from that dark place he'd been trapped inside.

He needed to bring up the subject himself, she'd acknowledged to Rafe.

He did. But for that to happen, they'd have to be in contact—in person, not on the phone—though now that she thought about it, she'd never seen him with a cell phone. What if he never came back to work? Would he go to Ray's, after he'd been so uncomfortable with the fuss made over him? She doubted it. Would he truly never return to the hospital to check on Freddie?

Why hadn't she made him tell her where he lived?

Because I was trying to respect his privacy.

She still should, but she didn't want to. She was worried about him.

As she checked her phone messages, Gabriel was still very much on her mind. Maybe Saint could help her figure out how to track him down. Gabriel had said he didn't live far from the jobsite, so if she canvassed the area…?

A glance at the clock had her rinsing out the carton hastily and dropping it in the recycling bin. A quick trip to brush her teeth and gather her things, then out the door.

Freddie's color was certainly better than the last time she'd seen him. "Thank you," she said to the night nurse, Cal, "for all you're doing. He doesn't have anyone."

"He seems to have you." Cal grinned. "One person can make all the difference."

She'd always believed that herself, that you had to light up your own corner of the world, that every person touched others and if you treated people in a kind manner, if you walked around with a positive attitude, it would impact others, and they would pass it along.

"I just hope the CPS people will see it that way."

"Yeah, I heard about that. You're trying to become his foster mother?" He arched an eyebrow. "You've got guts."

"He's not a bad kid. He's been thrown on his own, and he's done the best he could."

"Sad world out there," Cal said as he made notes and checked the PCA meter that measured out the pain meds Freddie was getting intravenously.

"Not all sad, though," she said. Sheesh. Could she sound any more like Pollyanna? "But I guess you see a lot of bad things in here."

"Yep." Cal nodded. "Good stuff, too. Plus a miracle, now

and again."

"I like that. That you believe in miracles, I mean."

"Sometimes there's no other explanation. Excuse me—I have to go make some notes," he said, and walked outside the cubicle, leaving her alone with Freddie.

She squeezed the hand she'd been holding. "You're doing great, Freddie. Just rest up, okay? I hope they decide to wake you soon, so we can see how you are." All the vital signs in the world wouldn't reveal the state of his brain function, she'd learned.

She wanted that plucky kid back, the one who had all kinds of terrible things thrown at him and still scrapped and fought to survive.

"The CPS lady said they're investigating Damien's situation," she told him. "At worst, Damien's mother has been put on notice that she's being observed. I'm sorry—it's the best I can do right now. I have to prove myself with you first, but when you're home with me, we'll go visit him and we'll keep an eye on him, okay?"

She was putting the cart before the horse. The social worker had told her that the special circumstances were being taken into consideration, but she'd made no promises. *It would be better if you'd had other children*, the woman had said. *Or if you weren't so young.*

Jilly had argued. Put her best foot forward, pointing out that she was responsible for the Foundation, that she had not only her own resources but a whole extended family to offer Freddie.

The woman wouldn't promise anything, though. Jilly guessed she understood, but…

If there was a father in the picture, that would help, the woman had told her.

Immediately Jilly thought of Gabriel.

For all the good that did. Teo hadn't seen him or heard from him. She was a long way from giving up on him, though, Rafe's advice notwithstanding. And not simply because he was troubled. He touched something in her no man ever had. Drew her like a compass to true north, the pull beyond her ability to resist.

Even if she wanted to.

"It's getting late," she said to Freddie. "But tomorrow's another day." Good grief. Now she was channeling Scarlett O'Hara.

Look how that had ended.

But she hadn't done anything to Gabriel to compare to how Scarlett had screwed over Rhett. If she were Rhett, she'd have left Scarlett, too. Only sooner.

Jilly laughed at herself. "Have you ever seen *Gone with the Wind*, Freddie?" She stroked his cheek. "One of these days we'll make a big tub of popcorn, and I'll torture you with it. My brothers all hate it, but Mom and I watch it once a year, without fail."

"Jilly, I'm sorry," said Cal from the door, "But it's time."

She nodded, then bent and pressed a kiss to Freddie's forehead. "Sweet dreams. I'll see you in the morning, okay?" With one last pat to his hand, she left. "Bye, Cal."

"Thanks for the goodies. I shared. Everyone loves you."

She grinned. "It's not enough to repay you for the important work that you do."

Cal smiled back. "It sure doesn't hurt."

Jilly went through the double doors and down the hall out of the ICU/surgical area. When she reached the hospital lobby, she couldn't help contrasting her feelings with how crazy scared she'd been the night before.

Nothing was resolved, but Freddie was safe, and good people were caring for him.

That wasn't nothing.

She crossed to the parking garage and found her car. She was still not sleepy even though her body was weary, so she decided to stop at the store and pick up some groceries.

That made her smile. She'd get some things for growing teenage boys, sort of a good luck totem to ensure that in a few days, Freddie would be staying there with her.

That made her start thinking about what to do with her spare bedroom. What colors did Freddie like? How would he decorate it if he were choosing?

The juices started flowing again. That was something positive she could do...and maybe the leap of faith would help shift the balance.

Freddie would be staying with her, sooner or later.

Think positive.

Gabriel was restless. He'd slept fitfully after returning from the hospital, then finally given up and begun work at *Mama C's*. He'd decided to build new shelving for the garage out of the scrap lumber he'd saved. He'd worked until he'd lost the light, then moved into the house to tear out threadbare carpeting.

It was after nine now. He couldn't remember what he'd eaten and wasn't really hungry, but he needed to keep up his strength.

Why, though? The question stumped him. He set down his tools, let his hands fall to his sides.

What was he doing? Where was he headed?

For a long time after the crash, he'd been focused on not dying, then on getting on his feet again, then on building strength. There'd been months of wandering back roads, hitching rides, doing day work…

Letting *Mama C* die alone.

Learning that she was gone when he'd finally showed up had knocked him off his footing. He'd poured himself into making amends somehow by fixing everything that so sorely needed it, that—damn it—would have been such a boon and a pleasure to her. If only he hadn't abandoned her to spend months trying to escape the muddle inside his head.

Yeah, that had worked well.

Months had gone by now, and he'd made the place sound—for what? Was he going to sell it? Would he stay?

What the hell did he want out of life, now that he was back in the land of the living?

Besides…*her*. Jilly.

That, he could not have. Yes, his episodes had diminished in number, but he was afraid of doing physical damage when he was locked inside those flashbacks. That hadn't happened often, but Jilly was too precious to risk.

So what else was left? Stay a hermit? Get off his ass and take a chance?

She was so beautiful—pretty in that girl-next-door, all-American way on the outside but inside—where it counted—bone-deep gorgeous. She had the best heart he'd ever known, sunnier than *Mama C's* and every bit as large.

He wanted her with every breath, every cell, every thought.

He knew why he wanted her, but the question was, did she want him? Why on earth would she? All he'd done was bark at her and push her away—okay, except for a couple of kisses that meant nothing.

Except that they'd meant everything to him.

But, he returned to his original point, what did he have to

offer her? A screwed-up mind he couldn't trust? A body that was battered all to hell? A heart that was so rusty it was a lost cause?

He didn't have any answers. And he was afraid to ask her the questions.

He would go for a run. That helped when nothing else would, simply getting out and racing past everything he couldn't figure out and all that he was spending too much time obsessing over, letting fresh air clear out all the fog in his head until either he wore himself out—

Or something came clear.

He changed quickly and took off as though the hounds of hell were hot on his trail. A few blocks later, he found himself charting a new course.

One that would take him right past Jilly's.

You are pathetic, he chided himself. He wouldn't stop when he got there. But he could at least be sure she was home and safe.

Tomorrow she was going to seek out Gabriel, she decided as she pulled into her drive and stopped the car. The solution to finding him was embarrassingly simple—only her worry and exhaustion could explain why she'd forgotten that Ray and Fayrene knew exactly where Gabriel's grandmother's home was. *Duh, Jilly.* Surely he was staying there, wasn't he? What had he said about that? She tried to recall as she got out of the car and opened the back left door to retrieve her groceries.

Suddenly she was yanked backward and slammed against the vehicle. Groceries went flying.

"You call the cops on me, bitch?" Mako loomed over her,

his face in the streetlight a mask of fury, his eyes frightening.

Go for the soft areas, she remembered her brothers teaching her. She brought up her knee between his legs, but he dodged to the side with a grunt.

He retaliated with a blow to her head that had her ears ringing.

She tried to go for his eyes, but he slapped away her hand. Then his fist shot out and hit her head so hard she couldn't think. Her world became pain.

"I didn't call them—" *Have to buy time* was all she could think. But who would come for her? She opened her mouth to scream so her neighbors would hear her—

He slapped his hand over her mouth. Shoved her backward. Her head slammed into the roof, and for a second she blacked out.

When she came to an instant later, there was a pistol jammed beneath her jaw. "What about all your talk about second chances, huh? Gonna help me, you say? Crazy bitch, you didn't mean none of it. That boyfriend of yours, he threaten my boys. Talk shit about me."

"I—" Her knees collapsed beneath her.

He hauled her up by the front of her shirt. Jammed his face right in front of hers, spittle flying. "Don't talk to me, bitch!" He grabbed her breast and squeezed so hard she cried out. "Yeah. You scared now?" He closed his hand over the neck of her blouse and ripped it open. "Scared yet? He say I better be scared of him, huh?"

He grabbed her jeans and yanked on them but couldn't get them down with only one hand.

She managed to bring up her arms between his, keys extended between her fingers as she'd been taught, and went for his eyes.

Then it was Mako who screamed, grabbing his eyes, falling to his knees.

Jilly turned and ran.

Footsteps pounded behind her, closing fast. He rammed into her back and knocked her to the ground. Landed hard on top of her. Dragged her pants over her hips and down her legs while she fought with everything in her. *No! No…* She tried to find air to scream again. Kicked at his legs while she tried to get to her knees.

He tackled her again. Jammed her face in the grass. Held her down by the back of her neck as he fumbled for his zipper—

Jilly screamed and screamed. Bucked her hips, flailed her arms, trying to get out from under–

Suddenly his weight vanished, and he yelped in pain.

She scrambled away, pulling at her pants and sobbing as she turned over—

Mako shrieked again as a form took him down, as a bigger man punched his face, his belly, methodically reducing him to a whimpering mass—

"Gabriel." At last she recognized her rescuer. How was he here? How did he know?

How didn't matter. Jilly sobbed and bent double, retching into the dirt.

Mako stopped screaming abruptly.

Kill him.

Jilly. Hurt.

No more.

Kill.

Gabriel gloried in the crack of bone, the slickness of the

blood—

Something touched his leg. "Gabriel. Please."

He whirled, fists clenched, near-blind from rage—

"Gabriel, it's me. Jilly. Don't. I'm okay—I'm—" She dropped her face into her hands and sobbed.

He glanced back at the unmoving man on the ground. Then at his fists, so red. Sticky with blood.

And Jilly wept.

He closed his eyes, swallowed hard. *Breathe. Don't go back there.*

But the siren call of his fury was strong. He kept seeing her, over and over again, her clothes torn, fighting for her life.

Screaming. Like Sayidah's pure crystal tones.

"Gabriel…"

He opened his eyes. Fought his way back.

Saw her ravaged eyes, her pleading hand outstretched.

He moved to her, gently tucked her in his arms and sank to the ground with her in his lap.

She huddled against him. "Tighter." She curled into a ball. "Don't let go of me. Please don't let go."

She shook and she sobbed, and he never let go. He held her so close he wondered how she could breathe, but still she clung to him.

His entire frame shuddered once. Twice. He wanted to pound the bastard into the dirt again. The urge to kill was strong, but for her sake, he locked it down and focused on her. "You're safe," he said, over and over. "You're safe."

"Don't leave me, Gabriel…please don't…" She looked up at him, her eyes dark holes in her face, her tearstained face ravaged.

She snaked her hand up without ever losing contact, body to body, and she laid it against his jaw. He realized his face was wet, and she was wiping his cheek.

"It's my fault." Self-loathing swamped him, and he started to draw away.

"No!" She flung her arms around his neck and pressed her body to his. "It's not. It's not, Gabriel. You—you saved me. You..." She began to shiver uncontrollably, pressing her forehead against his throat. "Thank you."

He recoiled. "Thank you?" He took her arms down and set her aside, backing away. "I did this, Jilly. I don't know how he found you, but...this...I..."

"It's not your fault. You don't have to go. Please don't—" She bent double, wrecked and vulnerable and weak.

He had to get her to cover. He retrieved her keys from the ground nearby, then scooped her up and carried her to the side door. Somehow he managed to unlock the door without releasing her and took her inside, settling her on the sofa.

The automaton took over as he covered her with an afghan and retreated to call for help.

Jilly couldn't stop shivering, and he wouldn't look at her, and she was...oh, God...

His anguish jolted her from her own. What had she done? All of this started with the stupid notion that she could save Mako, that anyone could be rescued.

"Gabriel..." She was so alone. So scared.

He looked at her. He didn't leave.

But he kept his distance.

Until the ambulance showed up, along with the police.

Saint was right behind them, his face a mask of grief and pain. And then she was being checked over and poked and prodded and questioned and loaded in the ambulance and...

She searched for him, looked every direction.

But Gabriel was gone.

And no matter how much she asked for him—

No one would answer.

"Sir, I need to ask you some questions," said the patrol officer who'd first arrived.

"Tell me how she is."

"We don't know yet."

"I have to see her."

"Sir, we'll get you information as soon as we have it. Now, tell me—"

Gabriel shoved past him, hearing the sound of Jilly's screams, echoing over and over in his head. If he lived to be a thousand, those cries he'd heard from down the block would haunt him every second, every day. He'd run faster than he'd thought possible, but—

The tunnel beckoned once more, and everything around him receded until he felt nothing. Saw nothing, except…

Broken bodies. Jilly lying on the ground, stripped half-naked, beaten all to hell—

"No!" he roared and struck out.

Hands gripped him, restrained him.

He lashed out blindly. He had to get to her. Had to—

With a cry from the depths of his soul, he battled harder, beyond reason as he fought his way to her. "No! No one else dies because of me—"

"Get him down!"

"On the ground!"

He fought grimly with every tactic he knew. She was lying

there, and that bastard was going to—If only he could—

The taser hit him.

He went down hard.

Chapter Fifteen

Nothing seemed real to her.

She felt disconnected from her body, floating somewhere beyond the pain, the shame…the terror of knowing that no matter what she did—

Think about Gabriel. Think about being sheltered and safe, surrounded by his strength.

Don't think about this cold hospital room, about people seeing you like this, about…

She wanted to curl up in a safe, warm, quiet place but instead a nurse was taking photos of Jilly's injuries. She remained in place, but she couldn't seem to stop trembling.

"Hang in there," Clarice soothed from nearby.

Jilly was grateful for her presence. Saint had not left her side until Clarice arrived after getting a neighbor to watch their sleeping children. Patrician to her toes and a trained psychologist, Clarice kept her features smooth as glass, but Jilly saw her friend bite her lip once when Jilly's torso was bared.

"I'm okay," Jilly told her in a voice that didn't sound like hers. "Please, Clarice…Gabriel saved me, but no one will tell me where he is."

"He'll be all right," Clarice assured her. "Saint called into headquarters to make sure he didn't get booked."

"Booked? How could anyone think—?"

"He fought the officers who responded. Hurt one of them pretty badly."

"He would never—" Then she thought of him with Mako on the ground, punching and punching, over and over…

"You don't have to think about that now," Clarice soothed. "There will be time later."

At last the photographs were done. "May I please have my clothes back?" she asked the nurse.

"The police need them for evidence. We want to keep you here for a while for observation, anyway. Perhaps someone could bring you more from home." The woman hesitated. "Are you positive you don't want a rape kit?"

"I told you he didn't—" Was that her voice, so hateful? Jilly forced down the unreasoning anger. "I'm sorry. You're just doing your job, I—I know that."

Suddenly she could feel Mako grabbing her breast. Hurting her. Tearing open her jeans and—

A sob erupted from her. Clarice was by her side instantly, gripping her arm.

Jilly couldn't help recoiling.

"I'm sorry," Clarice said. "I won't touch you."

"No." Jilly pressed her lips together. "It just—I just…" She grabbed for Clarice's hand and squeezed. "I don't know what—I feel so—"

Clarice squeezed back. "Whatever you feel is okay, Jilly. Say whatever you need to."

"No. I don't—I can't—" She bent double. She wanted to throw up, she wanted to run away, she wanted—

Oh, God, she was going to be sick.

"Here," the nurse said, putting a basin in front of her while Jilly emptied what little was in her stomach.

Clarice stayed beside her, stroking her back and speaking

to her, words that made no sense.

Jilly sank to the bed and curled up. She was so tired. She wanted to go away somewhere and sleep and sleep and…

She wanted Gabriel.

But he was gone.

She started sobbing, but she covered her mouth to keep from making a sound.

Clarice gathered her up and held her.

They weren't the arms Jilly wanted.

But she gratefully accepted the comfort.

Finally she found her voice. "Did Gabriel kill him?" she asked.

Clarice seemed to understand that she meant Mako. "No, but he's hurt pretty badly."

"Good," Jilly said. The burning behind her breastbone wasn't eased by the news.

But a part of her she'd never known existed was savagely happy.

"Sorry," Saint said to Gabriel when he emerged from the holding cell. "I got caught up in taking care of Jilly and I didn't realize—" He swore. "I'm truly sorry. You didn't deserve to be put through that."

Hell if he didn't. If he hadn't taunted Mako, Jilly would be fine now. "How is she?" he asked, jaw locked.

"My wife is with her right now. She's a psychologist who's counseled a lot of victims of sexual abuse and rape."

Gabriel's head whipped around. "But I—" What if before he'd gotten there—

"She wasn't raped, thanks to you."

"Thanks to me?" Gabriel roared. "It's thanks to me that that sonofabitch attacked her!"

A muscle in Saint's jaw jumped. His gaze bored into Gabriel's. "Yeah. About that…what the hell did you do?"

Gabriel wanted badly to look away, but he didn't deserve to dodge. "I was pissed off because of what they'd done to Freddie, so—"

Saint held up his hand. "Never mind. You shouldn't be telling me any of this. You may yet need a lawyer." They made it through the front doors and outside.

"No." Gabriel shook his head. "What happens to me doesn't matter."

They were outside the station now, and Saint whirled on him, slammed him back against the wall. "It matters. Jilly cares about you, you sonofabitch."

Gabriel could see the barely-banked fury. They were a decent match for size, but even though Saint was a cop, Gabriel knew he could hurt the other man.

He wouldn't even try to defend himself, though. Let Saint beat the crap out of him. "Go ahead." He would welcome the punishment. It might erase that image from his brain, Jilly on the ground, her clothes torn away, Mako over her, about to—

"If I weren't a cop…"

"No one will know. Come on. You know you want to."

Saint halted, reason returning. "Shit." Hands on his hips, he hung his head and exhaled hard. "No. Whatever else you did, you saved her." He stepped back.

There would be no balancing of the scales. "Damn it." Gabriel ground the heels of his hands into his eyes. He wanted to be punished. Wanted something to take away the pain of knowing that it wasn't him who'd paid the price, once again…it was someone he cared about.

As he'd cared about no other. For an instant, he could

feel Jilly curled up in his lap, shaking violently. Begging him not to leave her.

I had to, Jilly. There is nothing but pain for you with me.

He lifted his head and looked at Saint with hopeless eyes. "Will she be all right?" He swore. Of course not. She was sunshine incarnate, and she'd just been blindsided by the reality that life was brutal. That her goodness couldn't save her. "Never mind." He looked away.

"She's strong. The whole family's coming in to be with her. Her brothers Alex and Dane are probably already there. Vanessa is getting her some clothes."

The unstated message was *She won't need you.* "Good." Too drained and weary to make any decisions, Gabriel just stood where he was and waited.

Saint exhaled. "She's asking for you."

Gabriel's head whipped up. "No. God, no. I'm the last person—" He shook his head violently.

"Jilly usually knows exactly what she wants."

Slowly he shook his head again. "Not this time she doesn't." He stared at Saint. "Tell me you think I'm any good for her."

The other man stared at him for a very long time before speaking. "I really don't know."

"I do." Gabriel stared at the interstate overpass above them, calculated how far it would be to walk home.

Home. Hah. Best thing he could do would be to pack up and light out.

"If you care about her at all, you won't desert her."

Gabriel turned tortured eyes to Saint. "Staying would be worse for her."

"You want to explain that?"

Gabriel only shook his head instead of speaking.

"Come on, I'll take you home."

Damn. After all had happened, he wanted to be nice to Gabriel?

Gabriel sidestepped. "If I'm free to go, I'd prefer to get there on my own."

Saint studied him. "You're gonna break her heart if you leave her."

"You're wrong. Leaving is the best thing for her."

"Then maybe you really don't deserve her." Saint turned on his heel and walked away into the darkness.

There was never any doubt about that, Gabriel thought as he watched the man go.

Gabriel made it in under an hour, even with the circuitous route that took him through the worst neighborhoods. Every step he had taunted fate to bring on the scum, the gangbangers looking for trouble. The violence simmering beneath his skin would welcome the battle.

But though he passed more than a few candidates, no one responded, as though his face conveyed his eagerness to unload some of the murderous rage onto whoever crossed his path. No one approached. Silence accompanied his passage.

No one gave him the relief of offloading his pain with his fists.

Jilly's face…her pale skin exposed…her broken sobs as she clung to him…

He had to stop to be sick in some bushes.

But nothing could clear out the poison inside him.

Grimly he began to run, as if he could outrace the reality of what he'd unleashed on the person who least deserved it. Jilly was all that was good and sweet and now she was—

Broken.

On the deserted, cracked sidewalk in front of his grandmother's house, Gabriel fell to his knees.

A boy nearly dead.

A woman whose bright innocence was forever lost.

Ahmed, bleeding out. Sayidah, broken like a cast-off doll.

Mama C, dying alone.

Is it so wrong to want to believe in the good, Gabriel?

The tunnel beckoned, drawing him closer and closer to blessed oblivion.

You're gonna break her heart if you leave her.

Jilly laughing, ponytail swinging. Small and fierce and determined until—

Don't leave me, Gabriel. I need you.

"I'm fine," Jilly insisted. If she didn't get out of here where every single look conveyed pity or worry, she would scream. "I want to go home."

Her brother Alex appeared in the doorway with what she thought of as his FBI face firmly in place.

But his eyes were pure big brother. "Alex…" She held out her arms and swiftly he crossed to her, his broad shoulders blocking out the light as he hugged her. "Get me out of here," she whispered in his ear. "Please."

Alex drew back and studied her. As with Rafe, Alex had been grown by the time she appeared on the scene, yet he'd always treated her not as an imposition or a pest but as someone for whom he would always have time. He'd played dolls with her and taken her exploring the savage land that surrounded them. He'd taught her to paint—well, tried to—

and though she possessed absolutely nothing of his astonishing gift, he'd shared with her his eye, the one that he and Dane both possessed, the gift for seeing beyond the surface impression, of observing the world so closely that its hidden secrets were revealed.

Now that eye was turned on her. "Are you afraid to go back home, since that's where it happened?" He knew, better than most, the price extracted by violence. He'd been a hostage negotiator for years, and it had taken a toll on him. "You can come stay with us."

Yes, she was afraid, but she couldn't let herself give into that fear. "I'm okay, thanks to Gabriel."

One dark eyebrow cocked. "Gabriel?"

"He's the one who rescued me," she said. "Now no one seems to know where he is, except that Saint is supposed to be keeping him out of jail."

At that moment, Saint appeared in the doorway.

She craned to look past him. "Is Gabriel…"

Saint frowned. Shook his head.

She sat up too fast, and her head swum.

"Doesn't look to me as though you're quite ready to head home," Alex noted.

She gripped his arm. "Come on, guys. I'm okay. I just haven't had anything to eat."

"I'll see about getting you something," Dane offered, looking relieved to have something to do. He'd spent several months in the hospital and rehabilitation, not that long ago. Hospitals were not his favorite places.

"No." She put every ounce of strength she had into the pronouncement. "Listen to me, everyone. I. Am. Fine." But she couldn't seem to stop her eyes from welling. "I just want to go home." She looked at Saint. "And I want Gabriel. Where is he?"

He and Alex exchanged glances, then he sighed and returned his gaze to hers. "He's out of holding. He's gone home."

"Why was he there? He saved my life."

"I know." Saint kept his poker face intact.

"Saint..."

"He just...went a little crazy when he didn't know if you were okay."

"Is he all right? Does he know I'm fine?"

All of them stared at her. "You're not fine, honey," Saint said.

"I'm not badly hurt, I was just—" She had to shut her mind down. "I want to see him. I need to."

"Jilly," Saint said gently. "I don't think that's a good idea right now."

"He needs me, too," she insisted.

Alex turned to Saint. "Where does he live?"

Saint shook his head. "No idea."

He's not coming. He's...not coming. It shouldn't hurt so much, but it did, the unspoken part of Saint's message.

"You can ask Ray and Fayrene at Ray's BBQ on South First. They knew his grandmother, and that's where he's staying, I think." She swallowed hard, her hands gripping each other as she worked not to show how devastated she felt by Saint's news.

Why, Gabriel? I need you.

But clearly she couldn't afford to.

She cleared her throat and pushed back the sheet, sliding her legs over the bed. "I'm going home, even if I have to do it in this stupid gown."

"Hey, there," Dane objected. "Nobody said you could go yet."

From somewhere she found a semblance of who she used

to be and glared at him. "I don't care what anyone says. I want my clothes, and I want them now and—" She couldn't swallow past the ball of tears in her throat.

Just then Vanessa entered with a shopping bag in her hand. Vanessa had been her best friend before Dane ever knew the woman he was about to marry.

At the sight of her, Vanessa's eyes welled, but almost instantly, the woman who'd been a powerful executive reassembled her features and put on what Jilly thought of as her hostess face. "I could hear you in the hall. I'm guessing these might come in handy." Her pregnant belly preceding her, Vanessa deposited the bag on the bed. Inside Jilly could see new items, the tags still on them. How Vanessa would know that she craved that newness, especially when it meant shopping in the wee hours of the morning, she had no idea, but her gratitude made her eyes sting.

No. If you cry, you will never get out of here.

So Jilly managed not to. "Thank you."

Vanessa smiled, though her gaze held concern. "You're welcome." She glanced around at the men, all highly competent, all of whom practically shuffled their feet in their discomfort. They were used to Jilly being plucky and strong and cheerful. They didn't know what to do with her when she was hurting and weak.

So she wouldn't be.

"Scram, you guys." She cleared her throat. "Somebody see to breaking me out of here or I'm walking out, anyway."

Relieved to have something to do, they cleared the room in seconds, these men who loved her.

"Impressive," Vanessa said, busy removing price tags. "So tell me how you really are."

Jilly looked up at her taller friend, knowing Vanessa would listen if she wanted to talk, just as Clarice would. She glanced from one to the other gratefully, but she didn't dare, not now. "I'm fine," she said, pasting on a smile, then quickly turning her attention to the bag of new clothes with no memories attached to them.

It was just as well that the other clothes were needed as evidence. At the thought of donning them ever again—even the jeans, which were her favorite pair—a little shiver ran through her. She'd rather burn them. Soak them in lye. Pour a gallon of disinfectant on them, maybe.

As she slid the new jeans up her legs, an image of her old ones being jerked down blasted into her brain, and she lost her balance. She gripped the sheets and held on for dear life. *No. No. You don't get to do this to me. It's over. You're done.*

She didn't look at either of her friends but simply focused on zipping her jeans, then shaking out the shirt Vanessa had brought.

"I want to see Freddie before I go," she said when the men returned with the news that she was free to leave.

Clarice and Vanessa exchanged glances.

Alex spoke up. "Honey, have you looked in a mirror?"

She frowned. "No."

"Maybe you'd better."

Vanessa dug a compact out of her purse and handed it over.

Even such a minuscule glance made Jilly gasp. She stared at the visual evidence, and suddenly Mako loomed over her again, face twisted with hate, arm flying at her—

She swayed on her feet.

Alex grabbed her, tucked her into his side. "You need to be back in that bed."

She closed her eyes, but that only made the whole thing more real. She snapped them open. "No." She bit her lip. "Please, Alex, I just want to go home."

A hesitation. Around her every face bore sorrow. Fury. It was painful to see them so miserable.

She straightened and somehow found a smile, brittle though it was. "Good thing Freddie's sedated, huh? If he woke up now, I might scare him right back into the dark." She swallowed hard and handed the compact back to Vanessa.

"Saint said he would check on him," Clarice said gently. "Let's just get you home before the rest of the family arrives."

The rest of the family. She both wanted them desperately and had no idea how she would bear all the sympathy and the helpless rage everyone felt.

"Oh, dear," she said, pasting on another smile. "I'm pretty sure my bed's not made."

When the atmosphere lightened a fraction, the effort she'd made seemed worth it. That's what they counted on her for, to be cheerful. Resilient.

Unbreakable.

One step at a time. Fake it 'til you make it.

Chapter Sixteen

Gabriel awoke, and he wasn't sure where he was.

When he moved, every muscle in his body hurt. What the hell had he done the night before?

With a rush, it all came back. He sat up fast, though his body protested. His shoulder glanced off something hard. He blinked and realized where he was.

Mama C's altar, the private one in a corner of her bedroom. He'd entered this room only once since he'd been back, during his general survey of the place to check out the condition.

But the scent of her, so beloved and familiar, had sent him packing. Now he was back, and it didn't take a genius to figure out why.

When you cannot see your way, mijo, she would say to him, *the Blessed Virgin will help you. She will listen, and she will intercede for you. La Virgen de Guadalupe, she belongs to us special. When you have nowhere to turn, remember that she is with you. That through her love, I am always with you, as well.*

Gabriel glanced at the statue of the woman before him, fierce and beautiful. *I wish I could believe, Mama C.*

But he was lost. For a long time now, he'd operated on autopilot, simply getting through one day, then the next, his direction only temporary, his goals few and finite, always in the belief that somehow, someday, the reason he was still alive would become evident. That one day some new purpose would make itself known, and he would understand the next step. He would be able to plan out a future, now that his old one was lost.

He no longer believed that.

Don't leave me, Gabriel.

Then maybe you really don't deserve her.

Of course he didn't. He'd always known that.

Whatever else you did, you saved her.

Hell if he had. He leaped to his feet. He'd caused the attack. Mako would have left her alone if not for him. If the creep had thought of her at all, it would have been as the woman who foolishly believed in second chances. She would not now be terrified and injured and forever changed.

He cast a glance of apology at the Virgin. *I'm sorry, Mama C.* For good measure, he crossed himself and backed away, as was proper.

There were no answers for him. He strode from the room, spotted the packed duffel on his bed. Crossed to it and hefted it over his shoulder. Headed for the door to—

Don't go, Gabriel. Don't leave me.

Jilly as he'd last seen her rose vividly in his mind. He could feel her against his chest, trembling. Sobbing. Keeping her body in contact with his, crying out when he set her down.

Try as he might, that was the only Jilly he could see. The lively one, the stubborn, determined optimist had receded so far into the distance that only a shimmering trace, like a mirage, teased him from afar.

He let the duffel slide from his shoulder with a thud.

If only he could see her one more time and know she was okay…

If he could check on her without having to talk to her.

See but not be seen.

You're gonna break her heart if you leave her.

There was nothing he could say to her. No way to make this right. No, he couldn't let her see him.

But he had to lay eyes on her, just once.

Tonight. Under the cover of darkness, his old friend.

From her perch on the overstuffed chair in one corner of her kitchen, Jilly peered around her at the gathering of people she loved. She'd demanded to be let out of her bed, but the compromise was to stay put while the gathering swirled around her.

Everyone was here—all her brothers and their families, Mom, Dad—crowding the kitchen which overflowed with dishes brought by the families she'd helped, the volunteers she'd worked with. A few came back to speak with her—Teo, nearly unrecognizable without his gimme cap and tool belt, had managed nearly fifteen minutes, but he had barely been able to look her in the eye. Most seemed unable to figure out what to say beyond *I'm so sorry* and *Hope you feel better soon.*

She, in turn, wasn't sure how to ease them. She didn't feel the slightest bit bubbly, but she did her best to imitate the person they were accustomed to seeing.

Meanwhile her family tried to fill in the gaps and keep the atmosphere light. Currently Dane was teasing Vanessa that their dog Skeeter deserved a special place in their wedding, since he was the agent of their first meeting. "If he were human, you'd let him," Dane complained. "I mean, I found him a lighted collar and everything."

Vanessa laughed as hard as any of them as she sat perched

on the arm of his chair.

They were doing their best to make everything feel normal, and the love in the air certainly was. How many times had she been in the company of this group of people, laughing and cutting up, sharing the wealth of love that had been the bounty she'd taken for granted?

Her gaze shifted to her mother, the source of it all, and her father, Hal, a bluff, hearty man's man who might not say the words as often…but he lived them.

Love was her legacy, and once Jilly had treated it as if it were her right…but no more. The caring of these people filled the very air around her, rich and vibrant and plentiful.

But somehow all of it went on at a distance, a chasm she couldn't seem to cross.

Her mother caught her eyes, and Celeste's brows lifted in question. *Are you all right?* Jilly managed a smile and nodded, then quickly shifted her gaze away.

Only to see that Rafe was watching her. That Clarice was perusing her. That despite the merriment, everyone here was operating on two levels, one, the honest exchange of joy and caring.

Two, *how is Jilly doing?*

She felt naked. Exposed. Alone, when never before in her life had she felt separate from these people.

They were only worried for her.

They wanted her to be okay.

Needed her to.

She would crack if she sat here one second longer. The hideous, quivering mess inside her would spill out.

She cast her most glittering smile as she rose. "Excuse me." She pointed vaguely toward the bathroom. "Be right back." She felt as much as saw everyone's eyes follow her. More than one person shifted as if to accompany her.

She turned. "I can manage to go to the bathroom by myself, thank you." She summoned a facsimile of her old sauciness and dared all of them to challenge her.

Awkwardly these people—with whom there had never been a moment's awkwardness in her entire life—one by one looked away from her.

And an odd and unfamiliar silence reigned. As she escaped down the hall, longing to lock herself in her room and not come out, at last someone spoke. Liam asked Annabelle if it was true she was going to star in a film about zombie robots next.

Annabelle's spluttering response generated laughter, hollow and forced, like the merriment at a wake.

But at least the conversation renewed. Jilly took her first deep breath in hours.

And escaped out the front door.

When the front door opened, Gabriel stirred from where he'd settled in the vacant lot across the street, screened by an overgrowth of vegetation.

When he saw it was Jilly, he rose to get a better look, keeping back from the glow of the streetlight.

She was moving stiffly, and his jaw clenched at the sight. She had her arms wrapped around her middle—had her ribs been hurt or…?

Then she approached the porch railing, and in better light, he got a glimpse of the damage to her face—and he wanted to beat the hell out of Mako all over again.

Except that he knew who was to blame for that fist-sized bruise on her cheek, for the cut at the edge of her beautiful mouth.

He turned to go, wrecked at the sight of the damage…

But she was out here alone. *Go back inside. Stay safe.* If it were up to him, she'd be locked away in a castle with high stone walls, protected by an army.

That house was full of people who would protect her, he reminded himself. What he wanted didn't matter.

She stared out into the darkness and looked so sad. So lost.

Every cell of him ached to go to her.

Don't leave me, Gabriel.

It's not your fault. You saved me.

But she was wrong, and he knew it.

He could have patched up her injuries himself and stayed there with her all night, shutting out the world, taking care of her, holding her close, placing his body between her and the world.

Damn, but he'd wanted to. Except that the people he loved died.

She was hurt because of him. Could have died because of him.

The best thing he could do would be to leave her to that gathering of people, that formidable family he'd heard laughing through the open windows, that group of big, competent men.

They're overprotective. They treat me like I'm a kid.

But that's what you need right now, sweetheart. All the protection they can provide.

For an instant he thought about crossing the street, about taking her into his arms. About joining the ranks of those who would guard her.

But there were minefields in his head. She could be hurt again.

He'd lost control, and she'd paid the price.

But she looked so sad. So alone.

Go back inside, he willed. *Go back to where you are so loved.*

She looked as lonely as he felt.

Then the front door opened, and a man stepped out.

Jilly pasted on a smile, big and fake and nothing like her.

Disturbed, Gabriel watched her accompany the man back inside. Couldn't they see that she was faking it?

He didn't know how to help her, and it gnawed at him.

Then he remembered Freddie. She was in no condition to do so, but at least there was one thing he could do for her: he could check on the boy.

Early the next morning Gabriel stood inside the ICU cubicle, his eyes locked on the boy lying so still. Around him, machinery beeped and breathed. The tube down his throat, the tubing in his nostrils taped to his too-young, gaunt cheek, the thin chest rising and falling.

Another boy's still face superimposed itself, another brown cheek—

This one torn and bleeding.

Gabriel locked his fingers around the edge of the privacy curtain. *He's not dead. He's breathing. He's alive.*

But he wasn't breathing on his own.

"I bet he's not that quiet normally," said the nurse from behind him.

Gabriel jolted at her voice, tried to still his racing heart. "He's not."

"It looks worse than it is," she assured. "Once he's taken off the sedative, we'll pull the breathing tube. It's a precaution as much as anything."

"But you don't know when that will be."

"Not for sure, no. We're keeping him sedated so his body can heal. When the swelling in his brain has come down enough, we'll withdraw the medication and pull the breathing tube. He's strong, though. He will come back."

"Kid's had a hard life, but he's got guts."

"He must have. That was a terrible beating." Then she studied him too closely for Gabriel's peace of mind. "Say, aren't you the one who brought him in? I was coming off shift that night, and I remember seeing you carrying him in."

Uncomfortable with the praise, Gabriel only shrugged.

"He would have died without you, Dr. Evans said."

"I have to go." He turned.

"Sorry. I don't mean to make you self-conscious. You're one of those, huh? Reluctant heroes? Don't need the credit?"

"I'm no hero," he said sharply.

"Okay, okay. Have it your way." She paused. "Listen, I don't want to ask anything you're not up for, but—"

He exhaled. "But what?" He desperately wanted out of here.

"Just…" She lifted one shoulder. "It might help him if you'd talk to him some. Let him hear your voice, since it's familiar. That woman who stayed with him the first night hasn't been back since the day after, and I don't know why. There's a cop who's dropped in a couple of times, but…" she hesitated. "We see it all the time. Having someone with them helps them. I think of it as anchoring them to this world." She rolled her eyes. "Probably sounds stupid."

He really looked at her then. She had some of Jilly's fresh beauty, her spark. She was someone who believed in the good. "Not stupid." He drew in a steadying breath. "I'll try." Though he was more than ready to be gone, if it would help the boy, he'd do his best.

"It doesn't matter what you say to them, I mean, it doesn't have to be profound. Just the sound of your voice and the touch of your hand…it makes a difference, I swear. I'll give you some privacy."

He heard her footsteps going away. Before she was outside, he spoke up. "The woman? She would be here if she could, but she—" His throat got tight. "She's been hurt."

A pause. "I'm sorry for that. Tell her we're taking good care of him for her, then."

Not likely he'd have the chance.

But he still nodded.

Then he took the last step to the bed. "Freddie," he said in a voice gone rough. He cleared his throat. "Listen, I know you're hurt and waking up will be a bitch." He knew that sensation all too well, awakening in a world where pain ruled and nothing made sense. "But here's the thing—Jilly needs you to get better. Mako's—" His hand clenched on the railing. "He can't hurt you now." His mind clamored with shouts and screams and flesh giving way and the barely-registered impact of bones against bones…

Gabriel shook his head hard to dislodge the melee. "You're in a safe place." But where would he be when he awoke? When he was well enough to leave? Jilly had had illusions that she would get custody of him, but surely that took time, even if she were in shape to do so.

Which she wasn't.

He thought of *Mama C's* house, sitting there empty. He had room, yes, but who the hell would let him take this boy home with him?

So what did he tell this kid who desperately didn't want to be sent to a foster home with strangers? Gabriel had no power to change that, and he couldn't make the boy into a fugitive, even if he were any kind of option himself.

His knuckles were white on the bedrail, he realized, and forced himself to relax them.

Once he would have been secure in knowing that Jilly would have answers for all those questions, would have Freddie's fate securely in her hands, but now?

She didn't need the pressure. One look at her last night told him she was inches from breaking.

"Sir?" said the nurse from the doorway. "I'm sorry. Visiting hours are over."

Gabriel put his hand on Freddie's, careful not to disturb the IV taped to the back of it. "You're not alone, Freddie," he said, though mostly he was lying through his teeth. He was no answer and Jilly couldn't be one. He had no solutions that made a lick of sense.

But maybe there was another thing he could do for Jilly when he couldn't do what he really wanted and steal her away. Shield her from every being harmed again.

He'd get in touch with Saint. First he'd let the detective ream him out all he wanted, then whenever the guy ran out of steam, he'd start asking questions about what was happening with the social workers. See if there was anything he could do.

"Sir, I'm sorry, but—"

Gabriel nodded and squeezed Freddie's hand lightly. *Blessed Mother, watch over the small ones*, he prayed to the Virgin as Mama C would have. "Hang in there, kid."

Then he left.

Jilly prowled her bedroom in the darkness. She'd tried to sleep, but however hard she worked at it, sleep wasn't happening. Every time she closed her eyes…

She just couldn't. The attack…the fear… Though that wasn't all of it. She was worried about Gabriel. And Freddie.

Freddie was in good hands, she knew that. Medical professionals monitored his every breath, the slightest change in him. But no one could predict what shape he'd be in when he awoke.

And Gabriel? He'd taken care of her. Defended her…gotten her help. She'd never felt safer than when she'd been curled up in his arms.

Who was watching over him? When she had so many people ready to do her slightest bidding, prepared to accomplish whatever she needed…who took care of Gabriel?

It's my fault. I did this, Jilly.

Yes, she'd heard from Saint about how Gabriel had gone after Mako's minions and dared Mako to show himself after what he'd done to Freddie. But why did he think he should have anticipated Mako coming after her? It was Mako who was messed up, Mako who was violent and enjoyed being cruel.

Gabriel was none of those.

He nearly killed Mako.

He just…went a little crazy when he didn't know if you were okay.

Don't leave me, she'd begged, but he had anyway, in order to summon help. That was only responsible. She didn't blame him.

But clearly he blamed himself.

She thought back to his expression as Ray and Fayrene spoke of his grandmother and sang his praises. What had happened to him in Iraq? What burdens did he bear?

My spirit was so troubled and I was so ashamed.

She'd told Rafe she wouldn't pry. His past was only her business if Gabriel allowed it to be, and thus far he did everything possible to keep himself apart from others.

Yet she knew—she *knew*—there was such goodness in him.

Come to me, Gabriel, she called out silently. *Talk to me.* Jilly looked out her window into the star-scattered night, wishing she could see the first star again.

She would make a wish on it.

Bring him back to me. Please bring him back.

And please…please keep him safe.

She turned again on the path of her pacing. One careful step after another, she walked her bedroom through a night that seemed fated never to end.

Gabriel's post allowed him a glimpse of the windows that he was pretty sure were hers. Though his muscles cramped from so long sitting, still he didn't move.

He'd seen a figure pass the windows. Though she didn't turn on the light, the ghostly white of her nightgown gave her away. He was all too familiar with sleepless nights, how they went on forever.

He could cross over. Most of her family had left. Only her parents remained, and their bedroom was on the other side of the house, he thought.

He could be as close as a window screen. Press his hand to the metal weave. Feel the warmth of hers on the other side.

And maybe in the darkness he could confess all the reasons why she should welcome his departure, should insist that he leave and never return.

That's how it would go if there were any justice.

But that was far from what he wanted. He yearned to pick

her up again, cradle her in his lap. Wrap his arms around her as tightly as she could wish. Press her head to his chest and bend his own over hers.

And whisper softly why he so very, very much wanted her. She was so kind. So sweet. So vulnerable. So trusting.

Every one of those was one more reason why he would leave her where she was, just as soon as dawn rose.

But for now he would wait and he would watch. He would be the sentry, the line of defense he'd failed to provide on that one night that would scar her forever.

His fault. Along with so many other failures that were always and forever to be laid at his feet.

Chapter Seventeen

"Everyone needs to go home," Jilly said the next morning. She'd finally fallen into a troubled sleep and slept too late. Now it was nearly noon and the troops had gathered again, all of them busy people, all of them with lives they'd interrupted to circle the wagons around her. "And I need to get back to work."

Protests bubbled up, boiled over.

"Sunshine, you're not well yet."

"I'm fine, Dad. Just fine."

"You just got out of the hospital," Liam protested.

She rolled her eyes. "The hospital my family insisted I stay in overnight. Aren't you in the middle of a film? What's this costing the production every day you're missing?"

"That's not the point," Liam grumbled.

"It is the point. Vanessa, I know you have someone learning to manage the hotel, but you're getting married. You'll be gone for three weeks on your honeymoon. Surely you have a list a mile long of things to be done before then."

"I'll help her." Dane's jaw muscle clenched.

"You're finishing Jaime's book." She turned to Rafe. "How many patients have come into the clinic while you've been here?"

He only arched one eyebrow. "Diana can go back without

me."

"Abuelita is back there alone, when you normally drop by to check on her every day. She's ninety-three years old. I'm barely thirty." She glanced at her mother, pleading.

Her mother's gaze narrowed, and she did that mother scan.

Increasingly desperate to be alone, Jilly clung to every ounce of resolution she could muster.

Even though a part of her was terrified at the prospect of them leaving.

"She's right," at last her mother spoke. "Everyone has work to do."

"I'm not finished with the window I was replacing," blustered her father.

Celeste glanced around. "I see six grown men who can help." But her sharp gaze arrowed in on Jilly as if still assessing.

I'll be okay, Mom, Jilly mouthed.

She would be. She had to be. People went through much worse than being knocked around.

Celeste simply let her gaze range the room, that *Because I said so* finely-plucked maternal eyebrow lifted.

"Well, boys, I think you have your orders," Liam's wife Raina said, rising from her chair. "Meanwhile, there's a ton of food that needs to be portioned out and stuck in the freezer for later."

Jilly opened her refrigerator and groaned. "I couldn't eat this in a million years. Jade and Clarice, please take some of this home, since you live here in town. Let's see what we can bundle up and take to the homeless shelter." Which reminded her of Freddie. "Saint?"

He stopped on his way out the door. "Yeah?"

"Have you heard from your CPS contact?"

He winced. "Yeah…about that. Jen, it's not going to be easy getting custody of Freddie. They really have a problem with you being a single woman and him being a teenage boy."

"That's just wrong. It's sexist."

He rolled his eyes. "He's half your age and taller. He lives in a violent world. He needs more supervision than you can provide."

"But—"

"I didn't say I'd given up, but don't kid yourself. It's not going to be easy, and there's no way to make this happen before he's released from the hospital. If we didn't already have two girls fostered with us in addition to our brood, I'd volunteer, but—"

"I appreciate that. Maybe there's enough time for me to get through the approval process, though. He could be in the hospital for a long time, right, Diana?"

Her surgeon sister-in-law Diana shook her head. "Tough to say at this point. I've checked with the docs I know from when I worked at Mercy. If there is much damage, he could be in a rehab situation for quite a while."

"Oh, no." Jilly pressed her fingers to her mouth, imagining the lively Freddie's light dimmed. "Is that likely?"

"There's no way to be sure yet. But if he winds up with special needs, that's yet another mark against you. You have a full-time job that consumes you already. How would you take care of him?"

Sean was looking at her, and she looked back. If she took his job offer, she'd add traveling to her schedule.

She jutted her chin. "I'd manage. He's terrified of going to foster care. Something happened to him before." Urgency gripped her. "I need to be at the hospital with him."

"Not yet," said her mother firmly. "He's in good hands you said, Diana?"

"Absolutely."

"But what about someone holding his hand or talking to him? The night nurse said that would help."

"I'm still dropping by," Saint said, then cleared his throat. "And apparently Gabriel is, too."

Jilly went still. Gabriel was looking after Freddie, yet he wouldn't come near her. That hurt.

But so be it. "What about Damien?" she asked. At the puzzled expressions, she explained to the others. "Freddie has a little brother, half-brother, actually. He's not an orphan, but from what Freddie told Gabriel, he's been taking care of Damien whenever Damien's mother pulls a disappearing act." She frowned. "I ran into her. It's not hard to imagine that she's neglecting him."

"Ran into her?" Dane questioned.

She glared back. "I was looking for Freddie. I went over there."

"Do we want to know where?" Dane pressed her.

"Probably not." She didn't back down.

"Jilly got a case opened on him," Saint said. "And she promised to butt out of it after that," he reminded her. "I'll get reports, and we'll see what develops. Just knowing that she's being watched may make his mother straighten up."

"I have contacts at CPS, as well," Clarice said. "I'll put in a word."

"As will I," Sean offered. "So just relax for now, kiddo. Let us help."

She subsided. She was sore and weary, and she knew each of them was as good as his word. "You are all so amazing," Jilly said, her heart squeezing. "You drop everything and come to help me, and you'd do this for Freddie and his little brother, just because…"

"Because we're family," Alex said. "It's what families do."

Chapter Eighteen

"Sunshine, we'd be back in two weeks, anyway. Why don't we just stay?" Her father had her tucked under his arm as they swung on her porch swing a little while later.

She longed to crawl into his lap as she had when she was a little girl. He was a big, bluff, hearty man whose shoulders had always seemed as broad as the world. Now his sons matched him in height and he had slowed some with age, but she knew to her bones that he would slay armies for her sake.

It was all she could do not to turn into his broad chest and weep. Beg him to stay or to take her home with him as he so badly wanted to do.

But that would be letting Mako win.

And her father would never stop worrying about her living alone then.

So Jilly bit back her tears. Became his Sunshine once again. "I'm fine, Dad."

"You're not. How could you be?" He shook his head. "I'm sure not."

From somewhere she found the strength to rise from his side and settle in his lap, not like a little girl but as someone who could offer solace. She put her arms around his shoulders. He needed comfort as badly as she did. Needed desperately to feel that he wasn't abandoning his little girl to a world he'd never trusted with her in the first place.

She pressed the side of her head to his. "You made me strong, Dad. You still do. I know to the depths of my soul that you will be here the second I need you, no matter how far you had to travel, no matter what you had to do." She couldn't stop one hot tear from trickling down her cheek.

He gripped her with his formidable strength. "You know it, baby girl. You know I will." His voice came out choked with the emotion he seldom revealed. To the world, Hal Sullivan was a cheerful man, a tower of strength, someone who had a good word for everyone. But he'd carved a ranch out of hostile land and made it succeed through the sweat of his brow and the unyielding determination she had inherited. He'd met the widowed Celeste Sandoval, who'd sworn never to marry again, and he'd convinced her to love him, to bring three more children into this world while treating her two boys as his own.

He was the best father, the best man she'd ever known. "You're my hero, you know. You always were."

For a moment they clung to each other, each reluctant to part. Jilly knew that for him to leave, he had to truly believe she was all right, and she wasn't sure where she would find the strength to prove it.

But she had to. She would not cost this good man another sleepless night like the last two. She'd heard his pacing as she, too, lay awake.

She forced herself to release him, to slip from his welcoming harbor and to blink her tears back. "You're not supposed to make me cry, Dad." Maybe it was better to acknowledge it.

He looked up, his own eyes red. "Don't tell a soul, but I'm about one blubber away from doing that myself."

"Like you said, it's only two weeks before you'll be back."

She wiped her eyes and found a smile that was easier because she was looking at his dear face. "And you've already knocked out more than half my wish list, so I'd better get busy adding to it."

His glance showed gratitude for the change of topic. "Vanessa's place is looking more attractive all the time," he blustered. "She doesn't make me work."

"Yeah, but you can get gourmet meals and luxury bedding anywhere, right? Vanessa can't provide barking dogs next door and Mrs. Lucero's rooster at five a.m."

Her father laughed and rose. "We should suggest both to her."

There. They had pulled back from the brink.

She hugged his waist and walked companionably with him toward the rental car where Liam, Raina, Rafe and Diana were waiting with her mother, with whom she'd already shared a long goodbye.

"I will ask you one thing, Sunshine." Her father's voice turned serious again.

She glanced up. "Anything for you."

"Would you give your old dad a call for the next few days? Let me know how you are?"

She made her smile brilliant, rose to her toes to hug him and kiss his weathered cheek. "Absolutely," she whispered to him. "I promise. I love you so much, Dad."

One more hug that lifted her off her feet, then he set her down and turned to his wife, who held out her hand.

It nearly broke Jilly's heart to see his shoulders round. "I'm working on that list already," she teased, though her throat was tight.

"Work, work, work," he grumbled as he climbed in.

Rafe shut their door and turned to her. "We can be here in a matter of hours, Bright Eyes."

"I know. Please don't make me cry again. I'll be all right, I swear."

He hesitated. "And will he? Your Gabriel?"

She smiled past her despair. "I don't think he's my Gabriel, and the answer is, I don't know. He's still told me almost nothing and now he's vanished altogether." Well, from her, at least.

"Would you like me to stay and talk to him?"

"I don't know if I'll ever see him again, truthfully."

He drew her close, pressed a kiss to her hair. "You can't save everyone, little sister. He may be one of them."

"I so don't want to believe that, but…you may be right."

"Focus on Jilly for now. I'm never but a phone call away."

"I know that."

"Here's something to look forward to. When I called Abuelita to tell her when we'd get in, she said perhaps she should attend the wedding after all."

"Really?" Jilly's smile was genuine. "That would be so fantastic!" And if somehow she could get Gabriel to meet Abuelita, and her grandmother could perform her magic on him as she had Rafe….

"Liam's had a standing offer to her that he would fly her down and make the trip much less difficult." He grinned. "She's never flown before."

"Wow. Can you imagine making your first flight at the age of ninety-three? I'd like to be on that plane with her." She bent to look into the car. "Even if Hotshot is the pilot." She made a face at Liam, who returned the favor.

"You two…" Rafe chuckled, and she imagined that he, too, drew relief from the things that hadn't changed, like Jilly and Liam, so much alike, tormenting each other playfully.

One more hug, then she stepped away. "I love you all. Now get out of here before you turn into pumpkins."

She stood in her driveway and watched them pull out, a smile firmly planted on her face as she waved until they were out of sight.

Then she sighed. Let her face relax.

And felt the loneliness steal from the shadows to settle leaden over her shoulders.

She turned to face the little house she had loved since the first day she saw it. She forced herself to look at the driveway, at the back passenger door of the car she hadn't yet driven. At the spot where something in her had changed forever.

A small shudder ran through her, but she wouldn't let herself run back into the house. Instead she kept her steps even and slow as she made the first shaky attempt at reclaiming her home. Her life.

Honey, are you sure you don't want us to stay one more night? Her mother's face was on her mind as she rose the next morning.

I wanted you to stay forever, Mom…but I couldn't let you. She had to find her way back to that person she'd been, to the fearlessness that had always been part of her.

After a very long night spent jumping at every random noise, daylight was a blessing. She went into her room and started pulling work clothes out of her closet. April had insisted that she had things in hand, but she was the intern, not the executive. She couldn't see the big picture, couldn't know—

Blast you, stop shaking, she ordered the fingers so ineptly trying to button her blouse.

Focus. One button. That's all, just one.

With the intense concentration of a five-year-old, she

worked the disc through the opening, smoothed the fabric across and beneath.

Okay. You can do this.

One button, then two…finally she managed to get herself dressed and to slip on a pair of heels that had always made her feel tall and in control. She grabbed her purse and her laptop case, looked around her to see what else she should take.

This house was so empty. She was so alone.

Never before in her life had she felt that she had no one. Oh, she could call Alex or Dane or Saint or Sean. Any of them would come escort her to her car or drive her instead.

But then she would truly be a victim. Definitely be as helpless as they all were inclined to believe.

You can do this. People survive far worse every day.

Which made her think of Gabriel for only about the ten thousandth time. *Where are you, Gabriel? Are you all right?*

Why won't you come see me?

Especially since, out of everyone she knew, somehow he was the only one she really wanted with her.

One hand on the doorknob, Jilly clasped an image to her, that of her mother who, despite her own diminutive stature, always stood so straight and regal. She thought of Lucia, who had never let life defeat her, no matter how difficult her circumstances.

Something inside Jilly that she'd taken for granted had been breached, and there was a gaping hole in her chest where her easy assurance had always been.

She'd always thought she was so strong.

Fake it 'til you make it. She could do that, of course. But how could she get back what she'd lost?

She had no idea. All she knew to do right now was to keep moving forward.

Jilly opened the door and walked out into a world that,

everywhere she looked, seemed forever altered.

Are you okay?

What are you doing back here so soon?

Don't you think you should…?

The questions continued all day. She knew her callers meant well, but she just wanted to put all this behind her. She was still working after night fell, trying to catch up on all she'd missed. The encroaching darkness made her nervous, yes, but she was going to do her best not to give in to her fear. April had a study group and couldn't stay, though she'd offered. Jilly's family had checked in on her, and she'd lied about her whereabouts, told them she was tucked in bed, resting, reading a good book.

She didn't have the concentration for any of that. She had to reread everything, sometimes twice or more. She'd turned on internet radio on her laptop once April left, just to have the company.

But then she'd snapped it off because she wouldn't be able to hear if someone was creeping up behind her…

Stupid. This is ridiculous, Jilly. Head in hands, she stared down at the battered desk.

She was ready to jump out of her skin.

And she still had to cross the gauntlet of the street outside, the darkened parking lot. The drive home and then—

She put a hand on the phone. She could call Saint right now, and he'd be here to escort her. Any of them would.

No. She removed her hand again. Curled her fingers into a fist.

You have to reclaim your life. You can't cower from the night. If she did, she might as well start packing for West Texas.

Mako was in jail, she knew that. But he had his posse…

That wasn't the point. The world was no more dangerous than it had been a few nights ago.

It was her. She was different. She'd lost that certainty that had always bolstered her. She'd never been truly afraid before.

Now she couldn't seem to be anything else.

If you don't do this on your own now, it will only get worse. She rose, clumsily going through the motions of the daily shut-down that had been second nature. *Turn off the copier. The printer. Wash out the coffee pot. Straighten your desk.*

Pick up your things, walk to the door.

Get out your keys.

She heard Mako's shriek of pain as she jammed the sharp points in his eyes. She dropped them, took off running…

Slammed hard into the ground where he tore away her clothes and—

Jilly sank against the wall, curled into herself. What little courage she'd summoned evaporated. She pressed her forehead to the door, heart beating so hard she felt faint.

I can't do this.

She crouched in the darkness of her office, huddled against the door, and every two seconds, she pulled out her phone and stared at it like the lifeline it was.

Her stomach hurt. Her head pounded. She tried very hard to remember her yoga breathing. To calm down.

After a long time, she managed to get to her feet. To pick up all that she'd dropped, her pace that of an old woman.

One step at a time. One thing. Just do this one thing.

Finally she made it outside, keys brandished between her knuckles, pepper spray in the other hand. She practically ran to her car, and once inside, she locked every door, started the engine, bolted out of the lot.

All the way home, her eyes saw nothing, her teeth clenched, jaws tight, fingers locked on the wheel.

At last she made it into her driveway.

But she couldn't make herself get out.

There. Finally. Gabriel took a deep breath for the first time in an hour.

He'd been going out of his mind, waiting. Imagining the worst. Three times he'd almost left, but he had no idea where to look for her. Where was her family? Why was she alone?

He watched for her to emerge from the car, but she didn't. He rose to his feet. Crossed the street and approached her vehicle.

At last she opened the door and got out.

"Are you all right?"

Jilly started screaming.

He should have thought—"Jilly, it's me." Swiftly he moved around her, keeping his distance as he put himself in her line of sight. Her face was pale as death, her eyes wide pools of horror. "Jilly, you're okay. It's me. Gabriel." He wanted to touch her, to hold her and reassure, but she was backing away like she couldn't recognize him.

"Jilly." He held his hands out, palms out. "Honey, it's only me. You're safe. No one's going to harm you."

She stared at him, but she was somewhere else.

Then finally, she spoke. "Gabriel?"

"Yes. I'm sorry I startled you. I didn't mean—"

"I'm so scared," she blurted, her voice a hoarse whisper. "I don't know what to do."

"I'm here." He extended one arm carefully. "Would you take my hand?"

She glanced down, but she still wasn't fully there, gripped in a nightmare he cursed himself for causing. She was in the same spot where he'd found her, where Mako—

The tunnel loomed, the hollow drone growing louder….

He squeezed his eyes shut for a second. *Get your head straight. Do not go there. She needs you.*

"Jilly," he said softly. "Will you let me hold you?"

When she looked up, her gaze was tortured. "I have to be okay by myself. Everybody counts on that. I'm never afraid…" Her voice faded with each word, then her face crumpled. "How do I feel strong again?" Barely a whisper now. "How do I get it back?"

He wasn't sure she knew that tears were sliding down her cheeks. Seeing them tore his heart out. "You don't have to be strong all the time," he began. "It's okay to feel scared."

"But everybody expects… It used to be so easy and now…" She cast her gaze to the ground. "I don't know how to smile anymore, not for real. I—tried. I went to work. I talked to people but I…" Her head lifted, and her eyes were pools of torment and confusion. "I…pretended. I'm not…me."

She was so small, so wounded. This was all on him, and he had no right to be here with her, but…

Hell if he was walking away when she was hurting. He took a slow, careful step toward her, and when she didn't shrink away, he took another. "You don't have to be sunny with me," he said.

Her head started shaking, and he realized that the rest of

her was trembling, too. He closed his arms around her, gently and cautiously. When she didn't resist, he gathered her in.

She remained stiff with silent misery.

Then suddenly she pressed into him and gripped him hard. Dug her fingers into his shirt.

He tightened his embrace and wished to hell he never had to let her go.

Her head tilted back, blue eyes soft and open. "I was so afraid I'd never see you again."

Heaven help him, he could no more resist her than stop breathing. "I'm here," was all he could manage.

"I shouldn't need you this much."

"You let everybody in the world lean on you…when do you get to lean?" he asked. "There's no shame in feeling weak after what you've been through."

She did just that, pressed her cheek to his chest, her whole body against the length of his. It was the most peaceful he'd felt in longer than he could remember.

"I'm afraid to be outside my house in the dark," she murmured, as if uttering the darkest of confessions.

He cast a glance toward the porch, swathed in shadows. "Why don't we go sit on the swing for a bit?"

Her glance upward was grateful. "Seems like cheating if I'm not doing it by myself."

"Just consider me a transition." Which was all he could ever be to her, but he seized the opportunity gladly. Slowly he turned her in his arms, keeping her firmly against his side, though he really wanted to sweep her up and bear her away. "You're too strong to feel weak forever, but tonight, let me help."

They walked across her yard and up the steps. Once their feet tangled, but he quickly steadied her. "Would you like a flashlight?"

"Yes, but…" She inhaled a ragged breath. "I'm not going to use one or I'm afraid I'll never…" She shook her head sadly. "I used to love sitting out here in the dark. I felt so safe…"

She settled on the swing, piled with cushions. When he hesitated, she looked up at him. "I'll be okay if you don't want to stay." But her voice trembled faintly.

"It's not that I don't want to…" he began. *But it wouldn't be good for you to get closer. To depend on me.* The rounding of her shoulders stopped him from uttering those words. "I'm not leaving until you're ready for me to go." He lowered himself to the cushions.

She sat beside him stiffly, hands clasped in her lap. She seemed small and fragile, bereft of that lion's heart that had always been such a part of her.

He was so afraid of hurting her. Of disappointing her.

But she was hurting already, and it tore at him.

Gingerly he placed an arm around her shoulders, then drew her close. In the same moment, he used his foot to send them swinging.

Jilly sighed and relaxed against him. Slowly her clenched fingers untangled. Her head came to rest on his shoulder. After a bit, she drew her legs up and turned a little more into him, resting her bent knees atop his thigh.

In the silence they rocked, the motion hypnotic and soothing, to him as much as her.

Then she tilted her head back. "Gabriel…" Her eyes in the fragments of moonlight were deep and mysterious, beautiful and glistening with a longing that echoed in his heart. "Would you kiss me?"

The words were so soft he could have imagined them. They might have come from his own soul-deep yearnings.

But it didn't seem to matter. Like iron filings to a magnet, he bent to her. Touched her lips with his own.

In that moment, the world went silent and still. The only sound was the quickening thump of his heart, the voice inside him crying out to have her, to keep her, to hold her like this forever.

Her kiss swiftly heated with a bittersweet desperation, with an aching power that had the hair rising up on his neck. He couldn't trust how badly he wanted to let go, to steep himself in her. "Jilly, I'm don't know if—"

"Sh-h," she murmured against his mouth. "I need this. I need you, Gabriel. Would you come inside?"

She rose and held out her hand.

Torn between what he thought was best for her and what she was asking of him, at last he took it and followed her into this house that felt more like home than anywhere he'd ever been.

And she was the reason.

She pulled away from him only long enough to light a lamp, then led him to her bedroom, her small hand swallowed in his. Once inside, she drew him forward until they stood by her bed, a confection of fluffy pillows over a quilt that only furthered his sense of coming home.

"Jilly…"

She rose to her toes and silenced him with her lips. "Please don't say you shouldn't be here."

"I shouldn't." But he wanted to be. Desperately.

He pulled back. Cradled her poor injured face. "I can't stand this," he said, getting a closer look at what had been done to her.

"Please," she said, eyes swimming. "I don't want to feel ugly or scared. I want to feel beautiful."

"You are more than beautiful," he answered. "So much more." She needed him. Maybe only for tonight, but if this was all he would have of her…all he could do for her… Gently he pressed a kiss to her bruised cheek. To the barely healed corner of her mouth. Rage rose in him, monstrous and choking out every last—

I should have killed him.

"Sh-h," she said, over and over, punctuating each breath with a kiss to his eyes, his cheeks, his ears, healing something inside him with each touch, when he was supposed to be taking care of her. "I'm all right, now that you're here."

He lost himself in the blue eyes that were his vision of heaven. He could say he was sorry until the end of time, and it wouldn't make a dent. And in the doing, she would never be allowed to forget what she'd suffered.

Or he could try to honor her courage and her beauty, to pay tribute with his body to a woman he admired. Cherished.

So Gabriel did his best to lock away every ounce of rage, every killing thought that could taint what he wanted to do for her. Be for her.

Slowly, reverently, he worshipped Jilly with his body, with soft, tender touches of his lips and his fingertips, slowly baring her, never pushing her beyond her eagerness…and her eagerness grew.

Soon she was stripping him with haste, and it was hard to tell who was more nervous, whose fingers trembled most.

When at last they were both naked, he paused, looking down at her and wondering how one woman could encapsulate every dream he'd ever had. "You are so beautiful," he said to her. He let his fingers trace the glories of her flesh, taunting and teasing, delighting in every curve. When he spotted the fingertip pattern of bruises on her breast, rage rose to choke him again. Stopped him in his tracks.

But he felt her falter. Sensed her shame, her need to be healed.

He caught her chin in his hand and let his eyes say what he didn't have the words to express. Then he bent and used his lips to cleanse each mark of the violence she should never have had to experience.

His big hands were so reverent, so tender. With slow, careful strokes he painted her body with a torturous sweetness, a maddening caution that made her feel both deeply protected and brought her tears dangerously near the surface.

When at last he broke through the scrim she'd been fighting to paste over the shreds of her confidence in the wake of that fear-ravaged night, she tried to roll away from him, to cover herself and the soul-deep flaw that had been exposed in her.

He wouldn't let her flee. Instead he made her lie back, vulnerable and shorn of defense, and he sheltered her with his big body, with the fierce, powerful wings of his protection.

For a moment she hovered on the edge of terror, of the yawning pit of darkness her luck-filled life had kept her from seeing, surrounded as she had always been by those who loved her. She had, for the first time ever, experienced the soul-destroying powerlessness that she instinctively knew others like Freddie lived with every day.

She was so frightened that she was unequal to the challenge, that all the strength she'd never doubted she possessed was now revealed as empty bluster, and she trembled from the terror of it.

Gabriel seemed to sense it, gathering her up and holding her close, his powerful frame surrounding her, shielding her, the warmth of his skin seeping into hers, feeding her his own strength until hers returned.

He understood. Whatever it was that had marked him, had scarred him so, he too had been sliced to the core—judging from the wounds on his body, far worse than she could even imagine. He knew what it was like to feel powerless, and her fear didn't faze him.

He saw, and he regretted, but he didn't stop touching her, and he didn't hold her apart as though she would break. Instead, as soon as she began to settle, his strokes turned from soothing to whisper-light teasing, to a delicious, spooled-out torment. In her heart of hearts, she came to see that she could trust this man not to be afraid of her weakness, and the relief of it was stunning.

He was here with her, truly here. He saw into her heart, and she had her first true glimpse into his. There was much she didn't know about him yet, but they were together now, and they would have time to learn.

As she understood that she could be who she was—strong or frightened, cheerful or despairing—and he wouldn't flinch, need came roaring back to her.

Her hands began to roam over his body, and she was consumed by a tenderness she'd never felt before, by a driving need to prove to this man who so resisted letting anyone close, that his scars and his wounds didn't bother her, either. She slipped from his arms and pushed him back on the mattress, then began at his feet, pressing kiss after kiss to the terrible evidence of what he had suffered.

"Jilly..." he protested, but she shoved him back and kept going, taking her time to caress every ridge of scar tissue, every micron of puckered flesh. He remained tense, unable to accept her ministry as he had so willingly shared his own, so she added the stroke of her fingers to the press of her mouth. Slowly she worked her way back up his body, and at last he began to yield, to accept what she desperately wanted to give.

He had fought for her, this man, not once but twice. He'd rescued a lost, injured boy who would have died. She wanted to know what had happened to render him unable to see who he was at his core: a scarred, beautiful warrior whose heart was buried under the weight of his past but still beat strong and true.

She traveled her way up his thighs and felt a new tension invade him. She let the ends of her hair brush over his groin as she turned her face up to him and smiled, then took him into her mouth.

With a gasp, he reacted as if she'd branded him.

Suddenly she was on her back again beneath a hot, hard man with smoldering eyes.

"Gabriel…" Even as she burned with him, she cradled his face in her hands.

In that moment, he was open to her, those beautiful, wounded eyes filled with powerful emotion.

Then he bent his head and kissed her with such passion and fury that she was lost in the magnetism of this man who, unlike any other, spoke to the deepest part of who she was.

At last, she thought. *Here you are, my one true love. I was afraid I'd never find you.*

Something shifted in her, and Gabriel felt it in himself. The darkness in her eased, and shades of the old Jilly soon appeared, the playful Jilly, the one with shining eyes. She rose in a silken undulation, pushing at his shoulder and toppling him, quickly straddling him, a Celtic queen in all her glory, a bright, beautiful fairy with mischief in her eyes and magic in her fingertips.

With a smile curving her lips, Jilly proceeded to lay siege to his every last defense. She tickled him and giggled when he flinched. Arched her lithe body and rubbed herself against him until he moaned. She kissed his armpits, trailed her tongue over his biceps, down his chest and over his belly, then took him in her mouth once more.

He hissed and hastily plucked her off, reversing their positions again, loving her with his body, with his tongue and his lips and his hands, until she was moaning too.

Then, hoping to heaven she was better prepared than he was, he stretched past her, admiring her pretty blush as he fished for a condom in the drawer next to the bed.

Thank the stars for women who liked to be in control.

Watching her eyes go wide, her pupils huge and dark, slowly he sheathed himself inside her, never taking his gaze from hers.

And they climbed together into a refuge, a heaven he'd never been to before, a glorious, beautiful oasis where no one hurt, no one died, no one suffered. A haven lit by Jilly's smile, with a sky the color of her eyes, with a sun nearly as bright as her courage and her kindness.

Where Gabriel found, for the first time in longer than he could remember, a place where his heart did not hurt. Where joy raced through his veins. Where his world was this woman, this beautiful, sweet woman he could so easily love all his days.

Chapter Nineteen

Cordite stung the air. He couldn't hear anything for a second—

Then all he could hear were screams.

Blood matted his face, gore spattered his chest—

Gabriel awoke gasping.

Disoriented, caught on the claws of gut-wrenching despair, he felt the presence of another and went on full alert until he realized where he was.

Jilly's bed. Jilly's house, not—

His heart slowed a little, his breathing gradually evening out. Carefully he turned to his side and watched her sleep, tempted beyond wisdom to touch her hair, to rub his fingers over the red-gold talisman of her goodness.

Mijo, there are angels where you least expect them, *Mama C* used to say. As a boy he'd been fascinated by the notion; as a worldly teen, he'd been dismissive. As a grown man, he'd been tolerant of her beliefs, but he'd never shared them.

Angels. As he yielded to his longing and let a lock of her hair slide through his fingers, he smiled to himself. He'd never thought of an angel being stubborn or sassy. An unlikely angel, yes, but for all her single-minded determination to make reality take the shape that she wanted, this woman had a heart as fierce and pure as any celestial being could claim.

If only he could be what she needed. One day, maybe, but that was a big *maybe*, a day so far off he couldn't see it. He yearned to be that man, but his heart was filled with darkness, his mind a cobweb of all the horror he couldn't find a way to forget, all the pain and loss he'd been part of, all the guilt he could not shake.

He was a bad bargain, and this stubborn, valiant woman would never give up on him if he stayed. He would drag her down with him, and of everything weighing on his conscience, that failure would break him.

To the end of his days, though, he would never forget what it was like to be lost in love with this woman who was as generous with her body as she was with her heart. He would carry it with him, a flame against the darkness, wherever he went.

But go he must, before she awoke. Before she tangled herself deeper in the quagmire that was his mind.

And she was the one who broke.

Slowly and carefully he left the bed that had, for a few short hours, been the closest he would get to paradise in this life.

Goodbye, angel, he said silently.

And left…after one long, last, yearning look.

Jilly awoke to a morning bright and beautiful. She felt newly-washed and clean, cleared of the remnants of horror, the bindings of fear.

And her body…oh, her body felt absolutely glorious. She opened her eyes and rolled over to watch Gabriel sleep.

Except the bed was empty. "Gabriel?" Only silence greeted her. She sat up to swing her legs over the side, when something captured her attention.

On the other pillow lay a note.

She lifted her hand, started to reach—just as quickly retracted it. She exhaled a puff of air and delayed the reckoning. It might be only a note saying he'd gone out for doughnuts and would be back.

But this was Gabriel, after all. Mr. Vanishing.

She'd always been a rip-off-the-bandage kind of person, though, so even with her heart sinking, she leaned across and plucked the paper from the pillow.

She'd never seen his handwriting before, a bold slash of letters spelling her name.

Biting her lip, she opened it.

I can't do this to you.

Gabriel

She dropped the note as if it were on fire and all but leaped from the bed. Halfway across the room, she turned to glare at the paper as if it were him.

For the first time this morning, she felt truly naked. A rush to her closet, a grab for her robe. Belting it tightly, she gripped the neckline in one fist as her heart sank. *What happened, Gabriel? It was beautiful. You were beautiful. I thought we—*

I will not cry. She'd shed too many tears already. If he didn't want her, then just...screw him. Welcome anger swept over her. With quick steps she reached the kitchen and mechanically began assembling a pot of coffee, then busied herself poring through her overstuffed refrigerator in search of...*there!*

Defiantly she yanked out the amazing coconut cream pie Lucia Marin had brought over. *I will have pie for breakfast, and be damned to you, Gabriel Coronado.*

I can't do this to you. The words rang in her head. He was protecting her.

Which made him no different than any of the other males in her life, after all. She'd thought he was different, believed he saw her as she was. Didn't need her to put on a cheerful mask to pretend.

She'd gotten it all wrong. Last night had been a sham. Last night had been…

Glorious. She dropped her fork in the sink after one bite that tasted of sawdust. She stared out her window and let every second play out.

Last night…she had kissed his scars.

He had let his guard down. Had looked at her with no shields, with only his own broken heart bleeding before her.

Oh, Gabriel…

Give him space but not too much. It's a hard place he's in, and a dark one.

Sometimes the light you crave is the light you can't allow yourself to enjoy.

But what about me, Rafe? Fear was a ball in her stomach, dread that Gabriel was leaving, that he would be gone before she found him.

Yet for a second, she felt a flicker or her old self surface. *You're too strong to feel weak forever.*

She would go looking, she realized. No way was she throwing in the towel yet. A genuine smile rose inside her, and she set her back ramrod straight. As she marched to her closet, she was already dialing the phone. "Fayrene? I'm so glad you're in. This is Jilly Sullivan, and I need your help."

Gabriel had covered the windows and turned off the water supply to sinks, tub and toilet. He'd done a thorough check of the door locks and each window.

His duffel was packed, and his truck was loaded with what little he intended to take, mostly tools so he could find work…wherever the hell he was headed.

The cat was nowhere to be found, but Chico had managed to survive before Gabriel's arrival and would likely do so once he was gone. There was nothing left to tie him to this place. He would sell it as soon as he figured out what he wanted—at least, out of what he could have.

Heaven only knows when that might ever happen.

One last tug at the lock on the garage that had been his home for the last several months. He would stop by the hospital on the way out of town and leave the note he'd written for Freddie, then he was done.

He turned toward the driveway—

And halted in his tracks.

"Going somewhere?" Jilly leaned on the grill of his truck, no one's vision of an angel now, in her short denim skirt and the snug top that bared a tantalizing strip of her belly.

He decided the safer route was to remain silent.

She shoved herself off the bumper and prowled toward him with the slender legs he could still feel wrapped around his waist. "I asked you a question."

He couldn't figure her mood. "Yeah."

"Want to explain this?" She waved the note he'd written only a few hours before.

"Seems self-evident to me." He'd chew his way through razor wire to get to her, damn it. *Go away.*

"Well, maybe I'm just not too bright," she said, continuing to narrow the distance between them until he couldn't get a good breath. "But I don't recall giving you power of attorney."

He blinked. "What?"

"To decide my life for me." She still had those damn sunglasses on, and he couldn't stand it.

He yanked them off her nose and tossed them to the ground.

Blue lightning greeted him. The crackle of thunderclouds. "Those were my favorite sunglasses."

"What?"

"You owe me some sunglasses," she said, pressing her chest to his.

Oh, man…he knew those curves, knew the sweet pale rose of her nipples, how they felt between his lips. "Sunglasses?" he echoed.

She smacked him hard in the sternum. "Catch up, damn you, Gabriel. Who the hell do you think you are?"

"I've never heard you curse."

"You're about to hear more, you stupid, stupid—" Then she did the worst thing she could possibly do to him.

She burst into tears. "Look at what you made me do," she said, whirling away and covering her face.

And there it was, the nightmare he would create for her. "I told you I was no good for you, Jilly."

She wheeled around, eyes sparking. "You said I didn't have to be sunny for you. Did you lie?"

"No."

She brandished the note. "Then what is it that you can't do to me? Be real? Be honest? What is it you won't share, that you hold up like a shield between you and the rest of the world?"

"You don't want to know."

She lifted anger-bright eyes to his, and in them he could see the depth of her hurt. "You have no idea what I want."

No. But oh, how he yearned to.

Nearly as much as he feared finding out.

She fell silent, and the quiet hung like a dark, heavy cloud between them. "But you won't ask, will you? Because doing so might force you to care, and you're all about not caring, aren't you? Except there's the big, fat lie in all of this…you care far too much."

He flinched from the truth in her words.

"My brother Rafe nearly died from his injuries in Afghanistan. The rest of his team did. He was on a mission of mercy to provide medical care to a bunch of kids he'd all but adopted."

Gabriel swallowed hard and looked away.

"You lost people, too, Fayrene told me."

He flicked a glance at her but said nothing. *Don't*, he begged silently.

"Rafe didn't want to live. He nearly willed himself to die, but—"

Gabriel closed his eyes so she couldn't look. And he waited for the rest.

"Rafe had a whole big, loving family who refused to let him go. He fought all of us, but we fought back harder."

Gabriel swallowed and struggled to remain still.

"But you didn't have anybody to fight for you, did you? You survived, but you keep trying to be dead."

"I should be," he blurted before he stopped himself.

Jilly took a step closer, and he could feel her body's warmth. Felt himself leaning toward her as a flower seeks the sun.

She took his hand in hers, holding it lightly. "Who died, Gabriel? Who took your heart with them?"

He jerked his hand from hers and turned to put distance between them. He made it only a few steps before she plastered herself against his back, her slender arms stealing around his waist. "Tell me," she said softly. "You need to."

"No." He shook his head violently. "I don't."

She clasped him more tightly, and it should have felt like a restraint, like an unwelcome shackle.

But it didn't. The first warmth he'd felt in his belly in two years soaked into him. He covered her hands with one of his.

And held on.

Inside he was shaking apart because the pictures were coming too fast and he couldn't shove them away. Couldn't bury them.

"They were…children." The words tumbled out before he could stop them. "Innocent…kids. Orphans nobody wanted. They needed…someone." Every word was a stone on his heart. "Sayidah had the most beautiful voice, and Ahmed was…shy. But when he laughed—"

He wanted to buckle then, but Jilly held on.

More spilled from him. "The zealots didn't like them being with an infidel. Thought I would taint them. I was warned, and I tried to leave them, but the children…wouldn't go. I…ignored them, but they…followed. They loved to hear stories of America. To make up their own. They would tell me about what we would do when the war…ended. When they came to visit me." Every breath was a struggle. "Finally one day I…relented. They gathered round me, and they even brought me pieces of the candy I'd given them. They wanted to share what they had with me, when I—when a piece of butterscotch was nothing to me but—" He fought the image that haunted every night and day. "A car came by, and I was so caught in the joy of seeing them and hearing the story Ahmed wanted to tell me that—" The words clawed their way up his throat until he thought he would choke. "I wasn't paying attention to anything but them. I should have seen, but—"

The weight of it would never leave him. He was so glad he couldn't see her expression as he showed her who it was she thought she wanted. "The extremists attacked, and I was the only one wearing body armor. They—their bodies were torn to pieces. Sayidah had been in my lap, and she—the shrapnel…" He tore himself from her grasp, roaring out his fury, his anguish, the bottomless depths of it. He was desperate to get away from her, from the images that clawed at his sanity. He bolted for the side of the garage where she couldn't see him. He sank to the grass, his back to the wall.

And he prayed for her to get the hell out.

Nearly as hard as he wanted to plead with her *Don't go.*

Jilly wished fervently that Rafe were here or Abuelita or…anyone who would know what to do next.

But Gabriel only had her.

He'd been there for her when she desperately needed him. However inadequate she felt to the task, she was not going to abandon him. Cautiously she followed his tracks and rounded the corner, halting at the sight of him, this big powerful male with his ravaged heart.

He didn't lift his head as she approached, but at last he spoke. "You have to leave."

When do you know you're pushing too much, Rafe? She had no idea. She only knew she couldn't leave him like this or his shell would scar over again and never heal.

"I can't do that, Gabriel. See, I have this problem. I love you."

His gaze flew to hers, and in it she saw both his fear and

his hope. Then it hardened. "No, you don't. You just can't help taking on charity cases." He let his head fall back against the wood, looking utterly weary. "Trust me, you don't need me. Or this mess in my head."

"Maybe I don't," she admitted. "But I want you."

His gaze whipped to hers. "It would be a mistake. You can't count on me."

"I think I can. You've already saved me twice, even before last night. You rescued Freddie. You're a born hero."

"Don't say that!" He flinched as if she'd shot him. He pointed at the house. "That woman gave up everything, and I let her die alone." From the pain on his face, he believed that. Then he said no more.

"Tell me the rest."

"There isn't any more. People die, that's all."

"They do. People we love, whether we're ready or not. So it's wrong for you to live because others didn't?"

"Don't patronize me."

"I'm not. Tell me what happened with her. Go ahead—show me how horrible you are."

His glare should have vaporized her on the spot.

Listen to your heart—listen carefully, Jilly. Not to your head.

Gabriel was…hurting. And striking out because she was too close.

Logic means nothing to someone in that dark place. When a life is lost and you play a role in that loss, however unintentional, a scar is left.

"Tell me about her, your *abuela.*"

He sighed. "Can't you just leave?"

She settled beside him, took one big hand in hers. "Apparently not."

He looked around him as if seeing the place for the first time. He pointed to a corner of the yard. "Over there? That's her prayer garden. She worked two jobs and did other women's hair after hours, all to be able to feed and clothe a growing boy whose mother didn't want him. And every Sunday after mass, she would fix a meal she shared with any lost soul she encountered. Then after everyone left and the kitchen was all cleaned up, she would take her few hours of pleasure in a life full of work and disappointment, over there in that corner." He cut her a glance. "Mostly praying over me." For a second his eye lit with a flicker of humor.

"Were you a handful?"

"Absolutely. I was the toughest of *hombres*, all full of swagger and bursting to prove how bad I was, and she—" His voice caught and he looked away. "She would never have had much money, but she could have been taking it easy by then, at least. Instead she had me. She took me in when no one else would." His voice roughened. "And the second I could, I left for adventure and danger, and I left her behind."

"Children are supposed to grow up and leave."

His gaze was brutal. "Men are supposed to protect. She was here all alone, and she wrote me and she sent cookies and—" He cleared his throat. "And I sent her money and cards and flowers." His voice was full of self-loathing. "But not myself. Which was all she wanted."

"Your job wasn't one with a regular schedule…"

"Don't make excuses for me, Jilly. After I was wounded, I was in the hospital a long time before the military finally gave up on me and sent me away with some nice medals and an honorable discharge." His eyes locked on hers. "She wanted me to come home because she couldn't travel, but I couldn't—I was so—" He tore his gaze away. "I couldn't be with anyone, not even the one person who'd loved me all my life, so I hit the road for nearly a year, and I didn't call and I didn't write. Then one day I finally phoned, only to learn that she'd died four months before. She'd been sick even before I was wounded, but she never said a word, and she let me run when she needed me and—"

He leaped to his feet, then turned and jabbed his finger in her direction. "I failed her. I failed those children. I failed you. So don't tell me I'm any goddamn hero."

She wanted to wrap him in her arms and soothe away the anguish in his eyes, but he was far beyond platitudes, and his pain was terrible and real.

She cast about for the right words—and a notion smacked her right in the face. She could give him back what he'd given her.

"Maybe you're not," she said slowly.

The light went out of his eyes.

"Maybe you're not," he heard her say, and he squeezed his eyes closed against the pain of what he knew to be true.

But wished were not.

"I happen to disagree," she continued, her voice drawing closer. "But that's not the point. Look at me, Gabriel."

He didn't want to see that she had finally accepted how very much he was flawed.

But she surprised him. "The point is that you don't have to be a hero to deserve to be loved. You didn't kill your grandmother, and you didn't kill those children. You're just the one who got left behind to miss them. To be the one who never has the luxury of forgetting how it all happened. Your lot is to live with the reality and to try to find some way to forgive yourself—"

"I can't—" he interrupted, shaking his head violently. "I don't—"

"—when you know every one of them would forgive you."

"I—"

"—I talked to Rafe about his experience," she rose and continued without letting up. "And he told me that you never forget that kind of loss, that at best, you reach an uneasy peace with it. That you learn to forgive yourself by accepting that however much you regret what happened, you can't change it. You can only look for ways to balance the scales." She reached for his hand again and brought it to her chest, cradling it between hers. "Seems to me you've been doing that already, with Freddie and with me. With the Marins."

"But I—"

"You can't go back and save those children or your grandmother, but they're not the ones hurting, you are. How long do you have to suffer, Gabriel, before you've paid enough for events you couldn't control?" Then she smiled at him ruefully. "Rafe told me that I should be a little less me with you than normal, that sometimes my light shines too bright."

"Never." That was an answer he didn't even have to consider.

"I wasn't shining last night, but you were okay with it. Do you know what that meant to me, not to have to pretend with you?"

He didn't answer, only stared at her solemnly.

But he was listening.

So she went on. "All my life I've believed that I was strong, but suddenly I was terrified that I was anything but. That I'd never come back to myself, that I'd always feel weak and shaky." Her eyes were warm and soft. "But you believed in me, and you stayed with me in that dark place. You helped me find my way out, but you didn't expect me to magically be cured. You understood what it was like to feel powerless." She cocked her head. "But it's not okay for me to be with you in your dark place? To walk with you as you find your way out?"

"It's not the same."

"So you're telling me I can't love you enough to accept you as you are?"

"Love?" he echoed, his heart giving one hard thump.

"You're not going to stand there and tell me you made love to me like that, and you don't feel anything for me, are you? Because I will call you a liar, flat out." Her eyes were bright with temper and spirit and challenge. Then her voice softened again. "Don't you want to come out of the darkness, Gabriel?"

He was so damned tired he wasn't sure he could take one more step. His gaze clung to hers like the last hope in the world. "I do."

"You've done so much for so many. Look at how much you've done for Freddie. Look at how you rescued me and helped me heal." She opened her arms wide and waited for him. "Please let me walk with you on your journey. I don't care how long it takes, just…let me be there."

"I'm not asking you to be my sunshine. Or to save me." Though she was, simply by force of her existence.

"That's good, because I don't know if I can be that sunlight anymore," she said quietly. "But I could probably manage being a candle, at least." Her lips curved in a smile, but her eyes were wide with yearning.

He'd said he didn't want to hurt her, but he realized that what he was doing was hurting her more.

It was he who would be the coward, if he walked away now.

He could help her heal, too—and heaven knows she was so stubborn that she would never give up on him, just as she'd refused to give up on Freddie or the Marins.

With a relief so deep his head went light, Gabriel began to believe that maybe he could have this woman he wanted so much. That he wouldn't be the worst thing that had ever happened to her, that there was hope for them, after all. He closed the gap and gathered her in, burying his face in her hair.

Jilly clung to him, a ray of light piercing the darkness that had for so long been all that was left of his heart.

When at last he reached for her, Jilly knew a gratitude deeper than anything she'd ever experienced.

He wasn't going to leave her.

He was going to let her in.

Please, please let me be worthy of him. Let me do this right.

Maybe a good first step was to give him a break from baring his soul. Start finding that path back to normal. "Would you show me your home, Gabriel?"

He lifted his head. "Yes." But he didn't release her.

She didn't mind. She was far from ready to let go herself.

Her cell phone rang, and she so very much didn't want to answer it, but if it was her family, they'd worry.

She looked at the display. "It's the hospital," she said as she took the call.

"Ms. Sullivan? This is Sheryl. I'm Freddie Miller's nurse. We've turned off the sedation and removed the breathing tube."

Jilly's eyes went wide as she shifted her gaze to Gabriel.

"Freddie is asking for the man named Gabriel. Do you know how we can reach him?"

She smiled broadly. "I sure do." She finished the call and looked at him. "Freddie's awake, and he wants to see you."

"Me?"

"Would you like me to go with you or—?"

He pulled her into him and laid a devastating kiss on her lips. "Does that answer your question?"

She smiled, and suddenly the day seemed as bright as diamonds. "Wanna race to the car?"

A smile unlike any she'd seen from him widened.

Her heart lightened at the sight of him. Acting on impulse, she took off running, feeling young and carefree again.

He quickly caught up to her, swept her up in his arms—

And kept going.

With her, not away from her.

And, miracle of miracles, laughing.

It was a sound she resolved to hear again. Often.

When they reached the hospital, they were directed to a different floor where Freddie had already been moved from ICU.

"I should stay outside," Jilly said. "I forgot my face looks terrible."

"You don't want to talk to him?"

"Of course I do. I just—"

"Trust me. The boy has seen worse." He hesitated, then made himself go on. "And I'd like you there."

Her smile was pure sunshine then. She squeezed his hand. "Thank you."

They walked inside, and Freddie's head turned toward them. Gabriel waited, thinking of all the wounded soldiers he'd seen who'd suffered head injuries. The boy had asked for him, but that didn't mean he wasn't suffering lasting damage. "Hi."

Big dark eyes studied him. Flicked toward Jilly, then back. "I don't remember any of it, but the nurses, they told me you saved my life. That I'd be in the ground right now 'cept for you." He frowned. "Why you do that, man? I ain't nothin' to you."

Gabriel could feel Jilly's eagerness to speak, but somehow she restrained herself. "You're not nothing to me, Freddie." Words jammed in his throat. "How do you feel?"

"They got me on some good drugs. I ain't feelin' no pain." He glanced over at Jilly. "What happened to you?" His expression clouded. "Oh, no. Mako." Tears rushed to his eyes. "I remember tellin' him to leave you alone, but he didn't, did he?"

She left Gabriel's side and went to the boy. She clasped his hand. "I'm okay, Freddie, really." She smiled. "Thank you for protecting me."

The boy turned his head to the window. "Did it all wrong. You wouldn't be hurt if—"

"What happened to her was my fault," Gabriel said, taking his place at Jilly's side. "Not yours."

Her gaze whipped to his. "No more of that," she said to him, then turned to Freddie. "From either of you. I'm fine. We're all going to be fine."

Freddie looked over her head at Gabriel. "She still don't get it, does she?"

"Actually, she does." Then Gabriel yielded to his need to touch her, placing one hand on her back. "And without her kind of faith, you and I would be in a bad way, kid."

Jilly leaned into his side, and he slid his arm around her shoulders.

Freddie looked back and forth between them, then grinned that cocky smile of his. "Guess you don't need pointers from me, after all, huh?"

Gabriel smiled. "Guess not."

Freddie watched them for a moment. "So what happens to me now?"

"You don't worry about it," Jilly said. "We're working on it."

"Don't want no foster home," he protested weakly.

Jilly stroked his forehead. "Let us worry about that, okay?"

The boy looked skeptical until Gabriel nodded his agreement, and some of Freddie's tension visibly eased. "Tired." His eyelids began to droop.

"You go ahead and sleep, son." Gabriel laid a hand on his shoulder. "You're safe now."

Freddie sighed and fell asleep then.

Jilly kissed his cheek, then turned to Gabriel, her eyes fierce. "I have phone calls to make."

He chuckled.

"What?"

"Nothing, just…" He shook his head slowly. "The world somehow feels right when Jilly's making plans."

She went on tiptoe and kissed him, then grabbed his hand and pulled him out the door.

He didn't even try to resist.

He would follow this small warrior to hell and back.

Epilogue

Two weeks later

Jilly reached her spot under the spreading oaks on the grounds of Hotel Serenity and glanced over at Dane, winking at her bridegroom brother before she turned to watch Vanessa stroll down the aisle with Jilly's dad at her side. Since Vanessa had no family, she'd asked Dad to give her away, and Dad had pronounced that a great deal, being able to give her away as a surrogate daughter, then get her right back as a daughter-in-law once she'd said her vows.

Her brothers were Dane's groomsmen, and she, Jade, Raina and Diana were Vanessa's attendants. Skeeter woofed from beside Dane, but a firm word kept him in place as his beloved mistress approached. He wasn't wearing the lighted collar Dane had threatened to buy, but there were flowers woven into a shiny new one.

His tail was wagging madly, and laughter moved like a soft wind through the assembled guests.

Dane looked gobsmacked when he caught sight of Vanessa in her simple, flowing ivory gown.

She looked pretty much the same when she saw him in his tux.

Jilly tore her gaze from the two of them to seek out the man she couldn't wait to be with as soon as the ceremony ended.

Gabriel was right where he was supposed to be, in the midst of her family, Freddie at his side in a suit he'd complained bitterly about wearing.

But she'd caught Freddie, more than once, admiring himself in the mirror.

On the other side of Freddie stood Alex and Jade's two children under the watchful eyes of Sean and Annabelle. Where Jilly hadn't been successful yet—*yet*, she resolved—at being approved as a foster parent, Alex and Jade, with their ranch and big house with plenty of room, with horses and other livestock and two kids as playmates, had been able to cut through some red tape with Saint and Clarice's aid. For the time being, they would serve as foster parents for Freddie.

Jilly and Gabriel intended, long term, to get themselves settled and begin the adoption process, once they could dot all the *I*s and cross all the *T*s. Meanwhile, Damien's mother was enrolled in parenting classes that Jilly had found for her. The woman, Delfina, was well aware that many eyes were on her, but she wasn't having to do it without the moral support of the Sullivan/Sandoval clan. Jilly's mom, in particular, had taken an interest in Delfina, and no one could be a better example as a mother.

Freddie, still thin but eating constantly and recovering nicely, tugged at his tie, grimaced and rolled his eyes at her. She arched her eyebrows at him.

Gabriel watched them both and grinned.

Would she ever grow tired of the sight of his smile? Not hardly.

He had begun seeing a counselor who specialized in PTSD, and she was seeing someone, too, though she considered what she'd been through on only one night to be so much less than Gabriel had endured over a period of years.

They'd both been warned that the process for Gabriel to rid himself of the lingering effects of his wartime experiences would take time and could not be rushed.

But already he seemed to have shed some burdens he'd carried for far too long.

And he smiled far more often as they spent all their free time together, living in her house while working on his place. They weren't sure yet if they'd live in either one or sell both and buy something else.

In the meantime, Gabriel was supervising the Delgado job, while Teo was handling the Fosters. His wife had agreed to wait until spring to travel. The Marins had moved in just in time for *Día de los Muertos*, and they'd invited the entire crew to be part of the celebration.

Sean and Annabelle were still waiting patiently for Jilly's decision about the job, but regardless of her decision, she'd already begun helping them get underway as she could find time.

Another smile beckoned her from the front row beside her parents. Abuelita had indeed made her first flight on Liam's plane and had loved it. She had loved Gabriel, too, from the first moment. The two had formed a special bond and spent a great deal of time together already.

Life wasn't perfect, no. Not every plan she'd made fell neatly into place. Likely never would.

But as Gabriel stared at her as though she were more beautiful than the breathtaking bride taking her place beside Jilly, she couldn't imagine asking for more than the bounty she'd been given.

"You may be seated," said the minister.

Jilly had to drag her attention away from Gabriel to perform her maid of honor duties.

But not before she caught his smoldering gaze on her. His

beautiful smile she never took for granted.

As she took Vanessa's bouquet, she sighed with pleasure. With relief. With deep, unending gratitude for her family, her life…for the very real sunshine that had returned with Gabriel's love.

She couldn't resist one quick glance back to blow him a surreptitious kiss.

Gabriel winked. Her family chuckled.

Freddie rolled his eyes.

~THE END~

Thank you for letting me share my stories with you!

If you enjoyed TEXAS RESCUE, I would be very grateful if you would help others find this book by recommending it to your friends in such places as Goodreads, BookBub and by writing a review. If you would like to be informed when my next release is available or get news of special deals on my books, please sign up for my newsletter by visiting my website at www.jeanbrashear.com and follow me on BookBub.

The Lone Star Lovers series began with TEXAS HEART-THROB, Jilly's brother Liam's story:

Hollywood's hottest heartthrob Liam Sullivan has escaped the paparazzi and celebrity gossips after a sensational tragedy, reexamining his high-flying lifestyle and his priorities. In disguise, traveling through the Smoky Mountains of North Carolina, he encounters a rail-thin, starving woman who has lost everything but the dilapidated cabin where she once lived with her grandmother in happier days. Raina Donovan is determined to make her stand there, but winter is coming, and Liam cannot desert her until he can make her safe, however much she tries to make him leave.

Day by day, they draw closer, but Raina has secrets and so does Liam. Before they can trust enough to confide in each other, the world catches up with them. Can they overcome the stunning shock of their deceptions to find a way to be together, or will the price of their lies ruin any chance they might have for a future?

Start reading TEXAS HEARTTHROB today!

I love hearing from you, so please contact me through any of the options at the end of this book.

Thanks!
Jean

If powerful and emotional stories are your cup of tea, you might also enjoy the Second Chances series:

GUARDING GABY

With his freedom and his life on the line, only one thing would draw Eli away from his search for the truth: Gaby's safety.

Even if that means he'll lose her forever.

BRINGING BELLA BACK

When James finally locates the woman who owns his heart, learning that she remembers nothing of their life together is both a curse and a blessing. Can James remind her of all the joy they shared and make her fall in love with him again?

Before her memory of his mistakes returns…and Bella stays away forever?

THE PRICE HE PAID

Second chances don't happen for convicted murderers, and when old enemies conspire to send David back into the hell he barely survived, the only one who can help him is Callie.

The last person on earth he's willing to ask for anything.

THE HOUSE THAT LOVE BUILT

Once they had it all: a home with a man who adored her, three children they cherished, a life filled with passion and promise.

Until one troubled child cost them everything.

(A companion story to ***The Road Back Home,*** *a different perspective of the story seen through Ria's eyes and going beyond)*

THE ROAD BACK HOME

Can her family forgive what she can't forgive herself?

(A companion to ***The House That Love Built,*** *a different perspective of the story seen through Ria's eyes and going beyond)*

DREAM HOUSE

Her dream house is the scene of his nightmares. Can he bear to see it in another woman's hands—especially one so different from his delicate lost love?

Please enjoy this excerpt from GUARDING GABY:

"There's a call for you from Texas," the receptionist said. "A Sheriff Anderson. He refuses to leave a message. Congratulations, by the way."

Sheriff Anderson? It had been nine years since she'd had contact with anyone back there.

"Okay, I'll take the call. And thanks."

She punched the flickering button. "Gaby Navarro."

"Gabriela?" So strange to be called Gabriela once more. And the voice was not the older one she expected. This was his son, Chad. Her former boyfriend.

"Chad? You're…the sheriff?"

He chuckled. "Amazing, huh? My dad passed away two years ago, and the voters saw fit to give me the job." Memories crashed in on her…Chad, the golden boy, literally. Blond, tall and handsome. Quarterback of the football team, student body president. All that a girl could dream.

Until Eli changed everything.

"Gabriela, I'm sorry, but this isn't a social call. I'm afraid I have bad news."

The past vanished with the warning in his tone. "Papa is all right, isn't he?"

A long silence. "That's why I'm calling. You need to come home."

"Is he sick? Hurt?" Papa had always seemed invincible.

"I wish I didn't have to do this on the phone. No easy way to break it: your father is gone, Gabriela."

"Gone?" she echoed. Dropped into her chair and opened the middle desk drawer, groping for the picture she kept there.

"There was a fire in one of the barns. He was alone."

"Where was Ramon?" The foreman had been with her father as long as she could remember.

A pause. "Your father had to let Ramon go several months back, so there was no one—" He cleared his throat. "By the time a passerby noticed the smoke, it was too late."

She hunched over her desk, clutching the photograph. She'd left in a fury. Thrown ugly words in her father's face, and now they would never—

She barely registered what Chad was saying. "—good man, but in the last few years, his health had deteriorated."

The knife slid in a little deeper. "I'll be on the first plane."

"Let me know which flight, and I'll pick you up."

"No, I—"

"Gabriela, please. I want to help you."

"I have to go now. I'll take care of it." She hung up before he could tell her anything else.

Before she had to hear more recrimination in his voice. Her father had wanted her to marry Chad and unite their adjoining ranches.

But she'd had other dreams, even before—

Eli. Outcast Eli Wolverton had been her dark secret.

Her one true love.

Or so she'd believed until he'd abandoned her. Vanished under a cloud of suspicion.

Eli was old history now, not worth a second's thought, but Papa…

What have I done?

She stroked one finger across the photo of Papa and herself on her seventh birthday, a dignified man smiling at the girl in the pink organdy dress. Ruthlessly, she pushed back the black demon that would devour her if she thought about never being able to make up for what she'd done to her father—

Stop it. Focus on the details. Get online and find a plane ticket. With a leaden heart, she reached for her keyboard drawer.

“Hey, girl, I got us—What’s wrong?” Beth at the door.

Gaby couldn’t figure out how to answer her. She’d never told a soul how she and her father had parted. She’d left her past behind in Texas.

“I just—” She crumpled. “My—my father—he’s—” She lifted stinging eyes. “He’s dead.”

“Oh, honey…” In minutes, Beth had the whole story and, in her inimitable mode, had swung into action. Before Gaby could blink, she was booked on a flight leaving in three hours and tucked into a cab, headed to pack her things and return home.

Except it hadn’t been home for nine years.

And now it never would.

…*Excerpt from* GUARDING GABY *by Jean Brashear © 2019*

Start reading GUARDING GABY today!

The Lone Star Lovers series includes:

TEXAS HEARTTHROB (Liam and Raina)

TEXAS HEALER (Rafe and Diana)

TEXAS PROTECTOR (Alex and Jade)

TEXAS DECEPTION (Diana's sister Franny and Nate)

TEXAS LOST (Diana and Franny's sister Clarice and Saint)

TEXAS WANDERER (Dane and Vanessa)

TEXAS BODYGUARD (Sean and Annabelle)

TEXAS RESCUE (Jilly and Gabriel)

BOOKS BY JEAN BRASHEAR:

SWEETGRASS SPRINGS

Nestled in the Texas Hill Country, tiny Sweetgrass Springs was founded by four veterans of the Texas Revolution, and for over a century the town and their ranches grew and prospered. Nowadays, however, too many of the town's children leave for the big city as soon as they can escape, and Sweetgrass is barely hanging on. The heart and soul of Sweetgrass is Ruby Gallagher. Her daughter vanished from Sweetgrass right after high school, but Ruby, owner of community gathering place Ruby's Café, remains, keeping vigil, hoping for her daughter's return. She is fighting to save her ancestors' legacy, but the town is dying, and it's breaking Ruby's heart.

Then the granddaughter she never knew existed arrives and sets in motion a new life for this eccentric, lovable spot in the road…where hope never fades and love never dies. Readers call it "a special place for hearts that need healing."

Texas Roots: A Paris-trained chef on the run finds Texas family she never knew existed and a sexy cowboy she doesn't dare love

Texas Wild: Sexy SEAL turned Hollywood stuntman returns home to find his buddy's little sister all grown up

Texas Dreams: Take two reluctant brides and two frustrated grooms, mix with both clans of Gallaghers and season with a SEAL or three, a movie star, a Hollywood Barbie and a country music giant—and get not one but two surprise weddings

Texas Rebel: A former rebellious teen turned billionaire's reunion with his teenage sweetheart and a secret baby he never knew about

Texas Blaze: What happens when a shark lawyer in stilettos has a fling with a hot firefighter determined to find Suzy Homemaker?

Texas Christmas Bride: All he wants is the girl he thought he'd lost forever.

The Book Babes: Five women began as a reading group and became family…but now change is rippling through the group.

Texas Hope: Can two brothers who never knew each other existed overcome the secrets of a woman who abandoned one son and lied to the other?

Texas Strong: Can a man who's never trusted anyone and a woman who's trusted all the wrong men defy the odds and open their hearts to each other?

Texas Sweet: When a stranger who holds the keys to her identity arrives in town, will the girl everyone knows as Brenda come to terms with her past or run again?

Be Mine This Christmas: The man he's become is not the boy she once knew—and he may never forgive her, once he knows the secret she's been concealing.

Texas Charm: He's a country superstar; she's a small town waitress. When the real world slams into their reverie, whose heart will be the one to break? (Contains an original song written for this book)

Texas Magic: One billionaire...one tomboy...one night of magic. Miracle or mirage?

Be My Midnight Kiss: It's New Year's Eve...and now or never for these two hearts

Boxed sets:

The Gallaghers Of Sweetgrass Springs Boxed Set 1 (Books 1-3)

The Gallaghers Of Sweetgrass Springs Boxed Set 2 (Books 4-6)

Finding Home Boxed Set One (Sweetgrass Springs Stories)

Finding Home Boxed Set Two (Sweetgrass Springs Stories)

THE GALLAGHERS OF MORNING STAR

(cousins of the Sweetgrass Springs clan)

Secrets will be revealed and the lives of four people will be shattered as they learn that who they are and where they come from is not at all what they always believed.

Texas Secrets: Former SEAL Boone Gallagher returns to the only home he's ever known only to find that the ranch has been willed to a stranger who doesn't want it—and he must keep her there for thirty days, or it will be lost to them both.

Texas Lonely: A loner who's lost faith in love is the only hope for a mother and child on the run

Texas Bad Boy: Disgraced bad boy has his chance for revenge against the beautiful society girl who chose money over his love

The Gallaghers Of Morning Star Boxed Set

LONE STAR LOVERS

Heart-tugging, action-packed and passionate stories of the close-knit Sullivan/Sandoval family of four brothers and one sister, plus the three Morgan sisters, orphaned and separated for many years, whose lives reconnect as they become part of the family circle.

Texas Heartthrob: Hollywood's hottest star is a man in disguise when he encounters a woman who's lost everything…but her secrets. When the world catches up to them, will the price of their lies cost them everything?

Texas Healer: Special Forces medic holds the power to heal both a doctor's injured body and her wounded heart…but she can't stay in his world—and he can't leave.

Texas Protector: A detective forever haunted by the night when he couldn't save a young girl from trauma—now she's a cop herself and he has to send her undercover to lure a murderer.

Texas Deception: A plucky crusader falls for a down-on-his-luck stranger—only to learn too late that he's the villain determined to destroy her town

Texas Lost: A hard-nosed detective targeted by internal affairs and the woman who's professional evaluation will make or break his career. A a growing attraction between them risks first his case…and then her life.

Texas Wanderer: When she's lost all her dreams and is finally finding a place to call home, will she place her trust—

and her heart—in the hands of a wanderer with secrets?

Texas Bodyguard: He's undercover as a bodyguard to a film star because her best friend is his top suspect. When she comes to mean too much to him, confessing his deception means risking his career—but not coming clean with her could risk her life

Texas Rescue: A haunted warrior who lives in the shadows encounters a small, valiant woman who's a champion of lost causes, and the vibrant light within her lures him from the darkness. When she is rocked by a brush with evil, can he make her feel safe again...and can she convince him that he deserves to live in the light?

Lone Star Lovers Boxed Set (Books 1-3)

THE MARSHALLS

Texas Refuge: Haunted former detective is the only sanctuary for an actress being stalked by a madman

Texas Star: Sexiest Man Alive becomes a white knight for a woman who keeps trying to escape him

Texas Danger: Down on his luck rancher is the only hope for a socialite on the run from the mob

The Marshalls Boxed Set

SECOND CHANCES series

Love deserves a second chance...

Guarding Gaby: Gabriela Navarro believed she and Eli

Wolverton would always be together…until he abandoned her.

Bringing Bella Back: They had the perfect marriage…until he lost his way. Then he lost Bella.

The Price He Paid: The golden boy and the rebel girl who cost him everything

The House That Love Built: Once they had it all: a home with a man who adored her, three children they cherished, a life filled with passion and promise. Until one troubled child cost them everything.

The Road Back Home: Can her family forgive what she can't forgive herself?

Dream House: Her dream house is the scene of his nightmares.

THE GODDESS OF FRIED OKRA

"Wholly original, funny and poignant"
~#1 New York Times bestselling author Susan Wiggs

Every life has signposts.
Every traveler has a history.
Sometimes a detour is the only way home

Lost and grieving, Eudora "Pea" O'Brien sets off on a road trip to find her sister, collecting an unlikely family of strays along the way to discovering where she truly belongs.

DANGEROUS TO LOVE stories

Is he her enemy…or will he save her?

Dark, deadly and dangerous, they operate in the shadows, guarding the women they love but cannot have.

The Choice: Only one of them can win—and if they cannot learn to trust each other, both of them could die.

Mercy: He went to prison for twenty years to save her…can he save her again?

The Light Walker: A brand-new detective. A mesmerizing, mysterious billionaire suspect. A powerful attraction that threatens the balance in a battle between the dark and the light

Dangerous To Love Boxed Set

About the Author

A letter to Rod Stewart resulting in a Cinderella 16th birthday for her daughter might have been the first step on Texas romance author Jean Brashear's path to being a *New York Times* and *USAToday* bestselling author of more than 50 novels in romance and women's fiction.

Jean's stories are hailed as "feel-good romance at its finest" and her quirky small towns are called "a special place for hearts that need healing." All are evidence of Jean's heartfelt belief that love is the most powerful force in the universe, and her stories reflect that bone-deep commitment to spreading her faith in the goodness that exists inside us all.

Connect With Jean

Visit Jean's website: www.jeanbrashear.com

Facebook: www.facebook.com/AuthorJeanBrashear

BookBub: www.bookbub.com/authors/jean-brashear

Pinterest: www.pinterest.com/JeanBrashear

Instagram: www.instagram.com/jeanbrashear

To be notified of new releases and special deals, sign up for Jean's newsletter on her website

CPSIA information can be obtained
at www.ICGtesting.com
Printed in the USA
LVHW090206080921
697304LV00012B/62

9 781942 653547